S0-AGU-260

A WORLDLY MISS

"Ah, you are dallying with me again. I am a female, so I suppose that means you can not help yourself." Lilly laughed, and it was a merry musical sound.

"Perhaps, it is because I mean to steal another kiss," the Earl answered and nearly sounded serious.

"Would you do that? Take advantage of a green girl from the country who might give her heart with that kiss?" Her eyes twinkled naughtily.

The laughter in those grey eyes unmanned him. He felt himself no more than a schoolboy being taunted by a woman-child. "Indeed, I have not yet begged your forgiveness. Perhaps I should, but I think not. I enjoyed that kiss Lilly Aulderbury. I enjoyed it too much to say that I regret it."

"Well done, my lord. Surely now I should swoon into your arms so that you can claim that second kiss?" She wagged a finger at him then, and her tone subtly changed. "The thing is; I am *not* a green girl any longer."

ELEGANT LOVE STILL FLOURISHES –
Wrap yourself in a Zebra Regency Romance.

A MATCHMAKER'S MATCH (3783, $3.50/$4.50)
by Nina Porter
To save herself from a loveless marriage, Lady Psyche Veringham pretends to be a bluestocking. Resigned to spinsterhood at twenty-three, Psyche sets her keen mind to snaring a husband for her young charge, Amanda. She sets her cap for long-time bachelor, Justin St. James. This man of the world has had his fill of frothy-headed debutantes and turns the tables on Psyche. Can a bluestocking and a man about town find true love?

FIRES IN THE SNOW (3809, $3.99/$4.99)
by Janis Laden
Because of an unhappy occurrence, Diana Ruskin knew that a secure marriage was not in her future. She was content to assist her physician father and follow in his footsteps . . . until now. After meeting Adam, Duke of Marchmaine, Diana's precise world is shattered. She would simply have to avoid the temptation of his gentle touch and stunning physique – and by doing so break her own heart!

FIRST SEASON (3810, $3.50/$4.50)
by Anne Baldwin
When country heiress Laetitia Biddle arrives in London for the Season, she harbors dreams of triumph and applause. Instead, she becomes the laughingstock of drawing rooms and ballrooms, alike. This headstrong miss blames the rakish Lord Wakeford for her miserable debut, and she vows to rise above her many faux pas. Vowing to become an Original, Letty proves that she's more than a match for this eligible, seasoned Lord.

AN UNCOMMON INTRIGUE (3701, $3.99/$4.99)
by Georgina Devon
Miss Mary Elizabeth Sinclair was rather startled when the British Home Office employed her as a spy. Posing as "Tasha," an exotic fortune-teller, she expected to encounter unforeseen dangers. However, nothing could have prepared her for Lord Eric Stewart, her dashing and infuriating partner. Giving her heart to this haughty rogue would be the most reckless hazard of all.

A MADDENING MINX (3702, $3.50/$4.50)
by Mary Kingsley
After a curricle accident, Miss Sarah Chadwick is literally thrust into the arms of Philip Thornton. While other women shy away from Thornton's eyepatch and aloof exterior, Sarah finds herself drawn to discover why this man is physically and emotionally scarred.

Available wherever paperbacks are sold, or order direct from the Publisher. Send cover price plus 50¢ per copy for mailing and handling to Zebra Books, Dept. 4443, 475 Park Avenue South, New York, N.Y. 10016. Residents of New York and Tennessee must include sales tax. DO NOT SEND CASH. For a free Zebra/ Pinnacle catalog please write to the above address.

A Daring Deceit

Claudette Williams

ZEBRA BOOKS
KENSINGTON PUBLISHING CORP.

ZEBRA BOOKS are published by

Kensington Publishing Corp.
475 Park Avenue South
New York, NY 10016

Copyright © 1994 by Claudette Williams
All rights reserved. No part of this book may be reproduced
in any form or by any means without the prior written con-
sent of the Publisher, excepting brief quotes used in reviews.

If you purchased this book without a cover you should be
aware that this book is stolen property. It was reported as
"unsold and destroyed" to the Publisher and neither the Author nor the Publisher has received any payment for this
"stripped book."

Zebra and the Z logo Reg. U.S. Pat & TM Off.

First Printing: January, 1994

Printed in the United States of America

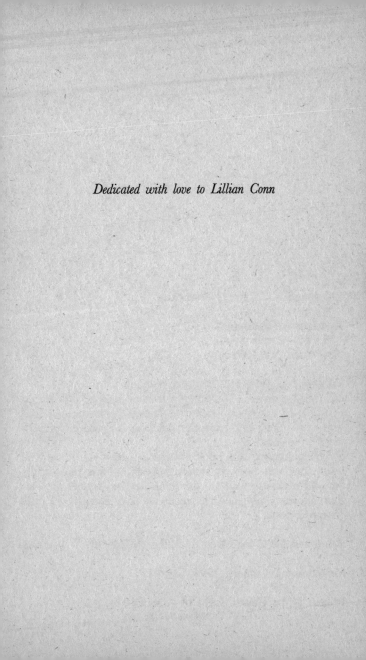

Dedicated with love to Lillian Conn

Chapter One

Miss Lillian Aulderbury peeped sideways at her companion as they strolled down the main avenue of Lymington Harbor. There was a warm light in her grey eyes, and the gentleman beside her grinned as he advised her, "Look at me just that way, Miss Aulderbury, and I will not be able to stop myself."

"Stop yourself from what?" returned Lilly, taking the bait.

A soft ocean breeze was blowing, and at that moment it whipped at her straw bonnet, caught her long black gleaming curls and sent her tresses across her cheek. She blinked slowly as her kid-gloved hand pushed away the wandering curls, and the gentleman caught her gloved hand to put her fingers to his lips and murmur, "Stop myself from this"—his kiss moved to her wrist—"and this . . ."

The lady snatched her hand away quickly before he could do more and was rewarded with his hearty laugh. He flicked her nose. "So afraid, innocent lamb?"

"I am not afraid, Sir Anthony, merely cautious, and *you* have avoided answering my question."

"Which was?"

She looked at him for a long thoughtful moment. He

was absolutely the most handsome beau she had ever had. His hair was thick, silky and the color of gold. His eyes were clear blue, and his mouth was full and sensual. He looked like an Adonis. Added to this was the fact that he was fashionably dressed, sophisticated, mysterious and at six and twenty a practiced flirt. Lilly was thoroughly enchanted, for the first time in her eighteen years.

"I put a question to you, sir, a reasonable question. Are you courting Cynthia Edwards? I should like a straightforward reply."

"Ah, Cynthia Edwards." He smiled audaciously at her, but said nothing further.

"So then, you don't mean to answer me," pursued the lady with a glint in her grey eyes.

"Why do you think that I am courting little Cynthia?" he asked warily.

Lilly did not see the caution in his vague blue eyes. "Stuart says you are. Stuart says you and Cynthia are often found together."

"Ah, Stuart. I was forgetting young Stuart. Do you always believe what Stuart says?"

"I see," answered Lilly turning away from him. She was young and perhaps unworldly, but it was obvious he was avoiding the question. Her cherry lips set gravely, and her fine black brows drew together with her sure concern.

He laughed it off and took her chin. "My pretty pretty Lilly. Why would I court Cynthia when all I can think about is you?"

Lillian Aulderbury blushed. She was indeed an innocent, just past eighteen and blossoming into a woman, but here was an experienced rogue and she was flustered by his delightful charms. "Stop that, you brazen

8

man!" Her wagging finger belied by her smile, soft and warm, "You do not mean it. You only—"

"I only," he interrupted her reprimand, "care for you. Indeed, Lilly, I do mean it." He took her gloved hand, and his kiss on her wrist was quite improperly warm. When he looked at her again it was to grin. "Come now, we told your aunt we would only be a few minutes."

With that, Lillian Aulderbury was returned to her aunt, who was shopping at the milliner's a short walk away, and Sir Anthony Meade briskly made his way to his leased carriage. Twenty minutes later he was bending low over Cynthia Edwards' soft white hand.

Lillian's few moments with Sir Anthony were tucked away as she and her aunt continued their day. Lymington Orphanage was one of their great passions, and a busy afternoon spent there with the children gave Lilly little time to consider Sir Anthony Meade's intentions. However, once back home, Lilly rushed about throwing her clothes on the bed. Then she slipped into breeches and dashed off to the stable where she saddled her own horse and mounted up.

Oh, it was good to be on her horse. Propriety insisted that she wear a lady's habit and use a sidesaddle now that she was of age, but every now and then she would pull on her old britches and ride astride her old comfortable saddle. She eyed the line fence that separated her aunt's property from the neighboring farmland. "Well then, Missy . . ." Lilly spoke softly to her mare as she urged her forward, steadily approaching the fence. The mare knew what her job was and took the fence with easy grace. Horse and rider landed deftly and proceeded across the field. Lilly laughed out loud and opened her horse for a gallop. "Yes, yes . . ." Lilly beamed as they picked up speed. It was always like this when she was on her horse. The world faded away until it was just the two of them running in the wind. Life these days was becoming too complicated, but, here all things fit into place.

Just ahead of them was a long coup separating one field from the next. Lilly checked her horse's speed, and then they were gliding over the width of this obstacle to land in the tall grass. They went lightly, easily, and moved swiftly as they sped across the wide rolling turf. Lilly's horse was fit and ready for more, but she spoke quietly to her mare as she reined her in and took her down to a trot. Just as Lilly leaned over to pat Missy's neck she heard a familiar voice calling.

"Lilly! Deuce take it girl, slow down," Stuart Langley shouted as he stood in his stirrups to get her attention. "That's it, here now."

Lilly's fine black brows went up as she directed a hard look and a cool reception toward her lifelong friend. She had a serious grievance to air with Mr. Stuart Langley. Sitting her chestnut mare erectly, she froze him with his own name, "Stuart."

"Ah then, miffed with me, eh?" Stuart was no laggard. He saw it at once. "The blasted fellow denied it? Tell me he denied it."

"If you are speaking of Sir Anthony," Lilly answered curtly, "I did indeed ask him this very morning about Cynthia Edwards, and yes, he denied it."

"Right then, what did you think? Did you think I've been making up great whopping tales? Did you think ol' Stuart was daft? Did you think I've been seeing things? What then, Lilly?"

She frowned. "What I think is that you are besotted

10

with Cynthia yourself and that you are jealous of any man who even speaks with her."

"Oh fiddle," retorted Stuart hotly. "Ay then, you know I'm . . . that I have a great regard for Cynthia. There isn't another soul knows it but you. Trusted you with that . . . thought you trusted me. Lilly, the man is a cheat. You've never been a ninny, don't become one now."

"Careful, Stuart," warned Lilly, her warm grey eyes ready to spark fire at him.

"Ay . . . spitfire you have always been! The trouble is your eyes are filled with stardust. Lilly, the blasted fellow is playing fast and loose with both of you. It's a game to him, nothing more."

Stuart was presently at an impasse. He was desperately in love with Cynthia Edwards, yet he had been watching her grow more and more infatuated with a man he knew to be an insincere rakehell. Now it would appear that his closest friend was also falling under Meade's spell. Would he yield to the forces of fate? No, by damn, he would not. He could not, however, take this conversation any further without revealing a confidence. What he knew to be a fact, it was not his place to repeat for he had been sworn to keep the secret of yet another friend who had been duped by the rakehell some years ago during a London season.

He shrugged his shoulders and attempted quiet reason. "The man is a devil. He has scores of hearts hanging from his cummerbund. You can believe me, or you can believe him. But answer me this. If he wants you, why am I forever finding him at Cynthia's house?"

Lilly took a moment to consider this point and frowned, "I . . . I don't know," she sighed at last.

"Right then. Lilly, you have known me most of your

11

life. I haven't a reason in the world to lie to you, but he has."

"Does he? What reason? Do you think he means to seduce me out of wedlock?"

"Stupid girl!" Stuart was exasperated.

"You don't like Sir Anthony, so perhaps you can not see beyond your dislike," she countered.

"If you will do but one thing for me, I shall be satisfied."

"What is it, you ridiculous lovesick boy?" She smiled kindly at him.

"Will you take my warning in good stead? Will you hold back just enough to watch him carefully as he plays his game?"

"Oh, Stuart, do stop."

"Do that for me—just that."

"Forget all this nonsense and tell me how your mother is? Better after that dreadful bout with the quinsy?"

"Ay then. We'll talk of other things. M'mother is it? She is better, much better, and did charge me with the errand of telling you and your aunt that she would be with you tomorrow to help sort out the books for the children's new library."

"Oh, Stuart, I nearly forgot!" exclaimed Lilly with a hand to her face. "You and your father won't have to go all the way to Christchurch after all. Apparently Gussie's nephew has arranged for an enormous quantity of books to be delivered by tomorrow."

"Well, I like that!" snapped Stuart testily. "I've been running about the countryside begging for books and—"

"And everything you brought in is absolutely wonderful," put in Lilly hurriedly. "However, it seems this nephew of Gussie's has quite a connection to the *beau*

12

monde and got up an impressive collection for the orphanage, so we needn't go begging anymore."

"Humph!" grumbled Stuart. "Which nephew is this?"

Lilly shrugged. "I have never met him. His name is Lord Raeburn."

"Rogue Raeburn?" Stuart appeared incredulous. "I don't believe it."

"And why not?"

"Lilly, Raeburn cares for nought but the cut of his coat, his horses, his sport, his wine, and his women—in that order, too! What has he to do with orphans?"

"Well, as to that, he seems to be a favorite with Lady Augusta, so you see how wrong it is to judge someone on rumour? Apparently, Lord Raeburn does care for more than his pleasures."

"Ha! No doubt he has a by-blow or two he feels guilty about. Perhaps they are even in our own little orphanage," returned Stuart pugnaciously.

"Stuart!" Lilly was genuinely shocked. "You are very odious today. What a dreadful thing to say about my godmother's favorite nephew!"

"Right then, forget it, Lilly. To the next fence!" Stuart gave up. The woman simply would not listen to reason!

Chapter Two

The Dowager Lady Westly intended her happy gathering to be nothing more than an intimate country affair. However, she was a kindhearted woman who derived pleasure from watching the young people enjoy themselves. Thus it was, when appealed to by several robust youths, she allowed the musicians to strike up the latest and most controversial dance, the waltz.

Lilly found her gloved hand in Sir Anthony's as he led her onto the floor. She felt heady, daring and sophisticated as he twirled her to the steps of the dance; however, she did not realize she was concentrating on her feet until he called her to order.

"You needn't go on counting, my beauty." His smile teased her.

Lilly bit her lip. "Oh dear, was it so obvious? I haven't waltzed very much . . . with men, that is. Only Stuart." She watched the rays of the flickering lights gleam against his golden waves of hair.

"Stuart again." He frowned.

"He is a friend, you see." She wasn't sure why she felt the need to explain this to him.

"Of course. I did not think otherwise." Sir Anthony glanced in Stuart's direction and then pointed his firm chin in another. "If it were Dowson over there that had been teaching you to waltz, I surely would have been jealous!"

"Jealous? Don't be absurd," Lilly giggled. "Jealous of dear sweet Douglas Dowson." Then as an afterthought struck her, she added, "That would be like me being jealous of you and Cynthia Edwards."

He grinned. "Ah, my little sugarplum, still baiting, are we?"

Lilly pouted in frustration. He was impossible. He would evade, always evade. Why? Why not just deny it outright? A liar, a rakehell would do that . . . wouldn't he? Stuart said Sir Anthony was cunning. Could it be so? No. She couldn't move in his arms like this . . . feel his admiration and think him less than what she knew him to be, could she? No. He was wonderful.

Sir Anthony looked at her and felt pure, almost unrestrained desire. He had been attempting to discover the extent of her inheritance and had, thus far, been unsuccessful. If Lilly turned out to be even half the heiress that Cynthia Edwards was, then it would be Lilly he would take. Most certainly it would be Lilly, for he wanted her in his bed. Perhaps, he could have it so still? Tricky business, though, bedding one of his own without marriage. However, if he were careful . . . perhaps? At any rate, she was a delectable piece and he had to have at least a kiss. With that thought he guided her towards the garden doors. "You need not be jealous, Lilly. You are far too beautiful to be jealous of any other female. May I take it that I need not be jealous of young Dowson?"

"No . . . no." She did not know what else to say when he was looking at her that way. It was thrilling, having his eyes caress her face. He led her outdoors and took her hand to hurry her to a dark lonely garden spot. "Lilly . . ." he said breathlessly.

She felt his arms go around her and waited for his kiss, which indeed came, sure and deft.

"Ah, Lilly . . I have never felt like this before." How many times had he uttered those words, how many women had so moved him? The notion that perhaps he wasn't capable of genuine sentiment flitted through his mind. However, the taste of cherry lips tickled his desire into a frenzy, and he pressed Lilly to him for yet another kiss.

She could hear people's voices. Yet the kiss was so exciting that for just a little while she enjoyed the naughtiness of kissing him in the garden. Yes, she wanted him to go on kissing her so she could remember exactly what his kiss felt like, later when she was alone, but they must go back. She pulled away and started for the door. He stopped her. "Lilly . . . ?"

"Yes?"

"You know you now belong to me? You can have no other." He was holding her to a promise. After all, she just might turn out to be the heiress he was counting on marrying.

"Belong to you?" Lilly was always high-spirited. "I think not." Her heart, however, silently protested that indeed she was getting closer and closer to belonging to him.

Even so, Sir Anthony felt sure of his conquest as he followed her back to the ballroom. It flashed through his mind that in leading Lilly to this point he might have gone one step too far too soon. However, he brushed this aside. What he had to do now was discover just what Lillian Aulderbury's fortune was in total. Then he would know how to proceed.

* * *

A knock sounded at Lilly's bedroom door. She had only just crawled beneath the covers and had not yet snuffed out her candle. "Yes?"

"Lilly, may I come in dear?" Lady Sarah called.

"Yes, of course."

Lady Sarah was a tall, elegant woman. She stepped within the bedchamber quietly and came to sit beside her niece, but there was no hiding the concern on her face. Lilly braced herself. "You are still angry with me because I walked with Sir Anthony in the garden, aren't you?"

"Angry? Dearest, I am not angry. I can remember doing much the same at your age." Lady Sarah smiled indulgently.

Lilly managed a smile in response, "Well then?"

"Lilly, there is something that does disturb me, for I expected with your good common sense you would not have been so easily taken in by the charms of an obvious rogue."

"Aunt Sarah . . . what can you mean?" Lilly knew exactly what her aunt was saying. She had known for weeks now that neither her aunt nor her godmother, Lady Augusta, found anything to like in Sir Anthony. No doubt they had been listening to Stuart!

"What can I mean? Child, can you tell me that you really don't know what I said?"

"Oh, I know you don't like Sir Anthony." Lilly sighed. "I can't imagine why. If only you knew him as I do—"

"Ha! You don't know him. You think you do because he is handsome, charming and older than any of the boys that have courted you."

Lilly's grey eyes sparkled angrily. How could she make her aunt see that it was more, so much more than his looks and charm that captivated her? "Please, Aunt

17

Sarah. He is so wonderful, so exciting and daring. I have never known anyone quite like him." Lilly's intensity of feeling was leading her into defiance. Aunt Sarah, Lady Augusta and Stuart were wrong, all of them. They simply did not know him.

Lady Sarah took a moment to collect her rising impatience. Lilly was eighteen, naive and far too ready to dive into something she knew nothing about. Yet, Lilly was her sister's only child. What to do? Sarah had taken on the girl's care six years ago when her sister and brother-in-law were lost at sea. It had been a labor of love, for she had no children of her own. It pained Sarah to hurt Lilly; but she wanted her to see the true Anthony Meade.

She attempted logic. "Precious, I want you to consider this carefully. Sir Anthony's finances are in a sorry state. Never mind how I know this; it is a fact. He must make a marriage of convenience. You understand what that means. He must marry a rich woman if he is to hold onto the style of living he enjoys so very much. It is not an uncommon situation. You have seen many examples of such marriages all around you. Lilly, you are not so innocent that you do not understand: people of our class more often than not must make a marriage of convenience?"

Lilly's chin was up, "Yes, I know that, but—"

"Sir Anthony's estates are mortgaged," Lady Sarah declared before Lilly could finish. "He is without funds. He has gambled away even his family's heirlooms. If he were genuinely attached to you, he could not offer for you. He is *not* in a position to court you. Therefore, his obvious pursuit of you tonight—his behavior, taking you into the garden as he did in light of what I have just told you—is the behavior of a cad. Do you not see it?" She could see by Lilly's face that the child did not quite believe her. How was this?

Lilly steadied herself. She had always met things head-on. From the moment she had been told about her parents' deaths, she had learned that life was an elusive promise. There was little to trust on this earth, but she wanted so very much to trust Sir Anthony. She looked at her aunt and asked on a quiet note, "Just how can you be sure of all this?"

"Suffice it to say, I know."

Here was a woman Lilly loved and respected. To her, Sarah was wisdom, loveliness, goodness and quiet strength. However, Lilly's heart spoke for her. "You are wrong." She shook her head, for she could see her aunt meant to argue further. "Sir Anthony cares for me. Tonight—"

"Tonight he was nought but a cad!" Sarah was at her wit's end.

"Why would he pursue me? I have no fortune."

"He thought you did until tonight. He mistook my circumstances. You see, he was under the impression that my fortune was far greater than the mere living I enjoy. We are quite comfortable, you and I, but there is no fortune."

"You said he learned otherwise tonight? How?"

"He was forward enough to ask, and he was answered." Lady Sarah replied softly, reaching for Lilly's hand for she could see the child was upset.

Lilly snatched her hand away. In the six years that she had lived under her aunt's guardianship and generosity she had never been made to feel like a poor relation. It hurt her now that she had been discussed as such.

"Who did Sir Anthony ask?" She was almost shaking.

19

"He discussed you, your circumstances, your parents' deaths with Lady Westly. Gussie overheard them."

"Fie, Aunt Sarah. I see what it is. You and Gussie have never liked him. Between the two of you—"

"Just a moment, young lady." Lady Sarah's tone was sharp as she cut her niece off to say, "Don't allow your emotions to run off with your good sense. Your godmother and I have only your welfare to consider."

"You think him a fortune hunter?" Lilly returned on a low note. There was a dare in her tone. "Fine then, you have managed to inform him that I have no fortune. He should bother with me no more."

Her aunt reached again for her niece's hand, but Lilly pulled away and turned to her pillow, "I am very tired, Aunt Sarah. Please forgive me if I say good night."

"Lilly, would that I could have spared you this hurt."

Lilly did not answer, and her aunt sighed as she left her to her own thoughts. Young love was often too painful to watch as it knew no bounds and had absolutely no rules!

Chapter Three

The Earl of Raeburn sat quietly at his newly installed Sheridan desk and inspected the gilt. It was a sleek structure beautifully lacquered, though a touch too ornate for his taste. Still, it was all the rage. Mail had been sorted into various stacks and neat piles by his man of business. He sighed over the quantity that he would still have to get to and quickly decided that all but one could be temporarily put aside. This particular epistle he held in his hand and skimmed for the third time. He dropped it onto his desk and sighed, let out a curse. "Damnation!"

The pretty collie lying at his heels picked up her head and looked at him inquiringly. He went on to explain to her, "You see, Sheba, this is what comes of going against one's instincts. When Gussie first wrote, she wanted books . . . books for her orphanage. Set about, got the blasted books, had them carted off in style and thought my duty well discharged." He raised a brow to the collie. Sheba sniffed. "Exactly so. I did not quibble, I did not put her off. I did my duty as a loving nephew. Did I think that my dearest Gussie would be emboldened by my lapse in character to go on and actually request another favor so soon? I did not." This time the handsome

Earl of Raeburn sniffed. "See what comes of such weakness?"

Sheba whined a response. Her master took up the offending letter and waved it at the collie who cocked her head to one side and attempted to sympathize. Her master grumbled on. "Quite right. I shall wash my hands of the whole affair. What have I to do with green country girls pining over fortune hunters?" He pulled a face. "Ridiculous."

Sheba yelped a reply. Her master looked surprised. "What's that? Of course I love Gussie . . . always been fond of the ol' gal. There is Uncle Wizzy . . . Gussie . . . duty. One mustn't forget that."

Clearly her master was laboring over a problem. Sheba's bark was sharp and absolutely signified that whatever he decided, she most certainly would uphold it. She then rolled over onto her back and, with tail brushing the oriental carpet beneath her, invited her wondrous master to rub her belly. The Earl considered her ruefully, released a short laugh and complied with her urgent request.

"There . . ." he said, as he rubbed her belly with vigor and then patted her affectionately. "You are nought but a little whore!"

This domestic scene was interrupted by the Earl's butler, an elderly fellow of uncertain years whose slim frame appeared in the open doorway. Though no smile lit his face, a twinkle lurked in his old faded eyes. Resonantly he announced, "Sir Harold."

"Eh, Harry, you say?" exclaimed the Earl, happily getting to his feet, "Thought he'd be here about now."

A tall husky gentleman immaculately dressed in a style more suited to the fashion of the day than to his substantial proportions strode briskly into the room. "Aha! There you are, you dog!" Harry scowled as he took the grey top hat from his head exposing carrot-colored and unruly curls. He handed his hat to the butler saying, "I shouldn't be giving this to you, I should be slamming it into your lord's face."

"Yes, sir," said the butler, who then quietly withdrew.

"Harry." The Earl laughed. "I am sorry. Forgive me, I . . . er . . . lost track of time."

Harry eyed his friend suspiciously. "Never say so . . ." And then with grievance, he added, "I have been waiting for you at Tattersall's for more than an hour!"

"Harry, what can I say?" The Earl was holding out his hands, moving over to shake his large friend by the shoulders. The apology on his lips was most certainly belied by the glitter in the Earl's deep blue eyes.

This was not lost on his friend, whose own eyes narrowed. "What can you say? Ha! You did this deliberately. Now where shall I ever find another matched set of prime goers like those greys of Wainwright?"

"If you will leave it to me, I shall find you such a pair and they will be a sight better than Wainwright's."

Sir Harold eyed him thoughtfully. "Why, what do you know that I don't?"

"Harry, those matched greys were more flash than anything else."

"Flash you say? Damn, but they were prime horse-flesh. There wasn't a horseman about that didn't want those two bloods!"

"That may be so, but I had a feeling Wainwright was letting them go for a reason. Harry, consider this. Wainwright is plump in the pocket. Doesn't need the blunt. Why then let such a pair go? Why haven't we seen him leading those greys about town lately? Broken down, that's why. Chronic problems, I'm sure of it. 'Tis no wonder when you think about the way he drives! Lord, he is forever getting flash horses and breaking them
23

down." The Earl snorted at this last statement. "Look, nodcock, if you wanted them so badly, you are horseman enough, you could have just gone ahead and purchased the pair without me there to hold your hand."

"Ay, well, you've always had an eye. I don't have that. You look at a leg, feel it over once and you know. I'll say that much for you, there is none that knows prime blood better than you."

"Trust me in this, Harry. I know Wainwright. I know the way the man drives his horses. You are well out of it."

Harry grumbled, but the Earl laughed, slapped his friend on the shoulder and suggested, "Come on then, there is an exhibition match set for noon at Manton's."

Diverted Harry brightened. "Is there? Jackson sparring?"

"No, Tibbs and Gentleman John."

"Well then, what are we waiting for?"

The Earl took up hat and gloves from a hall table as he led his friend out. Nettles appeared and handed Sir Harold his top hat and gloves before quietly receding.

"Good man," Harry called after him, then turned and followed his friend outdoors. It was a short walk to the main thoroughfare, where they hailed a hackney cab and climbed within. Harry settled himself and remembered that his mother had been asking after the Earl's aunt. "How does Lady Augusta go on? M'mother says its been an age since she has heard from her and she wants her news. Likes it in the country, doesn't she? Stays there for months on end. Odd that." He frowned over this, for he had always been happier on the town. Even the lure of fox hunting could never keep him far from London for very long.

"Hmmm, seems to. Never gave it much thought. In-volved with that orphanage of hers and Uncle Wizzy enjoys seeing to his estates. I suppose that keeps them there." The Earl shrugged this off, growing bored with the subject, and resignedly remarked, "But I fancy they will be along very shortly."

"Do you? Well, m'mother will be pleased enough to hear it." He eyed the Earl. "Though I can see you don't fancy the notion much. What's towards? Thought you liked Wizzy and Gussie?

"Don't be daft. I adore Gussie and my uncle, but damnation—I won't be drawn into my aunt's schemes, and mark me, Harry, she has mischief planned."

Harry didn't like the sound of this and immediately shot his friend a worried look. "Schemes? What schemes?"

"I can't tell, but I have this peculiar feeling that my loving Gussie means to draw me into her plans. This last letter of hers has sent chills up my spine."

Harry was near panic. "We'll go out of town. Only thing to do." There wasn't the slightest doubt in his mind that if the Earl was going to be drawn into Lady Augusta's machinations, he too would be drawn into them.

"Harry . . . look there." The Earl's tone suddenly changed as he noticed a strikingly lovely female in a red velvet walking ensemble with silver frogging. He sig-nalled for the hack to come to a halt and immediately alighted.

"Cameron!" complained Harry indignantly as he fol-lowed his friend out of the cab. "Devil a bit . . . what are you at now?" It was then that he observed a perfectly beautiful creature batting her lovely eyes in a most sug-gestive manner at them both. "Well, I say . . ."

Manton's boxing match was momentarily forgotten as

the two men took up a flirtation with this lovely woman, who was as adept as they in the very fine art of dalliance.

Chapter Four

Sir Anthony took Lilly's chin and tilted her face for his kiss. She had no fortune, but he meant to have her now, in the woods, with no one the wiser. What did it matter? He would soon be married to Cynthia Edwards and safely out of reach. Lilly's relatives would not want it known that she was a fallen woman. Perhaps he could even have her as his mistress in the future. He would certainly have money enough to keep her for as long as he wanted.

Pulled into his arms, Lilly allowed him the kiss, but as it increased in intensity she pulled away. "Stop, Anthony. I shouldn't be here."

"Yet you are."

She blushed. She was surprised at herself. Why had she agreed to meet him this way? It was wrong. Why had he asked it of her? She felt his arm go round her again, felt his hand on her slim waist. This was dreadfully wrong. She pulled away from him. "No. I must go home . . ."

"You are frightened. You needn't be," he coaxed. Again, he had her in his arms. This time his kiss insisted on a response, and he won one. He had the advantage, for Lilly believed that he loved her. She also believed that she loved him. He started to move his hand up from her waist. Like a splash of cold water in her face, that made Lilly react. She pulled angrily out of his grasp.

"Anthony! I must go." She turned, ignoring the voice calling to *her, and quickly untethered her horse, nimbly hoisting herself onto the sidesaddle. She was angry and confused, and did not look back as she rode away.*

That had been five days ago. Five days and she had not heard a word from him. It was beginning to hurt. The notion that he was indeed a fortune hunter, a cad, a rogue of the worst kind was taking root in her mind. Her aunt and her godmother might just be right. Then again, perhaps he was displeased with her for the childish way she had ridden off. No, he should not have tried to seduce her. It had been wrong. Gentlemen did not treat the women they loved in that manner. Did they? Confusion set in. Because of false hopes. Five bleak days and no Anthony. However, Stuart had called and had spent a goodly time complaining that Sir Anthony nearly lived at Cynthia Edwards' home these days.

Lilly was riding, wearing britches and a short riding coat, for she needed to ride hard and jump free, but as she approached a wide fallen tree she mistimed her pace and took the jump badly. Softly she berated herself before patting her chestnut mare's neck and murmuring, "Not your fault, lovey."

Lilly slowed her horse down to a walk. There was a lovely spring breeze, and it played with the long black curls framing her face. The sun's rays filtered through the forest, creating irregular patches of light on the pine needles and new spring growth. Lilly smiled at the beauty of the place and then stopped her horse abruptly. Ahead were two people just off the bridle path. She really didn't feel very much like chatting. Then a movement, a glint of gold, and she knew. Sir Anthony. The sun's light gleamed on his bright tresses. Cynthia was enfolded in his embrace as she herself had been only five days before. Lilly spun her horse around and clucked the mare into motion.

Stuart had been right. Sir Anthony Meade had been playing fast and loose with her and with Cynthia. Her aunt and her dearest Gussie had been right. She had wronged them. All of those around her had known, yet she had been nought but a stupid green girl! It was humiliating. It was . . . Oh, faith, it was very nearly breaking her heart. Tears streamed down her cheeks. Stupid, stupid girl, she berated herself. Suddenly a fence loomed before her. Timing, her timing was all wrong. Her mare shied, throwing her off center, and then popped the line fence like an amateur. Lilly went flying over her horses's neck and landed with a thump!

Missy whinnied with concern and nimbly inched her way to Lilly's slumped form. Her mistress was crying, and the sound distressed the mare. As she nuzzled her, Lilly pushed herself up from the ground. She was bruised, but nothing was broken. She touched her mare's nose, held it for a moment and then burst into heart-wrenching sobs. It was the end, the harsh end of her first real dream.

Lady Augusta Wizbough put her cup of tea down on the coffee table and got to her feet. Sarah watched her friend pace. Gussie was Lilly's godmother. She was a warmhearted, gentle creature of magnificent height and imposing presence adored by her considerable number of friends and by her family, but there was no gainsaying the fact that she was a totally domineering woman who felt Lilly was within her domain. This, both Lilly and Sarah had allowed, as Gussie had lost her only child, a daughter, to a fatal illness and had been childless since. However, at this moment Sarah was losing patience with her good friend.

"Just what would you have me do, Gussie?"

"Put your foot down. Tell her she can not, must not allow this awful cad to single her out as he has been doing. It is so very odious of him. Sarah, I know for a fact that the Edwardses believe he means to make an offer for Cynthia."

"Gussie, do sit, please." Sarah patted a place beside herself on the yellow damask sofa. "You quite tower above me when you are standing, and it is putting a strain on my neck." This from Sarah whose height was ample.

Lady Augusta sniffed and took up the proffered position beside her friend. Quiet for the moment as she thought the matter over, Lady Sarah smiled to herself. At fifty, Augusta was very alluring. She had never been a beauty precisely, yet there was that in her features, in her style, that was very arresting, as were her frankness of manner and her polished charm. Sarah had been pleased to watch Lilly learn a great deal from the Lady Augusta.

Gussie touched Lady Sarah's soft hand. "We must take hold of the matter, my dear. We must tell her what we know about Sir Anthony." Gussie shook her head. "There is no more sparing her feelings. In fact, we should tell Mr. Edwards about Sir Anthony's duplicity. I don't think he should have Cynthia . . . do you?"

"Gussie, don't meddle." Sarah shook her head. "As to Lilly, I don't think anything we say will make a difference. I do believe she feels she is in love with him. We know 'tis only her first infatuation, but to her 'tis quite real."

The morning-room door opened, and Lilly stood on its threshold. She was disheveled and sullied from her fall. Her long black tresses were in a wild mass round her head and her tear-stained cheeks told a story all its own. Both women jumped to their feet and ran to her.

"Dearest . . . oh love . . . What has happened? Have you had a fall?"

Lilly burst into tears again. "Oh yes, oh yes . . ."

Sarah and Gussie exchanged glances, but this was no time for speculation. They enfolded Lilly in their arms and began the business of assuaging her hurts.

Lilly got a hold of herself and touched their hands. "I'm fine . . . I think I'll just go and have a long hot bath. 'Tis a good thing I didn't injure Missy. I . . . I took the fence so very poorly you see . . ." Lilly moved away from them, unable to confide in them her real hurt. She had always done so in the past, but this, this was different.

They watched her go and Gussie turned a wagging finger. "You see, I knew it would come to this! Sarah, our girl is going into a decline. Something is wrong, and I mean to discover just what is towards, see if I don't!"

Chapter Five

Lilly took a stack of books and set them aside. A breeze filtered through her long black hair, and she took a moment to look out of the window towards the children's spring garden. Here at Lymington Orphanage, gardening was one of the chief occupations these children were geared to learn. There, too, sewing and housekeeping were taught to the girls, and because it was a country "home," a barnyard of sorts was maintained through donations, thus enabling the boys to learn occupations in livery and barnyard management.

The children were quietly busy at their afternoon chores as Lilly worked alone, setting the last of the many books they had compiled into a semblance of order. She liked working in solitude and was glad for the quiet, happy that her aunt and godmother were otherwise occupied this afternoon. She needed to be with herself.

A young housemaid peeped in at the library entrance to smile a greeting at Lilly. "All alone are ye, miss?"

"Suzy, hallo. Yes, I've been at these books for an age. Hopefully, my aunt will catalog the last of them tomorrow morning." Lilly smiled.

The girl walked into the room and reached for one of the leather-bound books that rested on the children's round work tables. She held it for a moment before venturing the piece of gossip she had in mind. " 'Tis said the children have handsome Lord Raeburn to thank for these."

Lilly studied her for a moment. Something in the girl's voice caught her attention, and indeed, the maid's crooked little smile was oddly intriguing. "That is true enough. He is Lady Augusta's nephew, after all." The explanation given, Lilly expected this line of conversation to end.

She was wrong. Suzy swung her hip round the table to bring herself closer and say on a confidential note, "Ay then, oi know that right well. As tall as she is, he stands a good foot taller, too." She clucked her tongue in admiring tones. "The very broth of a man, he is!"

This was too tantalizing to pass. Lilly knew the rules. One did not gossip with the servants, but Suzy was almost her own age and somehow that spanned the difference in class. "Oh, have you met him, Suzy?"

"Lord love ye, miss, 'twas some years ago . . . and oi was but sixteen. I had just started working here when he came by with Lady Augusta to see the new wing." She sighed at this juncture. "When he smiled at me, oi thought oi would swoon, oi did."

Lilly smiled. "So then, he is handsome? I have never met him. When he was here visiting, my aunt and I were in Brighton."

"Well, miss, oi have never met a man to compare to him." She shook her mop-capped head of short brown curls. "Left me broken-hearted and no good to no other man."

"Suzy!" Lilly was shocked. "Upon my soul . . . never say so. Do you say he dallied dishonestly with you?"

Suzy giggled, "Not he, and oi didn't find a dishonest thing about him. Lord love ye, miss. Oi loiked him well enough to find meself tripping into him as much as oi could, and he did jest whot oi expected any red-blooded man to do . . . he kissed me." She sighed with the memory.

"Suzy . . . how awful for you. The beast!"

"Beast? No, no, you mistake my meaning, miss. Beast he would 'ave been if he left here without paying me any mind. He never meant me no 'arm. Never made me no promise . . . 'ow could he? Bumped 'im for a kiss, oi did, and was happy to 'ave it. Then off he went, never more thinking of me, but oi thinks of him oi do." She shook her head. "Lord love him."

Lilly thought of Sir Anthony. A very different case. He had pursued her and with intent to seduce her. He had broken her heart, and he had known what he was doing.

"Why would someone like Lord Raeburn be interested in an orphanage so far away from London?" Lilly frowned as she asked the question.

"Rumour has it that perhaps he has a guilty conscience."

"What does that mean?" Lilly bit her lip as soon as she asked the question. She was fast learning a great deal, and she knew the answer almost as soon as the words left her mouth.

"Well, a virile man like his lordship . . . with girls throwing themselves at him, as they must, well then, there is no saying how many little ones he has left in his wake!" summed up Suzy.

Lilly's present mood was unforgiving. Ah then, he was no better than Sir Anthony. These handsome rogues were cads. One had to be wary, forever wary. Three weeks had gone by since she had seen Sir Anthony kissing Cynthia. He had played her for a fool, he had tried to use her. If only she had the means to repay him for his cruelty. Lilly had never been spiteful, but here was a man who went about using innocent females. He should be taught a lesson. This was, however, not possible. More depressing still was the thought that he no doubt found her so easy to forget.

"Well then, miss, oi better get about my business before headmistress comes looking for me."

"Yes, thank you, Suzy, I enjoyed our chat."

Sarah paced to and fro across the intricate carpet that adorned the morning-room floor. She stopped at the window overlooking the drive, but there still was no sign of Lilly. She would be coming home from the orphanage soon. She put her hand up to a silver curl and unconsciously played with it a moment before tucking it behind her ear,

"Now, just what are we to do?"

"Bless our good fortune," retorted Augusta with an unladylike snort. "Wizzy says it is for the best. Indeed, I do feel sorry for poor young Cynthia, but that fine young man . . . you know . . . what is his name . . . ?"

"Stuart?"

"That's the one. Young Stuart is there to comfort her. Mrs. Edwards feels certain she was not really attached to that odious fellow, Meade!"

"I am glad of that. You know, Augusta, I was feeling very uneasy that we were allowing Cynthia Edwards to be courted by Sir Anthony?"

"Now, Sarah, that is wide of the mark!" Augusta huffed. "You said we shouldn't meddle."

"Well, that is true, too. Oh, I am just glad we are all out of the business. If only Lilly's poor heart wasn't taking such a dreadful beating . . . I really did not think she was so very attached to Sir Anthony Meade."

"She was not attached to him, she was attached to the notion of first love, her first knight in shining armour. He crumbled right before her eyes, and she felt the fool. Lilly does not like to play the fool," Augusta summed up wisely.

"What I don't understand is why would Sir Anthony suddenly rush off to London when it was obvious he meant to marry Cynthia's fortune?"

"You can't see it? Sarah, you are quite naive," Augusta exclaimed, "Cynthia's fortune is nought to that of the Hawkinses'. The Hawkinses' fortune is one of the greatest in all of England!"

"Yes, but how could Meade know for certain that he could have the Hawkinses' daughter? How could he know that?"

"My nephew writes that the gossip mongers have it that Sir Anthony long ago put out lures in that direction, but Mr. Hawkins was then not ready to bring his daughter out and have her married."

"Yes, but—"

"Cameron . . ." Augusta stopped herself and eyed Sarah for a moment. "Do you remember my nephew? I think you only met him once many years ago. Before his title. He was then Cameron Mitchell?"

"Nooo . . ."

Augusta cut her off. "Never mind. The thing is, my nephew knows all one must know to survive in the *beau monde*. I wrote him, you see, and inquired about Sir Anthony, and his reply was that Mr. Hawkins is in the market for a title . . . and bets are being taken that Sir Anthony will appear on the scene."

"Well, I must say it was dastardly. He was all but bethrothed to Cynthia Edwards and then off he went."

"Exactly so. My nephew writes that Sir Anthony has a very good chance of winning Elizabeth Hawkins' hand in marriage before the month is out." Augusta lowered her voice. "Mr. Hawkins has installed his family in Kensington for the London season."

"Sir Anthony may be titled, but he is quite, quite vulgar."

"So it is. Wizzy is forever telling me that breeding has nought to do with birth, and he is quite right you know."

"What can have induced Sir Anthony to leave a . . . well . . . a situation that was at hand for something that may not take?"

"Ah, dearest, you haven't realized then? Mr. Hawkins may be the richest man in all of England, but his wealth is derived from trade!"

"Oh . . . oh . . . I see."

"Indeed, Hawkins made his fortune in wool. He means to settle all his estates on his only child, but he has a fancy to buy her a place in society. Meade's name is old and steeped in tradition. It is a logical connection for them both."

"Then Meade means to marry into trade," Lady Sarah said out loud as she thought this over. The aristocracy were raised to consider such an alliance a mésalliance, a taboo.

"Does he, by Jove?" Lilly remarked brightly as she entered the room and greeted both women with a smile that held no warmth. "Well then, once again, you should be pleased with yourselves. Sir Anthony Meade, man of the hour, is even lower than I had decided him to be."

Sarah was exasperated with herself. She had watched at the window for the last fifteen minutes because she did not want Lilly to walk in on this conversation. How very annoying. She put a hand out to her niece and quietly responded, "Is that what you think, dear?"

37

Lilly went to her at once and hugged her. "No . . . of course not. But, Aunt Sarah, I was so blind. How could I have been so very blind?"

"Stuart said it over and over darling," Sarah answered gently, "You had stardust in your eyes. 'Tis allowed to youth. 'Tis a lesson some of us learn the hard way. You are well out of it. Poor Cynthia pays a dearer price."

Lilly moved to the window, dropping a kiss on Lady Augusta's cheek as she passed. "Yes . . . At least Stuart, patient Stuart, did not stray from his purpose. It will help her . . . perhaps." She turned to look at her godmother. "I heard part of what was said . . . Apparently Sir Anthony has left town—oh, yes, I knew that he was gone—to pursue a larger morsel."

"Apparently," said Lady Augusta. "At least you are seeing things clearly, my girl."

"How could I see them otherwise, Gussie?" Lilly's fine dark brows were up. "Sir Anthony is more than just a fortune hunter. I did not tell you, but knowing I had no fortune did not stop him from trying to get me to his bed. I didn't tell either of you that before. However, it is a truth I have faced up to in these last few weeks. He is—"

"A blackguard!" ejaculated Gussie angrily.

Lilly eyed her for a moment and then suddenly giggled.

"Yes, love, he is a blackguard." Her storybook knight had taken his last plunge. He had played hard with her heart, he had broken poor Cynthia's and why, because a larger fortune out there awaited his pleasure. He was beneath contempt! She would not spend another moment feeling sorry for herself. 'Twas over!

"Well then, our girl will do," said Augusta, pleased.

"It has to hurt, child, before it can heal." She was patting her side of the sofa. "Come here, Lilly."

Lilly moved away from the window and dropped heavily down beside her godmother who enveloped her in her arms a moment before patting her back bracingly, "There now. Wizzy has the solution. Don't know why I didn't see it myself, but Wizzy is such a wondrous clever fellow." Augusta eyed Lilly calculatingly. "You see, Wizzy thinks we should all go to London and enjoy the season ... and he wants us to leave immediately!"

Lilly's attention was caught. "London? I ... I can not ... the children's library?"

"We will have that completely done by tomorrow afternoon." Augusta snorted.

"Augusta, I am afraid that Lillian and I can not accept. We simply can not afford a London season. The cost of gowns and such are beyond my means." Sarah's voice was low, disturbed.

"What have you to do with this? It was Wizzy's idea and Wizzy means to cover us for the season. *He* can well afford it!" retorted Augusta majestically. Then quickly, before Sarah could make further objections, she added, "Lilly darling, we shall take you to Almack's, for you must know that your aunt and I are on the closest terms with the Jersey, and as I recall she was quite fond of your dear mother as well. We shall attend routs, soirées, the theatre and of course, Wizzy and I mean to throw you a ball. It will be grand!"

"A ball ... vouchers to Almack's?" Lilly was momentarily stunned.

"Yes, think of it, child. There will be gowns for every occasion. We have our own stables in London as well, so you may bring that lovely mare of yours to ride in Hyde Park. Sarah and I shall go about in our town phaeton and cut quite a picture. Famous good sport driving through the park at the fashionable hour and nodding to one's acquaintances. I am very, very excited for us all!"

"Augusta, this is impossible. I can not impose on Wizzy's generosity." Sarah's hand was on her hot cheek.

Gussie bent suddenly and looked at her friend. "Sarah ... 'tis just what I need. Do you realize my daughter would have been eighteen this summer? Don't say me nay in this—Lilly is like my own."

Sarah capitulated at once and threw a comforting arm around her friend.

"Dearest Gussie ... I am so sorry. Of course ..."

Lilly hugged her godmother as well, and there was a moment's silence broken only by sniffling before they all moved in search of handkerchieves.

"There is so much to do ..." Sarah fretted for a moment after she attended to her nose.

"It shall be done; mark me on this, Sarah. We will see to it that the ladies of Lymington attend properly to the children at the Home before we depart and with peace of mind, we shall go and take London by storm!"

Lilly thought of London. She had not been there since she was twelve. London with its fashion, its history, its sights ... its poor and its fortune hunters! She was going to London. *He* was in London. Would she see him there? Would it hurt to see him there? It would hurt to see him and not be able to kick him in the shins. A tear nearly left her eye, but anger prevented it. No more tears, she told herself. Not for such as he!

Chapter Six

London! Was she really here? She looked at herself in the ornately framed, long looking glass. Was that her reflection looking back? Could that fashionable miss really be Miss Lillian Aulderbury of Lymington? Her dusky curls had been cropped and styled in a perfection of fashionable disorder around her pretty face. The gown she wore—one of several Augusta had chosen for her season—clung alluringly to her firm provocative figure. The gown, a pale shade of pink, was somewhat lower scooped at the bodice than anything she had ever worn before, and she blushed to see herself so attractively exposed. A dark pink velvet, wide sash accentuated the high waist, and a matching velvet ribbon ornamented with a cluster of pearl drops adorned her fine neck. The total effect was very nearly outstanding she told herself silently, with a fleeting thought of Sir Anthony. Something inside of her wanted him to see her and regret his actions, wanted more, much more than his regret! Notions of justice, sweet justice, were forever plaguing her.

Lilly was expected to present herself downstairs as they were receiving any number of morning callers. Her aunt and Gussie seemed pleased enough with the schedule they had been maintaining since their emergence in

London some days ago. They had no idea that only yesterday Lilly had very nearly bumped into Sir Anthony and that something very dangerous had clicked in her mind. She closed her eyes now as she recalled sighting the blackguard. He was princely in appearance in his town finery. He had been chatting with a merry young pretty at his side, totally unconcerned for the young girls he had hurt in Lymington. Well, well, this could not go on!

A knock at Lilly's door nearly made her jump, and she quickly removed all thought of Sir Anthony from her mind. Sarah stuck in a smiling face. "Coming, love? Faith! You do make a stunning picture. Augusta was quite right; I am very glad we took that gown after all. Pink is certainly one of your colors."

Sarah's aura was, as ever, calm and collected. Little fazed her, and some of this special quality had extended itself to Lilly over the years. Sarah opened the door wide as Lilly approached and was pleased to see that her niece did not appear nervous or missish. She and Augusta had certainly given the girl social exposure, but that had been in the country and now Lilly was about to enter the *beau monde*.

Lilly stopped at the doorway and gave her aunt a saucy appraisal.

"Well and look at you ..." She touched the lace of her aunt's pretty white fichu. "Very becoming."

Sarah touched the wide lace and beamed. "And such a marvelous bargain as well. Gussie took me to the Parthenon yesterday when you were out riding with the Lady Jersey." She patted her niece's arm with sure approval. "Gussie tells me the Jersey was quite impressed with you. Said you were a delightful girl very much like your mother. She also said that I did an excellent job with you." Sarah was attempting to modestly hide some of the pride she felt by lowering her gaze to the oriental runner beneath their satin-covered feet.

Lilly laughed and touched her aunt's hand. "Indeed, no other could have whipped that wild young zany into a semblance of a female."

"Stop now, you were no zany. Wild . . . perhaps," Sarah conceded with a short laugh. "I must say, though, you were a handful. Very high-spirited, but always, always, within bounds. At any rate, the Jersey said she found you a refreshing miss with wit as well as a great deal of countenance. High praise indeed from Old Silence herself. Vouchers to Almack's are definitely on their way!"

Lilly giggled. "Faith! All this fuss about Almack's. 'Tis all such fustian. Dress code, time code, social code." Lilly waved her hand in the air. "Seems to me all the wrong things are prized."

Sarah sighed. "To be certain, but such is society and, my dear, if you are to be a success, you must conform."

"Conform you say?" Lilly's hand went to her forehead in mock dismay. "No, no, oh woe is me."

Sarah laughed and gave her niece's arm a gentle smack. "Enough! Now, put on your town manners, my love, we are about to meet Gussie's precious nephew. 'Tis all I have heard about for days. Cameron this, and the Earl that!"

Lilly wrinkled her nose. "I am dreading this. I have heard *such* things about him."

"Don't believe gossip, my love."

"Yes, but—"

"Lilly, gossip is a terrible thing to rely upon. Try always to wait till you can see for yourself just what a truth may be."

"Yes, but—" Lilly pursued.

"Enough!" warned Lady Sarah quietly.

Lilly, however, was now in a bantering mood and took a few unladylike strutting steps forward. "Ah then, is he here to look me over?"

"To what purpose, pray?"

"Well, perhaps Gussie means to marry me off to her nephew?"

"Dreadful child. Stop that at once."

"Shall I be smitten by the Earl of Raeburn and fall beneath his spell? They say all females are subject to his charms, you know."

"Lilly, you are incorrigible!" Sarah laughed. "Now come along, you silly puss. The Earl is nearly thirty, very sophisticated and very sought after. There probably isn't a woman in London that wouldn't set out snares to win him for herself or her daughter, but I doubt that you will fall under his spell."

"Will he perhaps fall under mine then?" Lilly was wiggling her shoulders.

Her aunt stopped her and firmly replied. "He will not. I have no fear of that."

Lilly considered this for a moment. "Good, then we all understand one another and no one is playing matchmaker?"

"What a nonsensical notion. Neither one of you would suit the other, of that you can be sure." Sarah opened the door to the Wizboughs' morning room and moved quietly within. The Earl of Raeburn and Sir Harold immediately jumped to their feet and moved forward. Sir Harold's appreciative glance rested on Lilly's face and he breathed a soft,

"By Jove . . . yes, by Jove!" Harry finally was able to take her hand, put it to his eager lips and advise the new beauty that he was, "Enchanted, Miss Aulderbury, completely and totally enchanted."

Lilly smiled warmly at him. She liked his freckled

face, his thick reddish brows and his mass of carrot-colored hair, but she was pulled along quickly by Augusta and presented to the Earl of Raeburn. She had a quick moment to take his measure and saw at once that he was certainly an attractive specimen of masculine form—just the sort to break hearts. She noted that his hair was light brown and sprinkled with silver. She had a quick hazy sensation of his height as he towered above her and a sure notion that he was broad and powerfully built. However, it was his deep blue eyes that caught her attention as he bent to perfunctorily kiss her hand.

The Earl of Raeburn had come at his aunt's command. He had no interest in meeting her godchild and was thoroughly disgusted at his having allowed himself to be ordered about by his aunt. He was momentarily surprised that the "country bumpkin" he had been summoned to meet was such a startling beauty, but he was not overly impressed. After all, beauty was a commodity he was subjected to wherever he went. It was the tool of womankind. He was ever on his guard when beauty was present.

Some of his ennui displayed itself on his face and in his cynical smile. Lilly's brows went up for she was an intuitive and sensitive miss. His expression was not lost on her. Feathers, which had already been ruffled by her aunt's earlier comments, fluffed to a peak now, and she turned almost curtly away from him as she quietly said, "Ah, I see you, too, are enchanted, completely and totally."

Cameron Mitchell, Earl of Raeburn, was momentarily taken aback. His distinctive brows went up and his blue eyes reexamined their prey. Well, just what was this? A country bumpkin with a tongue?

"Indeed," he answered easily, his sensuous lips curving ever so slightly. "How astute of you to notice." He

45

inclined his handsome head by way of acknowledging her hit.

"Nay, my lord. You made no secret of it," countered the lady. Lilly's sense of humour took over, and she laughed at this juncture, for clearly he did not know what to make of her. Her grey eyes flashed her understanding, but surely here was a conceited, rude rake of a fellow and she knew better than to allow him the benefit of the doubt. Never again would she be taken in by a rogue! She dismissed him and immediately took a chair beside Sir Harold, inviting him to join her in conversation.

Harry was awestruck, which was not uncommon for him. Pretty faces usually sent him reeling towards infatuation. He would find himself in and out of love nearly every other month. However, here was more than just a pretty face. Lilly's knowledge of hounds, horses and hunting was soon discovered. Fox hunting took over their conversation and led them quickly into a comfortable friendship. They found one another much in accord and conversation flowed between them easily and continuously.

The Earl sat back and idly chatted with his aunt and Lady Sarah about the latest *on-dit*, but he found himself straining to hear bits and pieces of Harry's conversation with his aunt's godchild. She was certainly a lively piece. He found it immensely irritating that she had summarily dismissed him, which he was fair enough to acknowledge to himself was what he had done to her even before they had met. Nonetheless, the Earl was used to very different treatment from the ladies of his acquaintance.

Lilly glanced only once in his direction. He inclined his head as though he knew she must look towards him. This annoyed her no end, and she turned her grey eyes once more to Harry, determined not to look the Earl's way again that morning. He was obviously arrogant, puffed up as to his own consequence. She had been led about by a cad of a rake and knew how the game was played. Well, she would not play with the Earl. It was her turn to hold the reins! Thus the Season began.

Chapter Seven

As it turned out, Lord Wizbough's arrival in London was delayed. His lady received an affectionate missive advising her that his northern estates needed his personal attention and he would not find himself with her for another two weeks. He advised her to call on their nephew, the Earl of Raeburn, for escort.

Augusta was not in the least daunted by her beloved's absence. In fact, it fit right in with her schemes. Cameron's escort could only help launch Lilly's entrance into the *beau monde*'s select camp. Gussie was very quick to do as her husband suggested, and a note was taken by hand to Raeburn's townhouse posthaste.

The Earl's response to his aunt's demands was explosive. He shook his aunt's letter at his collie. "Sheba, do you see? Did I not tell you how it would be?"

Sheba panted expressively in sympathy, lay down and put her head between her paws. Her master made a disgusted sound. "She wants me to give her and her houseguests escort to the Branden soirée? I wasn't going to attend the Branden soirée!"

He repeated his complaints to Harry later that morning and discovered his friend was more than willing to make up one of the party. Thus, it was he found himself and Harry later that evening taking a coach ride to the Branden soirée.

He studied Lilly as she chatted happily with Harry and ignored him. What a rude little country bumpkin she was. A beauty though, no denying that. Her black curls gleamed in the carriage's dim light, and her profile was certainly exquisite. Augusta mentioned Castlereagh, and Sarah's response was quick and angry. Politics was one of the Earl's passions. He soon discovered himself in the midst of a supremely interesting debate. Lilly surprised him with her opinions. Not only was she well informed on the current issues, she had an intriguing way of putting her opinions forward. It made one take note. Oddly enough, when the carriage ride was over, he was disappointed. However, once within the Branden townhouse, Lilly soon gathered a group of young men and women about her, and politics again took over the conversation. What would have been an insipid evening turned out to be a lively affair that the Earl enjoyed immensely.

Thus it was, when the Earl was called upon a few days later to give the ladies his escort to a Venetian Breakfast, he did not utter more than one or two complaints to his collie, Sheba. This time, she cocked her head inquiringly because his words and tone did not match.

Time and time again the Earl found himself quietly appraising Lilly as she animately conversed with one gentleman and then another. He watched how she conducted herself with society's debutantes and was intrigued to observe the natural manner in which she won these standoffish misses to her court. This was due in part to the fact that Lilly had acquired quite a collection of young admiring bachelors. There she had Lady Augusta as her sponsor; Augusta had long ago won over society's pinks of the *ton*.

The Earl needed no more than a slight dutiful prompting to take the ladies to the Great Parade in Hyde Park. His constant companion on these jaunts, Sir Harry, was otherwise engaged, but even this the Earl took with amiable acceptance.

It was a clear bright spring day. The sun's rays glowed on the yellow daffodils which lined flowerbeds along the Serpentine. As they walked the park's winding pathway and raved about the perfection of the day, Lady Augusta and Sarah were hailed by a bevy of acquaintants. While the ladies chatted happily, the Earl turned to offer his arm to Lilly. She certainly looked enticing in her pretty blue walking frock with its matching blue silk bonnet. He noticed her glittering grey eyes and thought for a brief moment that he had never witnessed such warmth; then Lilly destroyed the moment by cocking her head at him and pronouncing, "No . . . don't do it, my lord."

"Don't do it?"

"No, you must not." She wagged a finger.

"Very well, I shall not." He smiled. "If you but tell me what it is I must not do."

"Don't flirt with me," she returned frankly. "I won't have it."

"You won't?" Tongue in cheek. "What makes you think I was going to flirt with you?"

"Weren't you?"

"Brazen little hussy, you deserve that I do . . ." He was smiling now and noticing that her grey eyes were twinkling.

"There you are, thinking a great deal of yourself and deciding the tediousness of a spring day might better be explored with a bit of dallying. Ah, here I stand just waiting for you to pay me a compliment and flutter my heart," Lilly said in way of explanation. "I won't have it. It won't do. You are a rake, and I am but a green girl. Pity, but there it is."

He laughed. "What you are is a minx if ever there was one. Are you sure you were raised in the country?"

"Well, as to that I traveled quite a great deal with my parents before they died. Picked up cosmopolitan ways in Florence, Paris, and London. I was just a child, but children do learn things here and there," she answered thoughtfully, and then quickly added, "I think we should understand one another . . . since we are together so much, you see."

"I see . . . or do I?" rallied his lordship, bemused.

"You do. Look here, I am eighteen. A ripe age for plucking, but I do know a thing or two. Harry tells me there is no other he would call friend before you. That means something to me. That means there is probably a bit more to you than you want missish girls"—she batted her lashes at him expressively—"like me to see. However, I still believe you think yourself a dashing fellow and so you are, but I don't want your heart, your hand or your soul. I don't mean to fall under your spell, and I shan't cast any lures in your direction. If that is agreeable, we may continue tolerably comfortable with one another, don't you think?"

"Well, I don't know. You are, after all, a beauty; I thought I would add you to my collection of virgins." There was a steel glint of anger in his deep blue eyes.

Lilly was a bit surprised. "Ah, I have insulted you?"

"As it happens, Miss Aulderbury, I do not seduce virgins—of any class."

"Do you not? Not all rogues are so . . . thoughtful," Lilly answered quietly, sarcastically. "So then, we shall move forward. Harry did say you don't play games with missish types."

"I could, however, make an exception and stray from my well-ordered path. You see . . . you deserve my special attention."

"Ah, you are flirting, and I won't have it." Lilly giggled.

"Yes, for it would be so very interesting to seduce you. Such a challenge you see."

"Very well. If you must, have at me," retorted Lilly much amused.

"Agreed, Lillian Aulderbury. You will make no attempt to ensnare my heart, my hand or my soul. I on the other hand shall take every opportunity to seduce you."

"Sounds like famous good sport." Lilly laughed.

The next forty minutes were spent in taking Lilly over the grounds which were filled with various tents displaying wares of every imaginable sort. Lilly oohed and aahed. She clapped her hands and exclaimed enthusiastically over nearly everything. He found her childlike merriment entertaining until they were approached by a beggar. Here, his lordship attempted to steer her away from the ugliness of the world. He was honourbound as a gentleman to do just that when escorting a lady. Lilly would have none of it. She touched his lordship's hand, then tugged at his finger and whispered, "Please, my lord, he needs help. Please . . . don't you see he is missing an arm? Think what his life in this hard city must be like?" Her grey eyes raked his lordship's face.

The Earl's attention was fairly caught, and he found himself turning to put a substantial coin into the beggar's tin cup. One man's gaze met the other's and he was conscious of feeling something he had not felt in a long, long time. He took hold of Lilly's elbow then and gently steered her off. "Come then, child. He will do for one more day."

"Yes, but, my lord, 'tis wicked. Here we are, dressed in all our finery, and men like him—all over the city—are starving. These are our people, English people. They are starving on English streets. 'Tis unthinkable, unpardonable. Something must be done . . ."

"Ay then, we are agreed on that, but there is little we can do when a man like Castlereagh and his Tory faction control the blasted government," he answered on a harsh note.

Lilly looked at him for a long moment, intrigued by this new side of his personality. "Indeed, I used to be fascinated by the Regent and all his antics until he made Lord Liverpool Prime Minister. I mean, really! If ever there was a High Tory—"

"Ay then, a rare dust was kicked up over that one, but it is not Liverpool we Whigs abhor. 'Tis Castlereagh, my girl. That is a cold, narrow, obstinate and hard-headed fellow."

"Yes, Aunt Sarah says he is detested outside the Tory establishment." Lilly shook her head. "She and Augusta say we shall never have any help for our poor orphans while he is in power."

"Quite right. He is responsible for all the deep discontents of this country, and *I,* for one, put the rioting we have had to suffer at his door!"

"Why did the Regent go that route?"

"The Regent? My dear child, he may be a likeable fool, but fool he still is."

"That is rather harsh." Lilly smiled. "But, from what I have heard, it seems true enough, I suppose. I thought I might get a glimpse of him tonight, but Gussie says he is suffering a badly bruised foot."

He eyed Lilly and snapped caustically. "His suffering

is higher than the foot. A blister on the head might be more efficacious than a poultice on the ankle."

Lilly giggled and was just thinking that there was a great deal more to Augusta's conceited nephew than his good looks and title when she froze in place. Her kid-gloved hand reached for and clutched his lordship's superfine dark blue sleeve. The Earl looked at her and was surprised to see that her cheeks were white. He followed her line of vision and noted that she was staring fixedly at a gentleman standing some thirty feet away. He knew the man to be Sir Anthony Meade. His brows went up, but she was already tugging at him. "Please, my lord . . . please, we have to go." She breathed out the words as if in a panic. She didn't want Anthony to see her just yet.

"Do we?" the Earl quizzed.

"Yes, yes."

Puzzled by her sudden change of mood, he took her gloved hand firmly in his own and, though he did not quite understand what was wrong, smiled reassuringly. "Well, of course, if you like. Look there, an organ grinder."

As there was a small monkey perched on the organ grinder's shoulder this was a successful diversion and he led her in that direction. At their backs Sir Anthony Meade was left to stare at their receding forms.

Sir Anthony frowned for a moment as he attempted to place a name to the pretty face. Lilly was, after all in clothing designed by a modiste of the first stare, and her long black curls had been shaped and reorganized into the latest mode beneath her becoming bonnet. However, her name did come to Sir Anthony and his eyes narrowed into slits. Well, well, the little country beauty here? Lillian Aulderbury on the Earl of Raeburn's arm? What was this? Had the Earl succeeded where he had failed? Had the Earl made the woman his mistress? How else could she be here, dressed in expensive style? He had learned that such things were mightily against Lady Sarah's means to provide for her ward. Sir Anthony watched them for a length of time before he returned his attention to the two young women he had been entertaining. Miss Lillian Aulderbury ... Raeburn's mistress? This would take some looking into before the day was over.

Later, while Lilly was soaking in a soapy hot tub she thought of Sir Anthony, what she had felt when she'd seen him earlier in the park, what she felt now. Humiliation, anger, but love? No, there wasn't even a spark of the old feeling. That had died with the knight that had never been! This man, this Sir Anthony, the *real* Sir Anthony was a liar of no mean order. How could she achieve justice with such as he? He could not be made to feel ... he had no emotions. What did he have that she could use? Greed. He had left her for Cynthia. He had left Cynthia for some wealthy tradesman's daughter, and still he kept a string of lovelies about him—just in case, she supposed. Indeed, greed was the only thing that lighted Sir Anthony's heart. How then to pull those heartstrings? This needed thought, deep thought. She would come up with the solution. She was eighteen, and eighteen is an age that knows no bounds.

Hence, Lilly's next logical concept was a picture of Sir Anthony groveling at her dainty feet, begging for her hand in marriage, begging for her attention as she turned up her nose. Why would he want her as his wife now when he did not before? Money. Well, she had none. Abruptly this obstacle reared its hoary head. Reality was such an inconvenient thing. Lilly frowned.

He was here in London to court a wealthy tradesman's daughter. Yet, he had been in the park with women of quite another caliber. Oh, he was terrible. It would serve him right if the tradesman's daughter would not have him. Then he would be in a bind, wouldn't he? If only she could do something?

Today she had been a coward. She had not strolled up to him and slapped his pretty face. Indeed, it was pretty . . . too pretty now that she thought about it. Why had she run like that? Did she feel anything still? No, not really, but she didn't quite want to face Sir Anthony with the Earl beside her. She didn't quite want to expose herself in front of Raeburn. Raeburn? Humph! Why should she care for his opinion? He was just another rogue. Well, perhaps he was a bit better than that . . . perhaps?

An eighteen-year-old girl rarely considers the consequences of her plans. Her mind works on loftier plains. Success much valued has to be achieved. Her goal was to seek revenge—justice—to savor it and thus be at peace. Perhaps she could entrance Sir Anthony with her town manners? Perhaps Raeburn might be a help in this regard? Perhaps Raeburn might enjoy lending himself to her game? Game? What game? Well as to that, she would have to take it as it came. First, Sir Anthony must think that somehow her fortunes had been reversed . . . somehow. Second, he must be enchanted by her new town manners. Third, he must lose all chance of winning the tradesman's daughter. Then Sir Anthony would be hers for the taking! What would she do with him? Why throw him into the sea, the cold black sea!

Chapter Eight

Mrs. Tuthill looked about her with a great deal of satisfaction. Everyone she could hope would be present certainly was. Music flowed; flowers filled the receiving hall and were tastefully arranged throughout her music room. Champagne punch was being appreciated in great quantity, thus assuring her that her guests were all feeling merry. What more could she want? She looked towards Lilly Aulderbury and sighed. She could wish that her daughter had one ounce of that one's extraordinary beauty.

Lilly wore a sea green creation of silk, threaded throughout with seedlike pearls. Its heartshape bodice and high waist displayed her alluring figure with tantalizing style. Her cropped curls of gleaming black twirled round her pretty head, and her smile was as engaging as her manners. She had collected quite a number of friends in her short time in London and was thoroughly enjoying herself. However, Lilly had something on her mind. She had several times attempted to engage the Earl in private conversation, but had not yet found the opportunity to do this and proceed with her plan. She watched him now, and as though sensing her scrutiny from across the room, he turned, caught her glance and raised his glass to her.

Lilly's grey eyes twinkled at him, and his lips formed a soft smile as it occurred to him that the "little country bumpkin" was quickly acquiring "town ways." Was she flirting with him? What did she want?

It was obvious to him that she wanted something. Curious, he went towards her.

Excited by the fact that she had actually managed to catch and hold his attention, she went towards him. They met, and though there was nothing romantic in the meeting, each had forgotten that there were any others in the room with them.

"My lord . . ." started Lilly, almost breathless. "I do so want to talk to you about something."

"Yes, I rather thought you did." The Earl smiled indulgently and took her elbow to steer her into a private corner, for suddenly all senses came alive as the room buzzed around him.

"Did you? Well, that is very clever of you . . . but I was very clever too, was I not?"

"Were you?" teased the Earl.

"You came and I did so want you to, so I must have the knack of it down, don't you think?"

"The knack of calling a man to order with your eyes, you mean?" His own blue eyes were twinkling appreciatively. "Well, let us say that you need not practice the skill any longer—if that is what you have been doing."

She giggled. "Well, I have, but I never counted it before for all the others are such boys." She appraised him. "You on the other hand are quite a coup." Now she was teasing.

He laughed and pinched her nose without thinking. "Right then, little one, what is it that you want?"

She eyed him thoughtfully for a moment and then

tentatively offered, "At home, with my friends, I was quite in the habit of coming right to the point."

"Were you, by Jove? Now why does that not surprise me?"

She peered up as she smiled. "I suppose you would rather I do the polite things first?"

He threw back his head with a shout of laughter. "No, child, be as rude as you like."

" 'Tis more shocking than rude," she answered on a frown.

"Have at me then. It has been a long time since anything or anyone has been able to shock me. I am quite past that."

"Yes, well, you see ... I should like you to ... to make love to me."

The Earl nearly choked on the champagne he was sipping. He had just said he was beyond shocking, but Lilly had managed to shock him very well. "You what?"

"Well, as to that ... I don't really want you to make love to me; at least, not *really.*"

"You don't?" He eyed her more closely. "Now just how much of that punch have you had my girl?"

Lilly giggled. "Not very much, though I knew I wanted to speak with you about this, so I did take two glasses. Or was it three?" She shrugged. "But, I am not bosky, let me assure you."

"Yes, go ahead, assure me." He grinned at her.

"I have a reason for asking you for this favor."

"Favor? What favor are we speaking about?"

He was not making this easy. She looked up at him imploringly. "My lord, don't you understand?"

He frowned. "No, my little girl, I don't."

"I simply want you to make love to me ... in public of course, not in private," she confided.

"Do you, indeed? Only in public? My poor deluded,

bosky girl, it may interest you to know that this particular rake only makes love to his women in private, not in public."

"You still don't understand."

"No, I do not. Just the other day you forbade me even a flirtation . . ." He was wagging his finger disapprovingly.

She laughed and grabbed his finger. "Do stop, my lord. You can't be serious. I mean really! I don't mean really make love to me."

"No, of course not. Just because you have asked that of me, why should I think it?" His brow rose mockingly. "I think perhaps it is not the punch. I think instead, you are mad."

She laughed again and realized she was still holding his gloved finger in her grip. Self-consciously, she released it. "Let me explain."

"Indeed, what an excellent notion."

"What I need you to do is to *pretend* that you are in love with me."

He regarded her as though he were sure she had lost her mind. "That is out of the question."

"Oh, please, don't say that just yet. So much depends on your part in this game. I need your help, my lord. Remember, you are quite safe with me. I shan't try to ensnare you, and I shan't fall a victim to your rakish charms, so we have nothing to fear from one another."

"On the contrary. I begin to fear you greatly." He eyed her with mock gravity, and then silently chided himself for asking the next question. "Why the devil do you want me to do such a thing anyway?"

"It is imperative to my plan," she whispered.

"A wondrous plan, is it?" Openly he mocked.

"Please, my lord, do take me seriously."

"I will, if you will but be serious. For one thing, it is

widely known that I do *not* seduce young women. I do not lead them on falsely or give them false hope. If I were seen in public attempting to win your favor, the gossip mongers would have a field day and in the end we would both be ruined."

"Oh," said Lilly somewhat daunted, "I had not thought of that." She brightened, "Right then, you could just appear taken with me, no more. People would just think you were mildly aroused, that is all."

The Earl was not sipping his champagne any longer, but he nearly choked again. "Mildly aroused? My dear child—"

She cut him off hurriedly. "Well, right then, not aroused . . . but mildly interested in me. Please, my lord, won't you do this for me?"

"Why?" He put the question on the table, and it came from the heart.

"Why should I do this for you, and more importantly, why do you need this thing done?"

"Well, you have reason, saving one, I am your favorite aunt's godchild." She saw this had not moved him. "Also . . . you could do it for a lark. After all, one London season to you must be much like another after having been through so many. This game I should like to play, perhaps it might divert you?"

"How will it do that?" She was absolutely adorable. She was an animated beauty full of spirit and caught his attention at every turn.

"Because, though you are—I am told—a rogue in your own right, apparently you are one with sure, set principles. The rogue I mean to bring down has not an ounce of honour."

"Ah, and who is this blackguard?" The Earl felt something stir his heart. Conflicting feelings momentarily confused his logic. He should end this conversation.

61

He could sense this was leading him into a dangerous complication.

Lilly suddenly stiffened beside him and even if he did not notice this, she then clutched his sleeve with a child-like motion. He followed the line of her gaze and noted that a familiar face had come upon the scene, Sir Anthony Meade. Well, well, he thought to himself. This was beginning to make sense. He remembered his aunt's letters inquiring about Meade, hinting at Miss Aulderbury's interest in the man. Well, well. So, it was because of him, eh? He looked at Lilly's face for a long moment, and he knew a sudden urge to plant Meade a facer. "Well, then," he said at last, summing up the matter, "you have it in mind to give Sir Anthony a set-down and believe I should participate for a lark? Have I got that accurately enough?"

She eyed him saucily. "Very nicely put. I want more than a set-down for that particular man . . . you notice I don't say gentleman?" Then before he could respond to this added, "But, yes, I do want you to help me—for a lark if it pleases you?"

"It doesn't. I am not going to be drawn into something which might very well end in disaster."

"Please," she said simply.

"No."

Something in her voice touched him as she fixed on his deep blue eyes. "You see, my lord, I have no other to turn to. I know you might think it ludicrous that I have turned to you, but I rather think you would stand me a good friend in this."

The desperation in her voice, in her darkly lit grey eyes yanked hard on feelings he'd long ago thought shot in the wind. "No," he managed again, but this time the word was not easy to say, so he explained. "I don't want all the world to think I am enraptured with a green chit of a girl." He smiled at her. "Think of my reputation, my sweet."

"The truth is," teased the lady, "it might do your reputation some good. After all, I am not at all despised by the *beau monde*. In fact, I am thought by many to be quite the thing!"

He burst out laughing and then flicked her nose. "What you are is an immodest imp of a child!"

"Then you will help me?"

"No, dearest creature. Ask one of the many young puppies forever following you about whenever we go into society."

"I can not," she answered on a serious note. "That would not be fair. As you say, they do follow me about. They might take me seriously if I flirted with them. You, on the other hand, don't want me. I don't want you. 'Tis perfect."

Her grey eyes were warm as they implored him, and he very nearly capitulated, but he was made of sterner stuff. "No. There is no point to it all. Sir Anthony is after a fortune—very nearly has it in hand. Your game won't serve."

"It would if he thought I had a fortune."

"Well, you don't!" retorted the Earl testily.

Sir Anthony walked into the Tuthills' music room and cast a disdainful eye over the proceedings. He discovered Catherine Tuthill readying herself to play the piano, but there was no sign of Catherine's good friend, Elizabeth Hawkins. He was surprised. The two girls had been attached at school, and he had quite expected to see Elizabeth during the course of this evening. He had not been making any real progress in his courtship of the Hawkins chit and was beginning to feel that he had thrown away the Edwards girl for nought.

He inched his way towards Catherine and was sure that more than a few women cast hungry glances in his direction. He smiled to himself. He was wearing a superfine dark blue coat that perfectly fit his lean hard form. His cravat was tied with easy expertise, and his hair of gold had been brushed à la Brutus. He was well satisfied with his appearance. Catherine Tuthill saw him and waved, pleased to have his company while so many envious eyes looked their way. It occurred to him as he approached her that she would end by looking prune-faced like her mother, but he bent gallantly over her gloved fingers and breathed, "Enchanted, my lovely. Your gown becomes you, as do the ribbons in your beautiful hair." He thought to himself that there were more yellow ribbons in her carrot-colored curls than in all the room, but never mind, she had what he wanted for the moment. She would know where Elizabeth Hawkins might be, for certainly it was too late now for her arrival. He had timed his own arrival so he would be one of the last to present himself to his hostess.

Catherine Tuthill blushed into her gloved hand and advised him that she was very nervous about the piece her mother wanted her to play for the assembled company that evening. He dutifully answered that she would sparkle at the piano and then casually said, "I rather thought your dear friend, Elizabeth, would be here to give you support."

"Lizzy is not in London," Cathrine answered as she waved her fingers at a group of friends she had not yet greeted. She was pleased to be standing with Sir Anthony and smiled brightly. "Mama's soirée is turning out to be a great success, don't you think? Look there ... Brummell is here, you know. He and Mama are very well acquainted," she added proudly. "Not in London, you say?" He was surprised into frowning. He had taken Elizabeth for a drive only two mornings ago and she had said nothing to him about leaving London. He was momentarily irritated into betraying an emotion, chagrin.

"Hmmm, yes. They left for Brighton to inspect her father's new townhouse." She looked at him full and then giggled, a knowing tease, "Lizzy will be back next week, you poor man. There, there, don't fret." So saying she giggled a great deal more, and he would have been supremely cross had he not then been diverted by the sight of Lillian Aulderbury across the room, stunningly lovely.

Well, well, he thought and excused himself to move in Lilly's direction. He had already learned that she was with the Lady Augusta and her aunt. She was no mistress to the Earl of Raeburn. Where then did she obtain the funds to clothe herself in the first stare of fashion? An interesting question, and curiosity regarding the answer certainly tickled his mind. He probably should stay clear of such a creature, but the notion of getting her to his bed still hit his fancy. This time, he would take her there more slowly.

Lilly saw him coming towards her, and her heart began beating furiously in her chest. She felt a shortness of breath. He was nearly there. What to do? What to say? Almost unconsciously she pressed against the Earl for protection.

Raeburn felt her tremble and frowned. The child was really distressed, and it was all because of Meade. Raeburn had very strong principles, and top on the list was the absolute rule that a gentleman did not play with an innocent girl's feelings. Such an action was beneath contempt. She seemed to lean toward him for protection, and as a gentleman of honour he felt he must lend her that. It was his duty to shield her and while a part of him balked at getting involved, he felt he had no choice. He stood ready.

"Miss Aulderbury. What a lovely surprise to find you here in London and looking as ravishing as ever." Sir Anthony was bending over her gloved fingers.

"Sir Anthony," greeted Lilly in her best town-mannered voice, "I believe you and the Earl must be acquainted?" She looked towards Raeburn and a plea for something, she did not know what, was in her grey eyes.

"Indeed," said the Earl, the hint of a sneer marring his perfect smile. "Sir Anthony and I have often bumped into one another . . . here, there." Raeburn's blue eyes were cold. "I fancy, however, that our interests . . . excepting perhaps one . . . more often than not, take us in very different directions."

Sir Anthony read the Earl as the Earl had intended. Their interest in Lilly was a mutual thing. What then? Was the Earl warning him off?

"Ah, true, otherwise I would have been pleased to pursue the acquaintanceship," replied Sir Anthony glibly. He was a Meade. He was *ton*. He would not allow the Earl to smile him a dismissal.

The Earl would not be charmed by name or manners; he made a show of sighing wearily and saying, "Apparently once again our divergent interests part us. I am afraid that *we* can not stay and chat. I was just taking Miss Aulderbury to her aunt." He turned to Lilly, "My dear, I believe we should take our seats as I see Miss Tuthill has already taken hers at the piano."

As Raeburn moved off with her, Lilly regarded him with admiringly grateful eyes, "Thank you, my lord. That was very well done of you. I know you must find escorting me about a dreadful bore, but thank you for this."

"Nonsense, child." It occurred to him that he might refuse to fall in with her wild-eyed schemes, but he could and would protect her from villains such as Meade. She was after all a veritable kitten, soft and innocent . . . his aunt's godchild. Reason enough to take charge of Lillian Aulderbury.

"Thank you . . . again and again," Lilly repeated, genuinely grateful.

"Again and again?" He smiled. "For what?"

"Please my lord, I think you know very well. Not so very long ago, I was a green girl, perhaps at heart 'tis all I still am. That man, hurt a green girl without a second thought and the town girl thinks he deserves a set-down. You were kind."

"Was I? It was not difficult to be kind to you," he assured her, wondering where the words came from.

She dimpled at him. "Would you like to continue to be kind to me, then?"

His head went backwards with his sudden laughter. What an imp of a girl! She actually awaited his response. What to do? Lilly had fancied herself in love with Meade. He found that fact momentarily annoying. He brushed that aside and attempted logic. This was not any of his concern. He would, of course, do what lay within his realm to see to it that no one hurt the child again, but he really did not want to become embroiled in nonsensical schemes. What had he to do with the absurdities, whimsies and frailties of an eighteen-year-old girl's imagination? The past was done; the future lay within her grasp if she would just forget Meade. Hearts get broken, and hearts mend. So it had been for his . . .

"Lily," he answered at length, "you are no match for

the likes of Meade. Let it go and walk away, nose in the air!"

But she was made of sterner stuff. Besides, she was eighteen. At eighteen, who listens to good advice? "I am going to take him on. He doesn't play fair and deserves some of his own." She looked at Raeburn. "Won't you stand my second in this battle?"

He knew he should run. What in thunder was he doing taking her elbow, bending to her will, saying, "Perhaps little one . . . perhaps."

Chapter Nine

Augusta stood on her toes, and though she was a tall woman she found she still had a reach to plant a kiss upon her nephew's cheek. Bidding him good night she made ready to take the stairs to her bedchamber, repeating, "Thank you, again, darling. You have been most obliging, and I know the Tuthill affair was just the sort of thing to bore you to tears, though I did see Brummell stayed for a few minutes and how nice that he actually chatted with Lilly. He seemed most amused. No doubt, I have you to thank for that as well?"

The Earl chuckled. "No, no acquit me. All I managed to do was introduce him to our Lilly. If he was amused, 'twas all her doing."

"Well, 'twas perfect . . . wasn't it, Sarah?"

Sarah agreed that it was, but added that she was so tired she could fall asleep right there on the stairs. However, she remembered a piece of gossip. "Oh, Gussie, did you see how fat Lady Willow has become. Why, I did not even know it was her when she first came over to me!"

"Indeed, Sarah, but that was nought to Mrs. Tangle's new turban! Faith, when our eyes met I very nearly burst out laughing right in her face. I did not know how to look at her after that."

The two ladies went up together, chatting happily and quite forgetting Lilly and the Earl who stood beside one another at the bottom of the stairs. Lilly had been strangely silent on the short trip home. She was experiencing a bevy of emotions she did not quite understand, but she knew beyond any shadow of a doubt that she wanted to speak again to Raeburn—alone.

"My lord, give me but one moment." She had taken his hand and pulled him along with her towards the study.

He stopped her abruptly suddenly realizing that it would not do for him to be seen by the servants taking her alone into an unlit room. She turned and frowned as she tugged at his hand and he would not budge. She moved to grip the lapels of the greatcoat he had not taken off as he had expected to be on his way to his own lodgings. "My lord . . . come into the study, do . . ."

He removed her small hand from his coat. "I don't know what it is about my garments that I am forever finding you clinging to them?"

Lilly giggled, but this was no time for jesting. "Please, my lord, we *must* talk."

The Earl knew this was his cue to run. She was an engaging creature, and he could feel himself being drawn into something too quickly. She had the soul of an innocent scamp and the trappings of a bewitching woman. A danger signal. However, he had an appointed role, and though it might prove tiresome, he found himself diving in headfirst. "Right then, talk . . . but here in the hall." To assuage her fears, he added, "There is no one about to overhear."

"Yes, but, my lord, no one must know what I am

70

planning. I confided in you earlier and I forgot to extract that promise from you."

"No one shall know. May I go now?" His blue eyes were twinkling.

"Not yet." She looked up at him as though searching for words. "My lord, you were very kind tonight."

"So you have advised me." His voice gave no hint of pliancy.

Lilly was not discouraged. She took his gloved hand into hers. "My lord, will you continue to help me? I know you said 'perhaps,' but I thought we might seal a bargain tonight."

Her warm grey eyes implored, but Raeburn had learned to dodge the wiles and tools of a woman. "I think what we both must do is go to our beds and think about this odd notion of yours by the light of day."

She pouted, and in spite of himself he chuckled. "Come then, my little one, walk me to the door, for apparently it is written that you and I should deal." He was committing himself to her. He was half-disgusted with it, completely surprised by it, but admitted the fact to himself.

"Oh, my lord." Her arms went round his middle, for she could not reach his neck.

He hesitated before gently tapping her shoulder and then setting her from him. "Listen to me, Lilly girl. I mean to protect you from the blackguard Meade—from yourself if need be. To that extent I shall lend myself to your plans. You work within the confines of those bounds and we shall deal famously. Step over the line and new decisions will have to be discussed. Understood?"

"Does this mean you will help me make him jealous?"

"Nonsensical child, you do not listen. Besides, men

71

like Meade don't allow themselves to feel jealousy or anything else."

"Yes, but——"

"I must go home now." He wagged a finger at her. "Sheba will have to be consulted."

"Sheba?"

"My collie," he answered as he moved towards the door.

Lilly laughed. "Will Sheba take my part in this?"

"I doubt it. Sheba always takes my part and my part alone. 'Tis why I keep her." He turned once more to her and touched her nose. "However, Sheba has always had a penchant for an incorrigible minx."

Lilly clapped her hands before clutching at him once more to say, "I must say, my lord, you are definitely much more pleasant than I first thought you."

"I am not sure I am glad to hear you think so," he retorted.

She eyed him naughtily for a moment and then said, "You see, my lord, it will all work out so easily. Here we are, you the rake, me the innocent, all alone with opportunity . . . and yet, we have kept each other at a distance."

"You mean *I* have kept *you* at a distance, don't you?"

"The point is, we can get on famously because we don't want one another."

"The point is, I don't seduce missy little brats, and I am not sure I get along with them either!" snapped the Earl opening the door wide, but he turned again and said quietly. "You are not the town girl you imagine yourself to be, my innocent Lillian Aulderbury. Why don't you go on up to your bed and dream about better things than winning the heart of a cad?"

"Indeed, there are better things, my lord, much better things to dream about, like breaking the heart of a cad!"

He laughed and shook his head. "Perhaps I should pity Meade." He left her then and some moments later found himself in his own library, stretched out in his comfortable chair by the fire, Sheba at his feet. She rolled onto her back and yelped. He groaned, but complied with her request to rub her belly. "There, little whore . . ." he said absently.

Thoughts of Anthea kept returning to his mind's eye. She had been a glorious light in his life, but he had certainly known her for what she was. Before Anthea there had been another, and she had had at him when he was but twenty and without his present title and wealth. He had learned a great deal about love in the years that had followed that first hard lesson. Those days were past . . . and now?

"What then Sheba? She is a minx of a girl . . . a child really."

His collie whined plaintively for him to go on rubbing her belly. He eyed her. "You are no help this evening. Don't you see, I think I gave her my word . . . in a manner of speaking. The question is . . . to what did I commit myself?"

He got up and strode purposefully towards the library door. The collie jumped up to follow. "No, you are not coming with me. I think I must go to Whites!"

That was it! His aunt had forced this little country chit into his well-ordered life, so be it! Meade was the enemy. One must know one's enemy . . .

Harry raised a glass, but his arm stopped in midair as he saw the Earl stroll into the brightly lit anteroom. "Cameron!"

"Harry." Raeburn grinned as he approached. "When did you get back to London?"

"Only an hour before." Harry sipped his brandy and winked at his friend. "Now this I'll wager never saw a customs house!" He sipped at it again. "Good stuff this, the frogs have some uses after all!"

Raeburn smiled ruefully. "The wonder is that you are right." He took up a proffered snifter from a passing flunky and his brow went up as he teased his friend, "Surprised you didn't pop in at Tuthill's soirée, tonight ol' boy."

"Ha! Managed to let that one slip by me," grinned Harry. "Can't think of you sitting quietly while the Tuthill chit pounded out her notes on the pianoforte." He touched his friend's forehead. "Going daft, lovey?"

The Earl's blue eyes glittered appreciatively. "Sneck-up, bottlehead. Brummell was there and the Tuthill chit wasn't half-bad at the keys. Introduced the Beau to our Lilly, by the way."

"Our Lilly? Not ours, Cameron. Mine! Brummell, eh? Never say so? So he was there? What did Lilly think of the Beau?"

"She thought him well dressed and . . . let me see, what did she say, ah yes, famous good fun."

"Little corker." Harry chuckled, then eyed his friend suspiciously. "Why did *you* go to Tuthill's?"

"Duty."

"Duty is it? Think you have an eye for my Lilly."

"Could be," bantered the Earl.

Sir Harry saw the jest in this and chuckled heartily. "And that my man might be true . . . an eye but not a heart. Right then, did Lilly ask for me?"

"Forget Lilly for the moment and tell me about Meade."

"Meade? What's to tell?"

"What new gossip? What old gossip buried away? What moves the man?"

Harry puckered over this. "I dunno . . . He must marry money to save himself. He wants the Hawkins chit. The father says yea, the mother says nay and no one knows what the chit says. 'Tis a deep game in that quarter."

"Now let me understand this, Harry. You believe that Mr. Hawkins is in favor of the match between his daughter, his only child, and this Meade person?" The Earl seemed incredulous.

"The thing is, you don't like Meade, I don't like Meade, but there ain't any denying that the fellow is *ton*. Old name . . . respected name. He is the first of his line to do the name poorly you know, and this Hawkins fellow wants a title for his daughter."

"Why?"

"They say he made his fortune in trade and then married above his station. His wife's family disowned her, at least in the beginning from what I hear tell, and now she won't have much to do with them. Means his daughter to have it all—fortune, title . . . social prestige." He mused over this. "Can't say I blame the fellow, and I saw his daughter some weeks ago at the Holland rout. Pretty enough, though she is a quiet thing. Tall and fair. She should do well I suppose. At any rate seems to be leading Meade an irritating dance. Ain't saying him yea, but don't know that she won't take him in the end."

"Is she the calculating sort? Mayhap she is waiting to see what better comes along?"

"I don't know . . . only spoke to her a moment or so . . . Tell you what, though, first impression?"

"Right then, first impression?"

"Don't think the chit wants Meade, don't think she is all that happy riding high in society and no, don't think

75

she is calculating. But there . . . can never tell with a female," mused Harry.

"Then it would appear our Meade will have to look elsewhere for a rich wife?"

"Perhaps . . ." Harry's eyes narrowed. "Eh? Never knew you to care a fig for such matters?"

"You are as ever very astute, my man, very astute," teased the Earl, " 'Tis for Lilly that I inquire."

"What?" shrieked Harry, loud enough to draw a few heads in their direction.

"Stubble it, Harry. What the deuce is wrong with you?"

"Ay, but you startled me, Cameron. What do you mean, you are asking about Meade for Lilly? What has Lilly to do with such a fellow?" Harry shook his head. "Think mayhap you've been drinking deep tonight."

"Haven't been drinking deep at all," said the Earl with a chuckle.

"Daft then?"

"Don't concern yourself, Harry, I have the matter well in hand."

"You have the matter well in hand? What matter?" Harry was nearly spluttering. "Am *I* going daft? Am I having this conversation with Rogue Raeburn?" He took his friend's shoulder in hand. "Cameron, you are the best of good friends, but I've often thought you a hard-headed, hard-hearted fellow. What do you care about Meade, or Hawkins, and what has any of this to do with my sweet Lilly?"

"I *am* exactly as you say, hard headed, hard hearted, make no mistake of that. When I bestir myself 'tis for myself," answered the Earl, and there was a glint in his blue eyes that gave truth to the statement.

Harry frowned and thought about this. "You know ol' boy, it wasn't always so."

"Was it not?" The Earl shrugged. "Well, time and experience have bent, twisted and trampled on feelings, so that the heart you speak of is as hard as a highlander's heelpiece." He looked off as though peering into another world. "Lilly is under my uncle and aunt's protection, and a sense of duty to them lends her my shield." He smiled at his friend. "Nothing more."

"Nothing more? I wonder," said Harry studying him a moment.

"And my own amusement, perhaps, for a time," added the Earl.

Harry grimaced. "Do you know that if you had made such a speech only a week ago, I would most certainly have believed you."

"And tonight?" Raeburn's eyebrow rose disdainfully.

"And tonight take me to the card table!" Harry grinned.

Chapter Ten

On Bond Street nestled between two exclusive men's shops was Appleby's House of Jewels. Here in quiet elegance the aristocracy purchased their finest ornaments. There as well, the gentry would come from time to time as their fortunes changed hands over the gaming tables, discreetly, to see Mr. Appleby in his private office. In that elegant backroom and with great solemnity such persons would sell their rare pieces.

Sir Anthony gave the item he had just sold Mr. Appleby one last look and attempted a parting smile. So be it. He had hoped for a coin or two more, but he had done well enough, he supposed. He took the wad from the table, tucked it into his leather pouch and deposited this into the recesses of his many-tiered greatcoat. He rose abruptly, nodded a cool dismissal to the little man who stood across the wide, dark, gothic desk and turned away.

At Sir Anthony's back, Mr. Appleby stood in silent contempt. Slowly he took up the purchase he had just made. It was a gold beautifully worked pocket watch and chain. Sir Anthony's great-grandfather's; it had been handed down from father to son, yet Sir Anthony had parted with it as though it had been nought. Heirlooms did come into Appleby's shop, but he had rarely received any with such cold abandon. The man had no sense of family. Gaming and drinking were obviously all this Meade cared about. Shame, shame.

Sir Anthony walked out of Appleby's office without another thought to the watch his father had so fondly placed in his hands when he had still been a boy at school. It was gone, but with the fortune he would make, he would buy dozens of gold pocket watches should he want any! The spring air's light freshness touched his face, and he took a moment to enjoy the fragrant breeze. It occurred to him that still he had his mother's diamonds, but those he might have to give his future bride. He couldn't chance doing anything wrong now that he was so close to his goal, though the Hawkins chit was not proving to be one of his easy conquests. This was puzzling and certainly irritating. He had given up Cynthia Edwards' decent fortune to ensnare Hawkins and all her riches. What must he now do?

Across the street from Appleby's House of Jewels, Madame Toussant serviced most of the aristocratic ladies of London. She was at the moment attempting to encourage Lady Augusta to purchase the ivory lace and satin gown for Lilly. Lady Sarah was objecting strongly to the extravagance and saying that the yellow gown which was very nearly half the price would do very well.

"Indeed, the yellow will serve, and it is ours," snapped Augusta testily. "Lilly must have both . . ."

"Gussie . . . the cost," Sarah whispered her cheeks very red.

Augusta snapped her fingers in the air. "Wizzy and I would have spent this and more, so much more had my daughter lived."

"Stop it, Gussie! You are forever compromising my

principles with that particular line of argument. 'Tis unfair."

"Yet, 'tis true," returned Gussie on a softer note. She patted Lady Sarah's shoulder. "There, there. Go and talk with Lady Holland while Lilly and I finish up here."

Instead, Lady Holland came over to them, and after the amenities were exchanged, she plopped herself into a nearby chair and exclaimed, "Ah, la, but such a morning I have had. Dreadful, absolutely dreadful."

"Why, what have you been doing, dear?" Lady Sarah sympathized sweetly.

"Sophy Milbanke," Lady Holland announced in disgusted accents. "Never allow Sophy to get her hands on you. Odious woman. Abuses one and abuses all."

"You like Sophy!" Augusta was much surprised.

"You mean I *liked* Sophy," grumbled Lady Holland. "Then she took me to this miserable place . . . a home for poor orphans. 'Tis in Soho." She allowed her tone to display the horror she had felt. She shuddered, "Sophy is forever dragging one into her schemes. A most tiring woman. She doesn't give a fig for those dirty little creatures, but, 'tis her cause of the week you see."

"Oh, surely you are too harsh on Sophy," exclaimed Lady Sarah more than mildly shocked by such an attitude.

"Harsh? No, I am not harsh enough. Understand me, Sarah, I am as kindhearted as any other woman, perhaps kinder. I have always contributed funds to such things . . . poor little creatures. I mean, one would have to be heartless not to feel for their plight, but one does not have to actually go there to work in the home to do one's part." She shook her head. "Sophy got it into her head that we must go there ourselves and measure the brats for new clothing. Brats I call them and brats they are! Wild little things." She eyed now the three set faces staring at her. "Can you imagine?"

Augusta broke the sudden tension. "No, I can not imagine *you* doing anything of the sort."

"Just where is this home?" Lilly had found her voice. Until now she had been riveted by shock. She liked Lady Holland. How could someone she liked be so very cold-blooded. The woman was speaking about children who had lived on the street, in the freezing weather, without food, without parents.

"Indeed," put in Lady Sarah softly, "just exactly where is this place in Soho?"

Lady Holland fished about in her reticule and pulled out a card, handing it to Lady Sarah. "That is the address. I spent about twenty minutes there before I told Sophy I was leaving."

"Did you? My word," remarked Lady Sarah, scarcely able to hide her disapproval.

"I did," returned Holland defiantly. "And Sophy gave it up as well and left with me."

"What of the children?" Lilly's dismay was all over her face.

" 'Tis a perfectly squalid neighborhood. I will never go there again, as I told Sophy. Next she will no doubt drag me off to Cruikshank's Home for the Needy!"

"Yes, but what of these children. Who will see to their clothing if you and Sophy have given it up?" Lilly pursued.

Lady Augusta hushed her with a glare. "I am certain their measurements will be taken and the donations for their clothing will be arranged?"

"Are you certain? Humph!" grumbled Holland. "Sophy is scatterbrained. She will forget all about the children by morning."

"Then we must remind her," said Lady Sarah quietly.

"Indeed. Oh, Gussie, we must go there immediately," cried Lilly.

"Darling, go outside for a moment, do. We will just finish up in here and join you. 'Tis a lovely day . . . enjoy the air," said Gussie quietly. She could see Lady Holland was bristling and did not want Lilly to come under fire.

Lilly stepped outdoors just as Sir Anthony was crossing the street, and their eyes immediately locked!

Damnation, but this chit was a stunning piece of fancy! Sir Anthony could not help but stare at Lilly in her warm pink walking ensemble with its matching hat set rakishly on her pretty black curls. It was certainly a damn shame that she wasn't an heiress. She looked a diamond of the first water in her finery, and just where did she get the money to purchase such expensive finery? He knew a renewed desire to own her. If only he could . . .

He frowned to himself as he moved towards her? Had his information been correct? Perhaps Lady Sarah was wealthier than he had been led to understand? Could she have somehow received a sizeable inheritance? He was very nearly within touching distance now, and he smiled warmly as he tipped his beaver tophat. Where was the harm? The Hawkins chit was still out of town, so who was to know if he enjoyed himself with Lillian Aulderbury?

"Lilly, my sweet love, zounds but you do take my breath away and make me forget all else."

"Do I?" Lilly's tone was dubious, and there was a bright light in her grey eyes. She had learned a thing or two in town.

An intuitive man might have been wary. Sir Anthony's confidence in himself sent his caution to the wind, and he plunged forward.

"Now, love, you know that you do. When I look at you I feel as though my soul is being spirited away."

Lilly felt sick. How had she imagined him a hero? She lowered her lashes and then raised them to answer, "Really . . . spirited away, by me?" She pursed her lips to pout the words softly. "And how far do I take it, sir?"

He wanted to ensnare her in his embrace, wanted to cover her face and neck with kisses. She was enticing him to abandon. Where was the country girl he had left behind? "So very much further than any other woman has ever taken it before," he answered softly.

"Ah, so then this thing that happens to your soul has happened before?" countered the lady, successfully throwing him momentarily off balance.

"Acquit me then most cherished being. No, no, only you have stolen my soul . . . my heart."

"You mistake, sir. I haven't stolen your soul. The truth is, I don't want it." She was now enacting a saucy woman as her eyes raked him.

He was mesmerized by her game. "Lilly, my country Lilly has turned into a polished woman. Am I so out of favor?"

"Should you be?" She was no longer the eager shy girl he had courted in the country. Her hurt, her anger had subsided into purpose. She was out for . . . justice, she thought in that moment, oh yes, sweet justice.

"I was called away unexpectedly. Forgive me?" he offered lamely. He took her gloved hand and set it to his lips. "Please, forgive me." He was begging, seduction in his eyes, in his throat.

"No, I don't think so," returned the lady softly.

"What must I do?" pursued the man now in the heat of the hunt. However, he took a step backwards as he spied Lilly's aunt and godmother step out of the shop.

"Quite right, sir," was all Lilly said as she followed his
83

line of vision. She laughed then at his confusion, for she wanted to bring him down, but some encouragement to the chase must be offered. "They, I know, don't mean to forgive you."

"Quickly, beloved, where, when can we meet again?" he whispered.

Again, she felt repulsed. He used such words without understanding their meaning. She raised languishing grey eyes to his face and purred, "No doubt we will meet again somewhere . . . soon."

He tipped his hat once more to her and without glancing towards her aunt and godmother hurriedly moved on to the street where he vanished between the slow on-going traffic.

The Earl of Raeburn had witnessed Sir Anthony's departure from the jeweler's. He had then seen Air Anthony and Lilly meet. He'd watched her play a game with her eyes, with her movements, that thoroughly surprised him. He had never seen her in the role of coquette. What was this? Was Lilly still in love with Meade? For some unexplainable reason this notion was supremely annoying. Everything she was doing was artful.

Then Lady Sarah and Augusta bore down on the pair. He should be off now that Lilly was safe. Right then, why was he moving in her direction? Turn about, free yourself, he was telling himself as he tipped his tophat to the ladies and heard Lady Sarah saying, "No, I am not telling you that you can't speak to that dreadful man. I am simply saying—"

"And what are my three lovely ladies at this morning?" Raeburn was all too aware of the grateful look Lilly shot him. It tickled him with pleasure.

"Cameron, darling." Lady Augusta was happy for the interruption. The conversation about Meade was becoming far too dangerous. She was sure Lilly was no longer interested in the blasted fellow, so there was no sense getting her into a position where she might look that way again. If she knew anything about the young, she knew they were a contrary set. "I am so glad you are here to save us from what would otherwise be a tediously boring afternoon."

He smiled ruefully. "No. Now this gets out of hand, Aunt Gussie. Where the deuce is my uncle? Does he mean to stay away for the entire season?"

"Such a dear boy . . ." Gussie patted his arm. "There is a coffee shoppe where all the poets go. I have been telling Lilly about it, and she so very much would like to go there, but you must see that it would not do for us to go unescorted?"

"Well, as to that . . ." The Earl suddenly felt trapped.

"Don't cry off, Cameron; please. You are such friends with Moore and Byron I thought you might find it entertaining yourself?" Gussie applied the pressure.

"Yes, but—"

"Don't bother the poor man," Sarah put in. "I am certain we can find adequate male escort amongst some of our friends, Gussie."

"Ah, am I not adequate?" The Earl couldn't stop the words. Somehow they were out. What was wrong with him. All the while he had been aware of Lilly's grey eyes quietly surveying his face.

"More than adequate." Lilly beamed. "Unless of course you really would like us to find better." Her grey eyes flickered with her tease.

"Brat," he returned in sharp accents much in contrast to the light in his blue eyes.

85

"So I am, but so I must be. You must see that?" Lilly baited him.

"Indeed, I suppose 'tis my duty now to ask you why?"

"No."

"Well, I mean to all the same. Why? Why must you be a brat?"

Lilly laughed. "How could I manage in this city of spoiled creatures if I were otherwise?"

"Precisely so," he said and took her arm to walk her to the curbing.

His aunt and Lady Sarah, he noted, were much pleased as they took up the rear together. The Earl hailed a passing hackney, and they all piled within its tight quarters for their little trip across town. It did not take Lilly long to drop her worldly airs and inquire in childlike accents as to whether Lord Byron was as wicked as they said he was.

"I would say he likes to think himself melancholy at times. I do not find him wicked, at least no more than any other man making his way on this earth."

"Yes, but—" started Lilly.

"Lilly, you must know that Byron and Cameron are dear friends. He won't say a word against him," confided Augusta by way of explanation.

"There isn't anything worth saying against him, Gussie. You, in your heart, must agree with that?"

"Yes, but, my lord, he seduced Lady Caroline Lamb away from her husband, and Lady Francis from hers and—" put in Lilly before being interrupted.

"And *they* were married, experienced women terribly impressed with his sudden fame, his auburn curls, his clubfoot. *They* pursued him and their husbands *chose* to look the other way until they could not. I do not put that at Byron's door, do you?"

"Well, to be fair . . . no, not if they chased him down

to earth as you seem to be implying. However, they say that he is a dreadful husband to that new young bride of his, you know, the Milbanke girl . . . ?" Lilly pursued.

"My Byron is married to a puritanical, self-righteous maid who does not tolerate his hedonistic tendencies. They will never suit—we had tried to tell him. We saw it, he could not. The world chooses to take sides with a marriage gone wrong, and they choose to see Byron as the villain. That does not put the truth to it."

"No, I don't suppose it does," answered Lilly.

"If Byron is there today, you may see for yourself what the man is made of."

Lady Sarah and Augusta were chatting quietly as Lilly and the Earl discussed Byron. Lilly fell silent for a moment and then suddenly remarked, eyeing the Earl sideways, "You know you didn't have to take us today if you really didn't wish to."

The Earl regarded her sharply. "There is not a soul on earth that can make me do what I don't wish to do."

She blinked at him. There was such a hard uncompromising set to his lips, to the sound of the words that she was taken aback. She must remember this moment. She had started to very nearly think that she rather liked him, but no, oh no, he was as arrogant and unfeeling as she had first thought he must be. She laughed, however, and lightened the mood. "Well then, since it must be what you want to do, come laugh with us and put away that sullen look you are wearing. Smollet says laughing is the sign of a rational animal, so quickly, let us laugh before they think us mad!"

"Absurd child," he answered, flicking her nose.

Sarah watched the two and felt a moment's uneasiness. Oh no. She really hoped Lilly was not forming an attachment for the Earl. She hoped the child was not taking kindness for anything else? He was a hardened

87

rakehell and she did not believe that his attentions to Lilly were anything more than gentlemanly care for his aunt's goddaughter. However, she noted the aloofness with which Lilly received his attentions and relaxed. No, Lilly had no interest there.

The Earl also felt Lilly's sudden withdrawal. A spark of contradicting sensations lit in his blood. He was pleased that the green country girl was not fawning over him, piqued that she did not seem to find him irresistible as did most of her kind. "Ah, here we are, my ladies," he announced as the cab pulled to a stop. "The poets await us!"

Chapter Eleven

Lilly saw the reflection of herself in the long, Gothic, framed mirror. She wore a deep red velvet gown delicately beaded with white seed pearls at the bodice and on the puff sleeves. Red velvet ribbon was threaded throughout her glistening black curls that had been piled waterfall style upon her well-shaped head. Tonight they were going to the theatre. Drury Theatre. It was all moving so fast. Who was she? Was this all a dream? Shouldn't she miss her home, her friends there? How dreadful that she had forgotten everyone in this whirlwind of pleasure. She should feel some shame, but somehow she didn't. She so loved the glitter. She even loved sitting with the dowagers and hearing stories about her mother and father's escapades amongst the *beau monde*. Her parents had been well liked and were fondly remembered. However, she had learned the truth about her father's losing his small inheritance on what one old dowager had called "nonsensical schemes to get rich."

She enjoyed watching her aunt and Lady Augusta move in these circles. Nothing seemed to astound those two, and although they did enjoy these hectic days and busy evenings, she could see they were both beginning to miss their home. Well, after today's experience she would be well satisfied to go back. She still trembled when she recalled how she had actually met some of the greatest poets of all time. Faith, Byron had walked out of the pages of *Childe Harold's Pilgrimage* and had actually bent over her fingers, taken a seat at their table. He had been beautiful in his aura of cool aloofness and overwhelming sorrow. She had been so very tongue-tied at first, but the Earl had managed to tease her out of her shyness.

She had watched Raeburn as he stood about jesting and exchanging quips with Thomas Moore and Lord Byron and then suddenly he was introducing them; they were taking chairs at the table, talking as though they were human beings and not the Gods of Poetry she had always envisioned.

Somehow the conversation had turned political, and corn laws had everyone talking at once. She listened with great interest and marveled that the Earl seemed to be working in the House of Lords to get a bill passed to help the hand weavers. She was impressed with the compassion he seemed to feel for the people. She watched as Raeburn worked himself into a temper and said to a gentleman sitting at a nearby table, "Those poor devils are much injured by our new Tory government, is it not so, Thomas?" He then turned to the poet Moore for confirmation.

Moore nodded, but was kept from replying by Byron, who waved his hand in disgust. "They are sacrificed to the views of certain individuals who have enriched themselves by those practices which have deprived the frame workers of employment."

"I don't understand?" Lilly ventured timidly, meek and unlike herself.

"Don't you? Well, my brat, that is because our

women are taught to pursue the frivolous life and we are forever encouraging one another to look the other way. How could you understand?"

"Well then . . . perhaps you would be kind enough to enlighten me?" Lilly's temper had been ruffled, and again her shyness had left.

" 'Tis simple enough. The new frame has been created in the name of progress and requires one man while six are then thrown out of employment. Further, the work done on this frame is inferior in quality, so it can only be sold overseas. It is a disgrace to a civilized country to see the state of these poor men out of work . . . our own English blood!"

"Ay, agreed, my friend." The man at the neighboring table nodded.

"The present bill they have at hand will push those poor devils into rebellion. Mark me on this," Thomas Moore stated gravely.

"What can be done for them?" Lilly was distressed now.

The Earl regarded her through thoughtful eyes. "At present the Tories have the Regent on their side. 'Tis a difficult situation to overcome."

"Difficult," put in Byron softly, "however, not impossible."

"It leaves our poor and their children in a terrible state. Where can they turn?" Lady Sarah's voice was accusingly grave.

"They turn to the workhouses," said Thomas Moore in disgust.

"I had a letter from Elizabeth Fry about her efforts to invoke change," said Byron, then, turning to the Earl, he asked, "Have you ever met her, Cameron?"

"No, but I have heard about her outstanding work. Now, there is a woman!"

Lilly stared at the Earl in wonder. It would never have occurred to her that rakehell Raeburn would find someone like Elizabeth Fry to be a female worthy of praise. She had assumed his tastes were . . . of another nature. "Indeed," said Lilly. She was certainly struck by this new side to the Earl. "Elizabeth Fry is a personal friend of Aunt Sarah's, you know, and the work she has inspired is far-reaching and seriously meaningful."

"Elizabeth Fry . . . 'tis all I hear from these two," said Lady Augusta, " 'tis they that are forever working at the orphanage at home."

"As do you!" put in Sarah at once.

"No, not I." Augusta laughed. "I have not the stamina for the little wretches. Cameron, now what must these two ladies do?"

Momentarily diverted he gave her the necessary "What?"

"Drag me off to work at some dreadful 'home' here in London—in Soho, if you will."

"I have yet seen the person that can drag you to anything you don't want," responded her nephew undutifully.

"Well, as to that, perhaps I do pity these poor little creatures, you know, but where shall we find the time during the season . . . ?"

"Gussie, how can you ask where we shall find the time to help feed, clothe and educate children who have nothing—absolutely nothing?" asked Lady Sarah.

"Indeed, we have so much, 'tis our way for repaying life's kindness. One must put back. 'Tis self-serving in the end, you know," added Lilly.

The Earl was surprised. He had been watching Lilly flit about London, acquire her town polish, and it had proved, thus far, to be both entertaining and stimulating seeing her point of view. He had not until now really suspected that she had any other interests. He made the mistake of saying so, and Lilly rounded on him, grey eyes sparkling.

"Ha! Just like a rakehell man to think a female has nought better to do than play with her clothes and her hair! Men go strutting about Parliament screeching at one another, blaming one another, shouting each other down, but children go about the streets hungry. And do you know who feeds them, clothes them, goes about the countryside seeking donations and books for them? The women of this country, that is who!" She folded her arms across her chest. "That takes more than words, doesn't it?"

The Earl was more than a little impressed with her address. "Yes, but—"

"No!" Lilly actually wagged a finger. "Elizabeth Fry and her kind speak up, but they also organize wherever they can. They collect women willing to give their time, their wits, their attention and whatever funding they can get a hold of to feed and house the needy. Don't you know, can't you see the pitiful conditions those children—the poor out there—must tolerate. What good is all this rhetoric when urchins fend for themselves in gutters? Whigs and Tories preen and screech, hanging beggars for stealing when what else can they do? They have rags to protect them from the cold, they scavenge for food. How can this be allowed in our civilized Christian society? 'Tis unthinkable."

"Our Lilly when impassioned paints us a very clear picture, does she not?" asked Lady Sarah quietly. "I am told that children live in gangs near the market of Covent Garden, sleeping under sheds and in baskets owned by the market traders. Subscriptions alone can not radically alter this appalling situation. 'Tis time our Tories and Whigs find a way of working together to accomplish a deed that will end in the betterment of our country, don't you think, gentlemen?"

The men seemed momentarily at a loss, but all agreed to the basic need. It wasn't long, however, before each man expressed his own view of just how this work should be accomplished. Lilly watched Raeburn. He certainly spoke in a manner that indicated he cared. He was working in the House of Lords to that end. Was it for his own glory? Or was it out of concern for those less fortunate? He could have chosen another, easier task to pave a way to glory?

The mirror glinted red velvet and brought her back to her surroundings. It had been a thought-provoking afternoon. A wonderful, wonderful afternoon. She would never forget it. She pulled a dark gleaming curl so that it hung to her shoulder over one ear. Tonight they were off for the theatre, but tomorrow there was work to be done—orphans to be cared for . . . and there was Sir Anthony. Oh yes, she must not forget Sir Anthony!

Chapter Twelve

Lilly's wide grey eyes looked out of Lady Wizbough's coach onto unbelievable scenes of squalor. In the three weeks they had traveled about London, she had never seen anything to equal the misery she was presently witnessing. Ahead of them a brick building carrying this etching in stone above its doors, The Philanthropic Society, seemed an oasis of hope in its grim surroundings. Everywhere Lilly looked she saw beggars in rags, children covered in filth eating filth, people huddled in groups passing about their bottles of gin. A uniformed beadle came along and ushered them off as he attempted to make room for the vehicles, including their own, that needed to pass through the avenue. Lilly's lips set with her resolution. She had never known there could be such poverty.

Lady Augusta's coach pulled up carefully, and the Wizboughs' livery opened the door for the ladies who had been unable to speak for the last few minutes. They took the short stone steps to the front door which was already being opened for them, their arrival being anxiously awaited. Lilly looked over her shoulder as they were hurried within and still could not believe the pitiful sight her own eyes beheld. If she did nothing else with her life, she would help as many of these people as she could.

The large woman in the grey, crisp linen uniform who had met them at the door was prattling at them as she led them down the hallway. She turned her head round suddenly as though unsure they were really listening and cocked a brow. "Ay then, oi know m'dears. 'Tis a sorry sight it is and quite toikes yer breath away, it does, oi know. But come now." She encouraged them along with a beaming smile.

Lilly's grey eyes met the older woman's in quiet understanding while her aunt apologized and identified herself.

"Ay, oi know, oi know. Mrs. Milbanke said ye would be coming this morning, she did, so then, oi've been waiting on ye oi have." She smoothed her white apron over her middle. "I be Mrs. Brooks, and though oi was hired as the housekeeper, being as that's me trade and always has been, well, oi been more a housemother than anything else, poor dears." She clucked her tongue as she shook her head. Then, shrugging this off, she beamed once more and Lilly was reminded of her grandmother whose cheeks had been plump and soft like Mrs. Brooks.

Once again Mrs. Brooks was moving in her ambling way down the corridor to another dimly lit passage. Lilly noted that while the walls were devoid of paper or paintings, they were freshly painted and clean. A double set of oak doors were opened wide, and Mrs. Brooks explained at the threshold, "Now then, this be the music room. Big tadoo over this there was, seeing as many of our subscribers didn't hold wit sech, but it does them a world of good, it does." She took a step within and allowed her guests to follow.

A young woman seated at the piano turned towards

them and smiled without interrupting her play as the children gathered round her were in the middle of a pretty ballad. Mrs. Brooks nodded towards the young woman, saying, "That be Miss Hawkins at the piano. We don't know what we would do without her and her dear mother." She thought it prudent at this juncture to lower her voice. "They are here all the time, one or the other, and the children love them." She sighed heavily and moved her large frame towards some hard-backed chairs against the wall. "Right then, why don't you ladies make yourselves comfortable until Mr. Reynolds arrives? 'Tis a nice thing for the children to have a bit of an audience when they are at their songs."

It was true, Lilly thought as she noted some of the children stealing glances their way. These children were hungry for attention. She turned to her aunt who patted her hand comfortingly, and they looked to Augusta. Augusta had always held back. She never wanted to become too attached. She wanted to give care, but she did not want to give anything of herself. She had her reasons.

This scene, for these orphans, was cheery and wholesome, but there was still so much to be done; so many children were dying in the streets. These were babes, but so were all the hopeless creatures who had not been taken to a "home" such as this. So much food was wasted as the gentry, such as herself, enjoyed their lives. One must be without heart to see such things and not help! Lilly knew a sure resolution to bring about change. She glanced at Miss Hawkins and guessed her to be about her own age. Well then, another step in the right direction. All young women her age must do their part. She would have to find a way to organize them. It was not enough to work alone. There was still such wide-eyed innocence on the faces of these children. It was heart-breaking to think of those others without shelter, without affection. No, it was a problem that must be dealt with by her own kind.

The door to the music room opened once more and a pleasant-looking gentleman of average height and modist fashion entered. Quickly he came to them and inclined his head. "Ladies, I am . . ." He then stopped himself as he realized that he knew one of the ladies looking up at him. He took both her hands and pulled Augusta from her chair to give her a warm embrace. "Gussie, dearest Gussie! How could *you* be in town and I not know it?"

She pinched his cheek. "Darling, I had no idea that you were involved in this." Her gloved hand moved expressively. "How wonderful to see you again, and how very sorry I was to learn about your mother. She was a great woman and a dear, dear friend." She turned to Sarah, and Lilly to hastily apologize. "My dears, this is Justin Reynolds. He often ran about in short pants at Wizbough and got into all sorts of trouble with Wizzy. A devil of a boy, Wizzy used to say of him." She smiled affectionately at her friend and then gave him Lilly and Sarah's names.

Mr. Reynolds smiled broadly. "How am I to redeem myself in your eyes, ladies, after such an introduction?"

"If you are responsible for this . . . haven, you need no other introduction," said Lady Sarah softly.

"And if you survived Uncle Wizzy's lectures, you are indeed quite a hero," declared Lilly brightly.

"Indeed surviving Lord Wizbough's reprimands was the making of me!" Mr. Reynolds laughed and touched Augusta's arm fondly. "But this place . . . ?" He shook his head. "This was all my mother's doing. She established it, she ran it. She browbeat her poor friends until they learned to love the place almost as much as she.

98

We miss her." He moved towards the door. "Come, we can have a nice chat in my office, ladies."

As Lilly followed everyone down the corridor to Justin Reynolds' office, she could not help but notice that he was certainly a man of the *ton*. Here was one of the *beau monde*'s own. Here was old family, old money, heritage. Here was a gentleman that did not follow the hedonistic pursuits of his peers. He spent his time in Soho with the poor. He spent his time with orphans. Here was a worthy man. Odd that this did not stimulate any romantic feeling towards him. He was pleasant looking. Quick to smile. Warm hearted. He had all the attributes she prized, yet nothing about him stimulated any of the feelings she had experienced when she had been with that cad of cads Sir Anthony. Why was that?

Justin stood behind his desk and waited for them all to be seated before he sank into his own chair and smiled to hear Augusta's immediate question: "How long have you been back?" She turned to her companions. "Justin has been abroad for any number of years."

"Two to be exact." He smiled indulgently and then sighed. "Two years too long, for, as you must be aware, I wasn't here for my mother in the end." He frowned as he recalled the helplessness he had felt when he had received the news of her death.

"Justin, it was so sudden. You had no way of knowing," offered Augusta.

"Perhaps not, but I do know that she was dedicated to these poor homeless waifs, and I mean to carry on her good work in her name." He smiled warmly. "And I am heartened that all of you have chosen to contribute your efforts to our cause."

Lady Sarah cleared her throat and quietly explained that she and Lilly were not in a position to do more than contribute their time and willing efforts at obtaining donations from those who could well afford them.

"Indeed, I plan to hold a breakfast for that express purpose," put in Lady Augusta. "I think I can promise you substantial subscriptions from a great many of my friends. Of course, my Wizzy and my nephew, Raeburn, will send in their donations as well."

"The Earl already donates quite a sum . . . and has been doing so for many years." Reynolds smiled.

"Yes, of course he does . . . where is my mind?" exclaimed Augusta. "You and he have been friends any number of years."

"Any number . . ." Justin Reynolds grinned.

Lilly listened to this interchange with acute interest. Raeburn a contributor? Rogue Raeburn a subscriber for many years? Was it because he cared, or was it because he had money enough and was merely doing a friend a favor? Why did it matter so long as the children benefited. These questions made a path through Lilly's thoughts, but there were no assuaging answers.

Justin Reynolds was saying, "That is very kind. Mrs. Brooks can work out a schedule with you to coordinate your time with that of our other regular volunteers. However, we do need funds, badly. In London, we have a problem far more unique to the city, and that problem affects us all."

"What can you mean?" Lady Sarah puzzled up as she scanned his face.

"What I mean is that time is crucial. Here in London we are plagued by Flash Houses, madam. Flash Houses!" Mr. Reynolds retorted grimly, "Worse than anything you could ever imagine. As English citizens we must see that in the end the state of such affairs affects all of us as individuals. We must make Parliament see this."

"Flash Houses?" Lilly eyed him doubtfully. She had never heard the term.

"Allow me to explain, though I am sure I would be censured for doing so to a gently bred female," answered Reynolds gravely. "We have orphans, abandoned children, thousands of society's unwanted—urchins—and these children live, sleep and survive in these dens. The children are given board and in turn are trained to be thieves, beggars, pickpockets . . . and prostitutes. The girls are perhaps no more than eleven or twelve years old, rarely older than fifteen, yet they are sent out to sell themselves. When one of them, usually a boy, is caught for stealing, he is sent to prison where he is flogged and then turned out without a penny. Right then, back he goes to the Flash House to survive. It is all he knows. He has not been given a choice." Reynolds sat back in his chair. "I have been working with Elizabeth Fry and members of the Select Committee, but we need the support of our own, of influential people, to insure that our efforts are not wasted."

A knock sounded and Reynolds excused himself to call out a welcome. The door opened and Miss Hawkins stood there shyly regarding them and apologizing. "I am so sorry to interrupt, but Mama has come for me. She wanted me to tell you that she gave Mrs. Brooks the writing supplies for the children and promises to be here tomorrow morning at nine o'clock."

Justin Reynolds had jumped to his feet to receive Miss Hawkins, and Lilly watched the two with mild interest. They were briefly introduced before Miss Hawkins excused herself and left them to join her mother. Some moments later they were taken back to Mrs. Brooks, and they spent a goodly hour working out their tentative volunteer work schedules.

On the ride home, Lilly found her aunt and godmother oddly distant and quiet until her aunt suddenly turned to Augusta and remarked, "I would think your nephew would use his influence regarding this dreadful problem."

"Why do you think he does not, Sarah?" Augusta's brows were up, and there was a warning light in her eyes.

"No, no. I did not mean it to sound quite so—"

"Critical?" Augusta was ready for a fight.

"Augusta, forgive me. 'Tis just so disheartening to see ... to hear about such abuses and know that one is a part of it simply by keeping silent. We can only accomplish anything through our men. *That* I find intolerable!"

"Agreed," said Augusta. "Still, one must give credit where 'tis due. My nephew does not flaunt his philanthropy about like a crown, but he is very good and I believe he tries very strongly to help those less fortunate."

"I am sure he does, as does dear Wizzy, as did my own darling husband."

"It would appear that we as women must always rely on a man to get anything done," said Lilly with a frown, " 'Tis another change that one day must come about."

The Earl was, in fact, making a statement about the problem of Flash Houses at a meeting of his colleagues. He was putting together a speech meant for the House of Lords. He would be cautious in his choice of wording, for thus far his views had not been positively received. There were still too many who believed the problem of Flash Houses was but a minor irritation, nothing more. However, he had on his side a growing number, for his name was old and highly respected and his was a wealthy family. His estates were extensive. He was admired for his efficient management of them. His fortune was very nearly the greatest amongst the aristocrats, and his power was strong amongst his peers. More than once he had extended a hand to a fellow gentleman "temporarily without," often to a top-ranking member in the House of Lords. In return these men were quite ready to lend their support to a cause they knew was worthwhile.

It was a modist gathering, but a hard-working one, and when the speech was written and then rewritten several times, the Earl stood to read it through to its end. It was concise, to the point; it drew on logic and it demanded compassion; at its conclusion the gathering of men jumped to their feet and their applause was deafening. They congratulated the Earl and one another with much backslapping and laughter.

The Earl regarded Sir Harry before turning to smile at his loyal colleagues. To the last man, they were fervent about this cause. He addressed them quietly. " 'Tis but a first step. We must get the bill passed. We must get the funding for more 'homes.' Without this bill, we as a people are no better than savages."

Chapter Thirteen

Almack's was full to overflowing with fashionable creatures of pleasure. The ballroom buzzed with the swaying
movements of their dance. Laughter and witty conversation could be heard in every corner, every corridor.
Thinly sliced ham sandwiches were nibbled at, then absently discarded. Lilly watched all this, and there was a
moment when she was physically ill. She had spent the
day with orphans and a poverty that still burned in her
mind. Here were wasteful people, uncaring creatures. A
frown descended over her pretty features, and she knew
an urge to run as guilt burned her cheeks.

"What is this, little one?" Raeburn tilted her face up
to his. He had watched the expressions flitting over her
face as she glanced round the brightly lit ballroom. Certes she was a beauty in her gown of pink and silver. As
quickly as this thought entered his mind, he chased it
away.

"This!" Lilly's hand went round the room. "All of this
. . . we are all so selfish. There are people starving in the
streets—children." She turned her face away.

"Ah, of course. You were at the orphanage in Soho
today," he answered.

Lilly looked at him, thinking he didn't care. "My lord, it was awful." She wanted him to see, to understand.

He did. He looked back into those grey eyes darkened with the intensity of her feelings, and he wanted suddenly to take her into his arms and hold her, just hold her. How was this? What was wrong with him? How long had it been since he had wanted to hold a woman simply to comfort her; why would he want that? He answered her softly and, in fact, could not resist putting his white gloved hand beneath her bare elbow and drawing her close. "Indeed, little one, it is unthinkable that such things exist in our enlightened world. We are the modern man, yet we allow atrocities to go unchecked." His other gloved hand found its way to her chin, and he tilted it up, noting that her cherry lips pursed adorably. He wanted to kiss her. He continued softly. "You are doing your part. I hope that I am doing mine."

His eyes were so blue . . . his touch, like magic, held her still. What was this? Ridiculous girl, stop at once, she told herself, and she shook the spell off to answer, "Are you?"

The doubt on her face irritated him. Just what did she think of him? He drew back from her. "Indeed, just as you are doing your part tonight."

"Tonight?" she repeated scathingly. "Tonight all we do is waste time, waste money on frivolous pursuits."

"Perhaps, but this life exists. It will not go away, and if you want to help, as you must, as we all must, then we must do our part by making ourselves pleasant company. These people are the ones whose assistance we need. They will be persuaded in the end far better by a friend . . . don't you think?"

It was a reality. Reluctantly she conceded. "I suppose . . ." She sighed and said, "I am sorry. I am no doubt boring you with my melancholy."

105

"No, you are not, little beauty. I have yet to find anything you do or say that is boring." His blue eyes were twinkling as he brought her wrist to his lips.

She peeped at him. "There you are doing it again, and we have agreed to—"

"To flirt outrageously whenever Sir Anthony is about, and my little one, he is about." The Earl indicated with a lift of his chin just where Sir Anthony stood.

"So he is," answered Lilly quietly. "I was quite forgetting Sir Anthony, and I really must not."

The Earl regarded her for a thoughtful moment. "Did he get so very close to my wild Lilly? Did he hurt you so completely?"

She shrugged, unwilling to bare her heart to him. "He behaved badly, suffice it to say that he should not be allowed to hurt others in the same fashion." She then smiled naughtily at the Earl and touched his lapel. "There . . . have I the knack, my lord? I am now dallying with you."

It was so adorably said that he was caught off guard and threw back his head with his laughter. "Indeed, imp, you have the knack!"

She smiled warmly at him before saying casually, "I met an old friend of yours today."

"Ah, Justin?"

"Yes, yes, how did you guess?" Then without waiting for his reply, she hurried on, "He is a wonderful person, dedicated, so well informed."

A twinge of something unnamed nearly made the Earl's eyelid twitch. He frowned, but managed to maintain his even temper. "Justin's efforts to continue his mother's work are to be applauded." Even to himself he sounded cool and crisp.

Lilly eyed him speculatively. "He said you are a subscriber to his orphanage, and you must be aware that I know how very much you have helped with our 'home' for orphans back at Lymington. You are very good."

"Goodness has nought to do with it," he answered gruffly.

Lilly frowned, for she took him at his word. She did not realize he was being modest.

"No? I suppose not," she answered quietly. There was no time to delve into it; for Harry appeared at that moment. "Well and zounds!" ejaculated the red-headed gentleman. "Do you mean to keep my Lilly to yourself all night?" Having chastised his friend, Harry turned to bow grandly to Lilly. "Stap me, love, you are the loveliest creature here . . . in all of England . . . in all of Europe."

Lilly laughed. The Earl responded testily, "Go away, Harry." The amiable light in his blue eyes softened the words, and Harry released a hearty laugh. "Not without darling Lilly."

Harry gleefully led Lilly to the floor while the Earl watched them. She moved gracefully to the music. Her smile was warm and bright and infinitely alluring. Her laughter reached the Earl's ears, and it was an infectious sound that swept through his entire body. He felt himself drawn towards her, but it was something he could not call desire. It was not desire . . . was it? He called a halt to such thoughts with an abruptness that left him frowning once more. This was absurd. What was wrong with him? He was past the stage at which a pretty face could enchant him to proceed towards anything but the bed, and Lilly was not meant for that road! Even as he banished all feeling, he looked in her direction, could not seem to look away . . .

* * *

Sir Anthony strolled leisurely around the ballroom of Almack's and surveyed the dancers on the floor. Elizabeth Hawkins and her mother were not present. He had not expected that they would be present at Almack's. Elizabeth's mother came from good aristocratic stock, but when she married into trade she gave up all chances of having her daughter issued vouchers to London's most exclusive club. Right then, what other little heiress could he pursue? Just to be on the safe side in case the Hawkins chit would not take his suit, and it was beginning to look—feel—as though she just might not fall for his charms. An odd thing that, but now and then it happened. So for his back-up, who then? There was Sophia Rothman idly conversing with some young pup. She had spots and dreadful taste in clothing. Her figure was plump, but then, so was her fortune. He moved towards the unsuspecting Sophia.

Lilly's giggle came to his ears, and he turned to find her on Sir Harry's arm and walking towards the Earl of Raeburn. Certes! There was no denying the chit was a beauty! She stood out in a room full of fashion. Her gown of pink and silver was a confection of froth that perfectly suited her provocative figure, and she moved with assurance and certain grace. Her black hair was done in high Grecian curls round her exquisite face; her cherry lips were pursed and looked ready to be kissed. Ay then, he thought, this one would have been perfect to carry his name if only she'd had the fortune to go with the face. He puzzled over this problem a moment. Her gown must have cost a goodly sum? The pearls at her neck and ears were an enviable set. Right then, how were such things funded if she was without means? Could he have been misled? Had they thrown him off the track on purpose? Lady Sarah had not approved of him. Could Lilly be an heiress?

This thought provoked yet another. Lilly's godmother was Lady Augusta. Now there was a fortune, and Lady Augusta was childless. There was an inheritance there, was there not? Of course, Lord Wizbough's fortune would go to his male heirs, but Lady Augusta had an independence that she may have bequeathed to Lilly in her will? Speculation, but certainly well worth looking into, and soon!

Sir Anthony knew just how to position himself so that he came upon Lilly before Sir Harry had a chance to return her to the Earl. He nodded a brief greeting at Sir Harry and bent a gallant bow to Lilly. "Dearest Miss Aulderbury, I am delighted to find you here, as I had no other reason to present myself at Almack's tonight, save in the hope, the single hope that I should find you here." He thought himself skilled at his art as he lowered his voice softly to add, "Won't you reward my efforts and grant me a moment of your time?"

"Take yourself off, knave." Harry grinned amicably. "I don't mean to share my Lilly with you or any other impudent dog."

Sir Anthony chose to ignore him and smiled his most tantalizing smile at the lady. "He calls you Lilly. I remember a day when I did so . . ."

She arched a look at him. "Yes, but, you fell out of favor, sir."

"Am I not forgiven? Then grant me the minute . . ." He was not above begging, he knew that he did it so well.

Lilly mentally sneered, but she showed him a pretty smile. "A minute, then, but you must return me to the safe-keeping of my aunt afterwards." She turned to touch Harry assuagingly. "I shan't be long, dear friend."

Her words softened the dismissal, and he quickly bent

over her fingers to fervently declare, "Were it forever, I would wait."

Lilly giggled and blew him a bold kiss as she turned to Sir Anthony and allowed him the warm light of her grey eyes. "Now, sir, you have but a moment."

He took her elbow and led her away from the crowd, managing a private corner near a wide white Roman-styled column. "A moment? 'Tis not enough, how could it be? A lifetime would not be enough to spend with you."

She laughed. "Sir Anthony Meade, I was a green girl in the country; mark me, I am no more!"

"You doubt me?" he asked as though incredulous that she could.

"No, how should I doubt you?" she bantered. "Do please tell me more. Do my eyes dazzle you? Do my lips beckon? Do you go mad at the thought of putting your hand at my waist and leading me into a waltz?"

He chuckled. Indeed, the child had attained some womanhood. "And you will have none of that? I am a fool, am I not? No, you must not be courted in the usual fashion, my wondrous girl. Tell me, how shall I court you?"

"Do you mean to?" she asked with a saucy toss of her curls.

"Until you are mine," he answered at once.

"Bold words," said a hard male voice coming from behind Sir Anthony. He whirled and found the Earl of Raeburn standing before him, and it occurred to him that the Earl looked as though he wanted to kill, looked as though he could.

"Indeed, but if they sound bold, they offer a gentle meaning," Sir Anthony offered to the stern mountainous man facing him down.

"Lilly, your aunt requires your company. Come, I will

take you to her," said the Earl, ignoring Sir Anthony as he bent his arm for Lilly's hand.

Lilly complied demurely, but she turned to give Sir Anthony a wildly flirtatious look. She left him feeling breathless and looking forward to their next encounter, and when she got out of his range, she giggled. "Why, my lord, you did that so well! *I* very nearly thought you were jealous."

Raeburn's impatience with himself, with the situation, was written across his brow. What was going on? Well, at least Lilly was not really interested in Sir Anthony again. From her tone, he could tell she had not fallen into the devil's trap this night. He eyed her sternly, "Playing deep, eh, m'girl?"

"I have him nearly baited, don't I?" returned Lilly, happy with herself.

"That is a singularly vulgar expression," admonished the Earl. "And yes, I am very certain that you do, but his intentions are *not* honourable, of that make no mistake."

"No, how can they be? He thinks I am penniless." Lilly sighed over the problem. "Still . . . he is wondering how I am able to afford this season, these clothes . . . jewels."

"How do you know that?"

"I know. I saw it in his eyes," she said almost sadly.

Did she still care about Meade? The notion stirred the Earl uncomfortably.

"The man is a cur. You must not forget that, Lilly. He is far more ruthless than you know how to be. He must be to survive, you see."

"He is despicable, more so than I ever imagined. Do you know, my lord, I really think he means to take me to his bed . . . me! How can he do such a thing? It would ruin me; still, he would do it!"

"I know, child." The Earl touched her arm. "Does that hurt you?"

"Because of him? No ... but it does shock me still that someone could be so heartless. I mean, after all, you would not do that, and you are quite a rakehell—or so I am told." She peeped up at him lest he be offended.

He was not, and displayed this with a chuckle. "Come then, little one. Your aunt does indeed await you."

She smiled at the Earl. "Odd, you know, I was determined not to like you, but I find that I do."

He was taken aback and realized that her words tickled something pleasurable inside him. "Outspoken to a fault, do you know that, brat?" And then, "I find that in spite of my determination to avoid contact with a green country girl, I am with her nearly all the time, and find her company tolerably acceptable."

"Ha! You like me very well, admit it!" teased Lilly, laughing.

"Never," he retorted and flicked her nose.

"I have heard such dreadful things about you, but I suppose many of those things were rumours," she mused out loud, as her mind took a new tangent.

"Ah, reputation, reputation, longer than I will it live," he said wryly.

"Indeed, rumours. 'Tis the very thing!" ejaculated Lilly.

"What is buzzing about in that pretty head of yours now?" He eyed her warily.

"Don't you see? That's what I need to tip the scales. A rumour. If Meade thought me an heiress, well then, the man would be mine, don't you think?"

"No."

"Of course he would."

"He knows you are not an heiress," said the Earl firmly.

"Does he? What he knows is what my aunt wished him and all other fortune hunters to know. 'Tis a guarded secret—my fortune, that is, do you see?"

"Where did it come from?"

"From my uncle—Wizzy, my godfather!"

"That won't work my girl, because Wizzy's fortune is entailed to his male heirs for the most part," he returned dampeningly.

"Right then, from Gussie—and perhaps, a distant uncle somewhere could have died and left me a sizeable portion that no one knew about." She was beaming excitedly, and exclaimed, "I am brilliant."

"You are a preposterous child," retorted the Earl scathingly. "Do you think this rumour will stand once it gets to my aunt's ears, or to your Aunt Sarah's?"

"Hmmmm." Lilly saw that this was an obstacle and gave it some consideration before putting up a finger to whisper. "Right then, my lord, we must be very careful how we give Meade the news."

"We? What do you mean we?"

"Well, I thought perhaps you could carry the tale to him . . . and perhaps you could caution him not to say a word." She narrowed her eyes as she went into deep thought. "He won't want anyone else to know, for he will want my fortune for himself."

"I am taking you to your aunt, where I hope you may come to your senses," he returned gravely.

"My lord . . . do not . . . I must think. Don't return me just yet. Please, my lord, I need you to help me in this?"

The Earl's jaw had dropped, and he shook his head as his blue eyes glinted with sure disapproval. "No, Lilly. A little flirting, perhaps, but this . . . no and again, no."

113

"Oh, my lord, 'tis the only way . . . please. Don't you see? He will make love to some poor girl—they say the Hawkins heiress—and she will believe he adores her when 'tis only her money he wants. She will end with a ring around her finger and no one to share her life with. 'Tis unfair. He doesn't play fair. He pretends an emotion he isn't capable of feeling. It isn't a marriage of convenience because he steals the heart of these girls. He doesn't make a deal with them honestly. No, he pretends, pursues and then leaves them. Allow me my game with Sir Anthony."

The Earl of Raeburn was frowning. This was all absurd, yet she drew on sensibilities he wasn't aware he still possessed. Her logic was off key and still drew him within its aura. "This sort of thing is not what I like," he offered, but he knew himself fairly trapped. Something in her grey eyes forbade reason. He should get away from her and her nonsense. What had he to do with such as this? Still he stayed to argue.

"You may not like the means, but the end, my lord, perhaps you will like the end?" bantered the lady.

He laughed and touched her chin. "You are a comely girl and you tempt a man to leave reason behind, but I have not attained my years without learning how to avoid doing what I don't wish to do."

"What if I begged you? What if I toad-eat?"

He put up a hand to interrupt her flow, "Enough. You are a sauce-box trying to turn me into a gull-catcher, but for now I mean to lead you onto the floor for a cotillion where this conversation can not continue without great difficulty."

Meekly, Lilly allowed him to turn her towards the dance floor, but she caught his attention once more by dropping the subject they had just been debating to say in her most adorable fashion, "Yes, my lord, but tell me, do, what is a gull-catcher?"

Chapter Fourteen

Lord Wizbough had just settled back down in his leather-bound winged chair to resume his reading after he stoked the fire. It seemed chilly and drafty to him this night, though spring was well on its way. The sound of happy female chatter filtered through, and he smiled as he got to his feet. Finally, his lady was home. He took quick long strides and hurriedly opened the library door wide to discover his wife in a bevy of high spirits. They had been married twenty-five years, and it never ceased to amaze him that the sight of her tall and lively form filled him with unmatchable pleasure. Since they had been apart nearly four weeks, he now felt much like a love-sick schoolboy. She was after all these years still very much his sweetheart. He went forward, hands extended.

Something, a feeling, a sense made Augusta spin round, for she had not been facing the library. She saw her husband at once, and with a joyful exclamation went to him and found her ample body taken in his embrace. "Wizzy," she said softly, "you have come."

"Did you doubt it, goose?" He chuckled.

"Well, you certainly took your time," Gussie said petulantly, and then smiled. "But, you are here now." She turned to Sarah and Lilly and allowed them to come forward and greet her husband. A few moments after their warm reunion, they were all seated near the fire taking turns at regaling Wizzy with their doings in London.

The last few weeks were recounted by three females from three different points of view, at length, with a great deal of animation, satisfaction and some pride. Lilly embellished every story with the dramatics of youth. She would jump to her feet, clap her hands, use gestures in describing this or that. She made faces and she mimicked until all were rollicking with laughter.

Lord Wizbough was much amused, but finally put up a hand. "No more, no more. I am thoroughly exhausted."

"Yes, but Uncle Wizzy," protested Lilly, "I was just coming to the part about—"

"Lady Duncan with the purple turban," Augusta put in. "Oh Wizzy, 'twas priceless."

"I am certain." He got to his feet. "However, 'tis late and I am old and need my rest." His eyes were twinkling at his wife. "I bid thee Sarah and dearest Lilly, good night."

Lilly watched them leave the room and sighed. Would she ever love like that? Would anyone ever love her like that? Would it be mutual?

As though reading her mind, her aunt touched her arm. "Indeed, my niece, they are very lucky. I was as well, and I am certain you, too, shall be."

So it was with the arrival of Lord Wizbough, the Earl of Raeburn's services as genial escort were no longer needed. Right then, he told himself as he considered this newfound freedom. He should be relieved and happy to be on his way. Certainly, his time was much in demand. He tossed the letter he had just had from his aunt into the wastepaper basket. The missive informed him that he was now at liberty to do as he pleased as his uncle was there to escort the ladies to the Venetian Breakfast they'd had Lady Hazelton put together to raise funds for the "home."

The Earl picked himself up, took his dark blue top hat, his greatcoat and gloves and made for his front doors. His man had them already opened as he approached. He was for Harry's lodgings. No doubt together they could find ways to amuse themselves this day. Still . . . there was this odd feeling pestering at him.

He walked the short distance to his friend's establishment, a bachelor's comfortable and adequate but simple abode no great distance from his own. There he found Harry just coming down the stone steps. "Cameron!" Harry exclaimed in some surprise. "You here?"

"Fool of a man." The Earl grinned. "You can see that I am. Where are you off to?"

"Lady Hazelton's Venetian . . . eh? Why aren't you escorting your aunt and Lilly there?" Then, as panic set in, "Never say they aren't going?"

"Take a damper, you lovesick fool. They have to be there; they are the ones who convinced Hazelton to sponsor this event to raise funds for Reynolds' orphanage. My uncle is in town. He is escorting them."

Harry had been finding his best friend very much in the way these past few weeks. It seemed as though the Earl was forever at Lilly's side, making it difficult to make any headway with her. This new piece of information was therefore quite welcome. With Lord Wizbough about, the Earl would not be expected to dance attendance on the ladies. Cameron would no doubt return to his old haunts and leave the path clear to court Lilly in

117

serious style. Harry put a solicitous hand on his friend's broad shoulder and sympathized.

"Cast aside, eh? Well, I'm off!"

It was obvious that Harry did not understand. The Earl glared at him. "What the devil do you mean you are off? Why are you still going? 'Tis bound to be a dull affair. We'll post our donations. No need to be there in person, Harry."

"What are you talking about?" Harry returned. "Don't you know? Haven't you seen that blackguard, Felix Winthrop, attempting to make mad love to Lilly whenever he can? If I don't keep on m'toes, he'll steal a march on me. And I am not going to lose Lilly to Felix!"

The Earl laughed, for Harry and Felix had been rivals over women since their days at Cambridge and the Earl had always suspected that they enjoyed the rivalry more than the women. "Certes, man, don't be a noddy. Lilly won't have either of you."

Harry eyed him narrowly. "Won't she, by Jove? Why not?"

"Bright girl, Lilly Aulderbury, too bright to be hoodwinked by the likes of you and Felix," bantered the Earl.

"Eh, well, and we'll have to see." Harry hesitated before saying on a deliberately casual note, "Julian and Anthea will be there."

The Earl's blue eyes lost their twinkle, and he studied the top of his friend's carrot-colored locks a long moment before replying,

"I did not know that Julian and his bride had returned from America."

"Ay, well, with the States in an uproar and warring with us again, he thought it best to bring her home. They have been in London the better part of the week."

The Earl's handsome features were touched by the

118

suspicion of a sneer. "And this piece of information should induce me to attend the breakfast or stay away, which dear friend?"

Harry was serious all at once. " 'Tis time you saw Julian . . . and Anthea. You and Julian were friends, and, Cameron, you didn't deserve what you had from him. You should not have extracted a promise from me to keep mum about what happened. He should have been told the truth."

"He thought I was trying to steal the woman he loved, and he did not think I even cared for her. He was right in that, for by the time I realized she was playing us one against the other, I no longer did care for her."

"You are telling yourself and me a lie. You loved her."

"That was not love. I wanted her . . . and did not know her."

"You should have told Julian what she was."

"Why? He would not have believed me. My aunt, Gussie, tried to tell *me* what the fair Anthea was beneath her beauteous skin. I didn't believe it."

"Still, Julian should have been told. You made a sacrifice for his sake."

The Earl's harsh laugh cut him off. "In the end it was no sacrifice, and perhaps I did Julian an injustice by allowing him to have her."

Harry readily agreed to this with a sure smirk. "Ay, he may have thought he saw her in your embrace, but she didn't take long after they were married to find the beds of most of his friends!" Again he shook his head with disgust. "You should have told him."

"Harry, told him what? Should I have said, Julian, we are warring over a tart? Should I have said that she followed me into the garden? Should I have said she forced her kiss on me. *That* would have been a lie. I wanted her then, so I don't know how much I discouraged that last kiss."

"You . . . she . . ."

"Stop, Harry. 'Tis done. Julian was a man then as well as now. He had eyes. He must have known in his heart of hearts what she was. If he wanted to blame me, well, then he was driven. He could not help himself."

"He was blind. He wanted Anthea."

"No doubt he is still blind . . . perhaps hopefully so." The Earl looked at Harry thoughtfully. "I know he no longer counts me friend, and I am reluctant to regain his friendship by bursting his tenuous bubble of happiness."

"Come then, Cameron, and that bubble of his . . . I have a notion 'tis already burst. Come and decide for yourself," said Harry grimly.

Lilly adored Lord Wizbough. She was completely and totally pleased to have his escort and grateful for the wondrous season he was giving her. It had not dawned on her until they reached the Hazelton household for the Venetian Breakfast that this would mean she would no longer have Lord Raeburn's company.

As this fact imbedded itself into her conscious thoughts she realized at once how very disappointing this was, to be sure. After all, he was always so intriguing and such good fun. Well, she told herself, Uncle Wizzy was good fun. Still she found herself asking her godmother,

"Does the Earl not attend the breakfast this morning?"

Augusta waved this off. "La, my dear child. Poor Cameron has been dutifully dancing attendance on us while Wizzy was away. I wrote the dear boy and told him he was quite free to pursue his own pleasures now that Wizzy has arrived." As an afterthought, she said, "Though I am certain he will contribute a respectable donation. He has always been very good about such things."

"Oh." It was all Lilly could think of to say. Why did the words "poor Cameron" bother her so very much? Well, she had been silly to imagine that the Earl had perhaps enjoyed her company. She was being foolish to think . . . What had she thought? Nothing. Lilly turned and started to flirt with the young man patiently awaiting her attention.

It was at this moment that the Earl of Raeburn with Sir Harry at his side entered the room. Lilly noted that he commanded attention with his handsome features, his broad shoulders, his air. His blue eyes found her and twinkled and she felt a rush of inexplicable pleasure. However, this was short-lived.

An elegant woman with glistening blond hair and exquisite beauty stepped between them. Lilly could see that she was a lady of fashion and that she and the Earl were very well acquainted. The woman touched his shoulder. He took her gloved hands and set her aside, no doubt, Lilly thought, so that he could better view her beauty. The woman laughed and linked her arm through his as she took him to another part of the room. Lilly turned away and gave her full attention to the patient young man still awaiting her response to his unheard question.

Raeburn looked into Anthea's china blue eyes and wondered what he had ever seen in the woman. Hell, there was no gainsaying she was beautiful, but there was a coldness in those eyes that reached down to her heart.

He remembered the first time he and Julian had sported for her favors. It had been a game, only a game, and then Julian had announced that he was in love, that he was serious. Raeburn remembered the feeling of cold shock. What to do? He rather thought he loved Anthea as well, but marriage? Marriage was something he still wanted to think about. He wasn't sure. Julian had accused him of playing fast and loose with Anthea's feelings, and so he had withdrawn from the game. He had tried to convince Julian of that.

Now he looked round the room for Julian. Instead he saw Lilly, doing very well for herself with some young buck. He watched her a moment, diverted by her antics, for he had never seen her flirt to such an extent. She looked his way, and he inclined his head. She scarcely acknowledged him.

"What?" Somewhere in the background he heard Anthea jibber-jabbering at him, "Oh, yes, the colonies." He felt a male hand on his shoulder, heard Julian's familiar voice greet Harry, who had suddenly returned, and then himself. He turned to see his old friend and warmly welcomed him.

Anthea took over this first meeting of theirs with a series of worthless babble, and Julian withdrew into silence as he watched her. Disgusted, the Earl gave Anthea his back, leaving Harry to do the polite as he took his old friend's elbow and steered him off. "Time," Raeburn said quietly, "heals all wounds I am told, so I must hope that I am forgiven my trespasses."

"It should be I asking for *your* forgiveness," Julian returned on a frown.

"The past is lost, but the future ... ah?" The Earl smiled, then rammed his shoulder none too gently into his friend's. "Or perhaps we may yet be saved from the future. Come then, I want you to meet my aunt's goddaughter. I have been dutifully squiring her about this season and have come to consider myself very nearly her guardian. I can see that she is misbehaving with nearly every drooling puppy in the room and must call her to order!"

"Guardian? Duty? No . . . Something has gone wrong with my hearing?" Julian laughed.

"Not at all. I think I am fast becoming a reformed rake," said the Earl somberly.

Julian's hazel eyes lit with amusement. "Impossible, you forget who it is you are talking to."

A moment later he found himself looking at a petite package of sassy beauty as he was introduced to Miss Lilly Aulderbury. He eyed Raeburn for a long moment, and there was a question in the look. This chit, though lovely, was obviously an innocent miss and one that was under the Earl's family's protection. Surely it was not the Earl's style to seduce such a maid? Julian bent low over Lilly's hand and softly said, "Well, and I am honoured to meet the woman who seems to be reforming my old friend."

"And from what quarter have you had such nonsense?" Lilly as always was direct to a fault. "Not a woman in all of England could do that, and besides, I rather think he is just fine the way he is." As this last was uttered she wondered at herself. She certainly did not approve of libertines, and yet, here she was giving his status her approval.

"Then I take it Cameron is still up to his usual wicked larks and has not been a good boy?"

Lilly laughed and eyed the Earl playfully. "I know not first-hand sir, but I am told that the Earl of Raeburn is always good at everything he chooses to do whether it be wicked or no."

The Earl inclined his head and took her chin. "Sauce-box. You are in need of a beating."

"Nay, unhand the beauty, brute!" Julian bowed dramatically for Lilly. "Shall I thrash him, my lady?"

"No . . . not yet. I may need his services—soon," Lilly returned eyeing the Earl once more and with meaning.

"You would not say so if you knew all his wicked crimes," confided Julian, enjoying himself immensely.

"Then quickly recount them to me," Lilly bantered merrily.

"La! My darlings," cut in Lady Anthea possessively as she approached with poor Harry in tow. "Lady Hazelton has kindly rearranged the seating at breakfast so that I may have you, Cameron, and Harry on either side." Of her husband's place she said nothing.

Julian detained her and politely introduced her to Lilly, who could not help but notice that with this woman's arrival something in the air had changed. Anthea was quick to ignore Lilly who bristled, but the other woman's skill was great as she seemed to flirt with all three gentlemen at once. Lilly felt a moment's bout of jealousy. Nonsensical girl, she told herself. You have been the center of attention these past weeks because you were new. It has all been very pleasant, but such experiences are tentative at best.

Some ten minutes later she found herself seated with Felix Winthrop on one side and a young admirer on the other. Directly across from her sat Harry. Next to Harry was Anthea, at her other side, the Earl. Julian was at the far end of the table. Lilly attempted to gain the Earl's attention for she wanted to speak to him about Sir Anthony, but he never appeared to look her way. She sighed and put this aside with some determination as she gave herself over to a naughty flirtation with Felix. Harry eyed his rival with absolute fury and frustration,

124

and when Felix attempted to feed Lilly a hothouse strawberry Harry nearly stood to attention and spat a threat across the table. Lilly laughed and wagged a finger at Harry as she advised Felix that she was perfectly capable of feeding herself. Thus, the morning moved into afternoon.

Chapter Fifteen

Lilly smiled to hear her godmother complaining bitterly to Lady Sarah as they climbed the steps to the front doors of the orphanage. Lady Augusta was becoming far too attached to the poor little urchins. This had happened in spite of the barrier she had put up to protect herself from just such a thing. One in particular seemed to hold her interest.

"He is a perfectly horrid little waif who is stealing my heart, and he will no doubt steal my purse if ever he gets the chance," snapped Augusta. "Do you remember Tom? Do you, Sarah?"

"Young Tom was a charmer, and I am afraid was already too set in his ways to change when you came across him, Gussie. He just could not help himself." Sarah sighed. "There can be no comparison here."

"No? Well . . . I tell you 'tis going to happen to me again, and I just can't seem to stop myself from caring about the little beast!" Gussie was quite caught up with this problem; it nearly had her in tears.

Lilly touched her shoulder. "Gussie . . . 'tis different, you are different, the situation is different. You will see."

They were met at the door by Reynolds who explained that Mrs. Brooks was out on a bargain spree with both Mrs. Hawkins and her daughter, Elizabeth. He went on to clasp their hands warmly and congratulate them on the Venetian Breakfast Fund and to comment on Raeburn's speech in the House of Lords.

They had moved down the corridor and Lilly was removing her gloves when she heard this last and stopped short to repeat questioningly, "Speech?"

"Indeed, a bold piece on the conditions of the needy and the reforms required to lend them aid. It was very well received," returned Justin Reynolds enthusiastically.

Lilly was pleasantly surprised. She had not realized that the Earl was inclined in that direction. However, she wasn't given any time to dwell on that as Reynolds led them about. She watched Justin as he spoke and noted that he smiled with his eyes as well as his mouth, and it was this that ultimately decided her; yes, she liked Justin Reynolds.

They were momentarily diverted by a small boy who came to stand in front of Augusta and regard her with large imploring eyes as he said in a frightened voice, "Please, oi be needing ye, oi do, fer oi can't manage wit 'is abuse no more and Mrs. Brooks said oi was to come for'ard if 'ee started on me again."

"You have done the right thing, Jess. Come along and we shall get to to bottom of this immediately," returned Augusta ready for war.

"Ay then," agreed young Jess, regarding his champion with adoring eyes.

As Augusta took the small boy's hand and the others followed, she inquired doubtfully, "Are you stating that his attack was unprovoked?"

"Well, don't know whot that means, but it was out of course a noddleheaded thing to do." He shrugged. "Stands to reason oi'd go fer help."

"You don't know what it means, eh?" stuck in Reynolds. "Well then, it means, did you do anything to cause this boy to er . . . have at you?"

"Whot? Do ye toike me for daft then? He be more than twice me size." Jess shook his head of dark curls.

"Right then, come along," said Mr. Reynolds, this time taking the lead.

Lilly watched Augusta with the small boy. In the last few visits young Jess and Augusta had gravitated towards one another. He was a charming little urchin with a sweet smile, and it was easy to understand why he looked up to Augusta.

The children enjoyed an hour of free time in the afternoons, and it was then that Jess had been encountering his problem, an older, bigger boy. Lilly watched as Reynolds approached this lad, and noted he was the largest in the room. He was also somber and perhaps the oldest in the home, but there was still the touch of innocence in his face for he was no more than ten years old. His movements showed that he had a stubborn streak, but when confronted by Augusta he lowered his eyes to the uncarpeted highly polished wood floor.

Lilly watched as the boy stood silent, listening to Justin Reynolds quiet scold before he raised his eyes and pointed at Jess. "Ye bleater! 'Tis all ye know—blab, blab, ye bottleheaded halfling!"

Now Jess began to whimper. Justin raised a brow and told him there was nought to cry about. The older boy contradicted Mr. Reynolds and said, "Ay, but there is and 'ee knows it. A bleater knows what comes 'is way in the end!"

Justin Reynolds challenged this in a voice close to anger as Jess continued to whimper. It was Augusta who finally silenced them all.

"Enough!" she said taking control.

Gussie turned to young Jess and firmly yet softly or-

You
can enjoy
more of
the newest
and best
Regency
Romance
novels.
Subscribe
now and...
**GET
3 FREE
REGENCY
ROMANCE
NOVELS—
A \$11.97
VALUE!**

TAKE ADVANTAGE OF THIS SPECIAL OFFER, AVAILABLE *ONLY* TO ZEBRA REGENCY ROMANCE READERS.

You are a reader who enjoys the very special kind of love story that can only be found in Zebra Regency Romances. You adore the fashionable English settings, the sparkling wit, the captivating intrigue, and the heart-stirring romance that are the hallmarks of each Zebra Regency Romance novel.

Now, you can have these delightful novels delivered right to your door each month and never have to worry about missing a new book. Zebra has made arrangements through its Home Subscription Service for you to preview the three latest Zebra Regency Romances as soon as they are published.

3 **FREE** REGENCIES TO GET STARTED!

To get your subscription started, we will send your first 3 books ABSOLUTELY FREE, as our introductory gift to you. NO OBLIGATION. We're sure that you will enjoy these books so much that you will want to read more of the very best romantic fiction published today.

SUBSCRIBERS SAVE EACH MONTH

Zebra Regency Home Subscribers will save money each month as they enjoy their latest Regencies. As a subscriber you will receive the 3 newest titles to preview FREE for ten days. Each shipment will be at least a $11.97 value (publisher's price). But home subscribers will be billed only $9.90 for all three books. You'll save over $2.00 each month. Of course, if you're not satisfied with any book, just return it for full credit.

FREE HOME DELIVERY

Zebra Home Subscribers get free home delivery. There are never any postage, shipping or handling charges. No hidden charges. What's more, there is no minimum number to buy and you can cancel your subscription at any time. No obligation and no questions asked.

TO GET YOUR 3 FREE BOOKS
LL OUT AND MAIL THE COUPON BELOW

3 FREE BOOKS

Mail to: Zebra Regency Home Subscription Service
120 Brighton Road
P.O. Box 5214
Clifton, New Jersey 07015-5214

YES! Start my Regency Romance Home Subscription and send me my 3 FREE BOOKS as my introductory gift. Then each month, I'll receive the 3 newest Zebra Regency Romances to preview FREE for ten days. I understand that if I'm not satisfied, I may return them and owe nothing. Otherwise, I'll pay the low members' price of just $9.90 for all 3 books and save over $2.00 off the publisher's price (a $11.97 value). There are no shipping, handling or other hidden charges. I may cancel my subscription at any time and there is no minimum number to buy. In any case, the 3 FREE books are mine to keep regardless of what I decide.

NAME _____

ADDRESS _____ APT NO. _____

CITY _____ STATE _____ ZIP _____

TELEPHONE ( ) _____

SIGNATURE _____ (if under 18 parent or guardian must sign)

RG0194

Terms and prices subject to change. Orders subject to acceptance by Zebra Home Subscription Service, Inc.

GET
3 FREE
REGENCY
ROMANCE
NOVELS—
A $11.97
VALUE!

ZEBRA HOME SUBSCRIPTION SERVICE, INC.
120 BRIGHTON ROAD
P.O. BOX 5214
CLIFTON, NEW JERSEY 07015-5214

AFFIX
STAMP
HERE

dered, "Go on then and return to your little game or your drawing or whatever it was you were doing before all this nonsense started."

"Oi was playing at ducks and drakes oi was . . . wit Jeremy," returned Jess on a whine.

"Right then, ducks and drakes it is," answered Lady Augusta who then rounded on the ten-year-old boy. "What may I ask is your name, young man?"

"Francis," he answered defiantly, "and right proud of it oi am."

"Well, and why shouldn't you be?" Augusta was surprised. "Francis is a fine name."

"There are them that thinks otherwise, m'lady," the ten-year-old grumbled.

"Are there? Well then, they have not enough education and must receive more." She looked round the room, squared off with Justin Reynolds who was looking tolerantly amused and said, "I am not at all comfortable here, and I don't think you are either. Would you like to go with me for a walk in the courtyard?"

Francis eyed her reluctantly. Of all things he wanted to go outdoors. There was not very much to do in the playroom, and his self-appointed job as bully had not allowed him friends. He mistrusted adults, yet something he could not understand drew him to Lady Augusta. He nodded his head in agreement. "Ay then."

"Well, Francis, what are we waiting for?" She reached for his hand. He refused it to her and grumbled that he was not a baby. She met Justin's eye and heard him whisper, "I do not believe in rewarding unacceptable behavior."

"Nor do I. However, one must at times get to the heart of the matter before making a judgment. Communication, Justin. 'Tis always wise to try."

Lilly watched Augusta go off with Francis and turned

129

to see her aunt in conversation with one of the young girls. She smiled to herself and then to Justin Reynolds. "Well then, 'tis a grand start, sir. What have you in store for me?"

"Hard work, Miss Aulderbury, very hard work. Our educator, Mr. Prim, advised me only this morning that he required some help with the grading of their last assignment. Do you think . . . ?"

"With the greatest of pleasure. Lead the way," Lilly agreed, beaming.

It was some hours later that Lilly descended the stairs of the Wizbough townhouse in thoughtful preoccupation about the events of her day. There was so much to do. They simply needed more volunteers, more housing. It was time the London aristocracy thought of more than their daily pleasures. Gold taffeta rustled as she moved, and she smoothed a gloved hand over the high-waisted lines of her gown. She wore Lady Augusta's topaz drops in her ears and a matching necklace round her pretty throat. As she approached the library she wondered who would be present for their little dinner party that evening. A moment's excitement swept through her when she thought the Earl of Raeburn would probably be among the gathering. Indeed, she thought. It would be perfect, for then she could have further conversation with him about her plans for Sir Anthony's immediate future. She opened the door to the sound of a warm crackling fire in the hearth and the soft tones of easy conversation.

The Earl of Raeburn stood, brandy glass in hand, by the fireplace. He wore a black velvet coat that fitted his athletic form with a quiet elegance. His white silk shirt and wondrously white satin shortcoat were only excelled by his wide white cravat tied in the Brummell style of the day. His muscular thighs were covered in black satin britches and white stockings shaded his firm hard calves. It was, therefore, not a surprising thing that someone entering the room should be quite riveted by the sight of such an arrestingly handsome presentation. At least, 'twas what Lilly told herself as she stopped to stare.

Lilly's grey eyes took in every detail of his powerful presence before they met his blue and glittering orbs. She felt herself very nearly dazzled and blushed to think she could have her head turned by a handsome rake. Silently she admonished herself. She came into the room then and went to her aunt, who was saying her name as she recounted their afternoon's work at the orphanage.

Lilly dropped a kiss upon her aunt's forehead, swept the others with a delightful smile and moved towards the Earl. After all, why should she feel shy of him? They had a pact, did they not? They meant nothing to one another. He was safe with her and she with him, right?

The Earl watched her as she made her way across the room to him. She was beautiful. Her dusky curls with the gold feather sweeping round one ear set off her piquant face. He smiled to himself. The poor feather would go the way of its predecessors he was sure. Just the other night she had worn a pretty aqua feather that had bothered her once too often. He had been astonished to watch her rip it from her curls and stuff it into her beaded reticule and say, "There, that's better." How he had chuckled. Her ruby lips parted now, and her sweet smile swept his face warmly as she approached. She was an enchanting mix of child and woman, but she was not going to ensnare his heart, he told himself resolutely.

"My lord," whispered the woman-child, "I have so

131

wanted to get you alone. Could we please find a quiet corner together as soon as possible?"

He restrained his laughter. What would she say next? She was forever making him smile. He teased her. "Dangerously put, but you need have no fear; I am too much a gentleman to take advantage of your most exciting offer."

"What?" Then dawning lit. "Oh, yes, gentleman you may be, however, you know there is no offer in the words."

"Alas, I know it to be so," Raeburn replied on a mockingly disheartened note.

She laughed and then touched his arm. "My lord, do try to be serious. 'Tis a matter that must be taken in hand and disposed of if I am ever to have any peace. And if you would like your peace returned to you . . . well, then?"

"You are child of hell," he answered her grimly, but his blue eyes twinkled.

"Yes, I am," she answered, "so you can not refuse me anything."

"Ah, then I must declare myself your very obedient servant, my sweetheart."

He was rewarded for this with a blinding smile, and he marveled at the quantity of pleasure such a meager reward awoke in him.

Chapter Sixteen

Vauxhall, the Regency's playground for the aristocracy and middleclass citizens alike was a place like no other in London. A magical arena of gardens and lights, music and entertainment, elegance and bawdiness. This was Lilly's first visit to Vauxhall and for some minutes she was enthralled with its grandeur and vivacity. Forgotten for the moment was her plan to change the world. Forgotten was her desire to win Sir Anthony's cold heart and feed it to the devil. There was only the moment captured by her youth, taken by the sights and sounds that surrounded her.

"And where do you mean to spirit me off to, my beauty?" inquired Raeburn as he bent his lips to her delicate ear.

"What? Whatever do you mean?" Lilly was instantly diverted.

"Are you not the same woman who just this evening advised me that she required my services alone in a hidden corner? I would think now is the time."

She giggled. "Oh yes, I forgot."

"Alas, my heart breaks." He put a hand to that organ's site and lowered his head.

She slapped him playfully. "Be serious."

"How can I be serious when the subject at hand is the elusive Sir Anthony."

"Well, he won't be so elusive when he discovers that I am an heiress," said the lady unashamedly.

"Indeed?" returned the Earl. "I felicitate you."

"Don't be nonsensical. You know I am not an heiress."

"I *thought* I knew that."

"I mean for *him* to think it," offered Lilly tentatively as she eyed him hopefully.

"Oh no . . . no . . ." started the Earl.

"Please my lord, 'tis absolutely necessary to my entire scheme."

"Lilly, the Earl was suddenly somber, "lies lead us into treacherous waters. Are you sure you want to go into them?" His blue eyes searched her face.

"I must. People should not be allowed to get away with . . . with the hurts they heartlessly inflict on others. Lessons must be taught. Crimes must be punished."

"With truths, not with lies."

"Well, I won't be the one telling him the lie—you will, and it won't be an outright lie, more . . . well . . . an insinuation. If he chooses to pursue me when he believes I am an heiress, then, well, does he not deserve what he gets?"

The Earl grimaced at her. "You are a she-devil if ever there was one."

"But you will do it?"

"Tell me exactly what it is you want me to do?" Just why was he allowing himself to be drawn into her plans? What had he to do with children's games? Had she been so in love with Sir Anthony? The notion that she had, made him frown. What was he doing? He asked the question and then had an urge to run. That's right, all he had to do was say no. It was an easy thing, surely.

He could just say he wouldn't be a party to her ridiculous plans and walk away from it all. Instead he allowed himself to be mesmerized by her soft grey eyes as she answered him. "What I want you to do is give him more than a hint, less than a statement of fact."

There, too, he consoled himself, if he didn't go along with her, she might think of another more outrageous plan and ask aid of someone who could not be trusted to keep her and the family name out of scandal. Now here was a reason to go along with her scheme. He sighed resignedly. "And these wondrous words to do the deed? Will they be yours or mine? Who has the writing of them?"

"You play the part, sir, I will pen the words," she answered saucily.

He tweaked her nose. "Understand me, my dearest wild Lilly. I don't mean to be manipulated by you or anyone else. If I agree to this absurd plan of yours, I will handle it in my way."

"Of course you will," agreed the lady all too pleased to see he might be bending. She knew better than to quibble. "The thing is, it might prove useful if he thinks that as Lady Augusta's godchild and Lord Wizbough's favorite, a handsome amount has been settled on me. After all, it may appear that way, for they *are* sponsoring my season . . . so in a manner of speaking, 'tis not even an outright lie."

"What will you do if he receives this piece of tenuous information and *still* pursues the Hawkins chit?"

"Then I must concede the point," answered the lady promptly. "Perhaps, that would mean he has formed a real attachment in that quarter." She cocked a pretty brow at him. "However, I hardly think that possibility a likely one, as I do not think the man capable of forming a genuine attachment for anyone."

135

He took her hand and held it to his lips, moved his kiss to her wrist. "Perhaps, my little one, if you are very good to me, I might fall in with your schemes."

"Ah," said the lady, gently withdrawing her hand, "I am good to you, for I do not fall in with yours!" Her grey eyes twinkled at him.

He laughed and inclined his head. "Touché, my girl."

Sir Harold arrived at that moment to slap the Earl on the back a mite harder than was friendly. "There you are! Come along, our box awaits and the concert will soon begin."

It was morning. Vauxhall felt like a dream she had had during the night. Reality was here among the children. Lilly shook off the evening's magic and returned to the present, choosing one of the younger girl's drawings to praise. "Well done. That is quite a wonderful-looking creature, isn't it?"

The little girl eyed her. "Aw, ye don't even know whot it is, do ye, Miss Lilly?"

"Nonsensical child, of course I do," answered Lilly, braving it out. She turned to Elizabeth Hawkins who stood near by and waved the sketch at her hopefully. "Look here, Miss Elizabeth, Sally has drawn a very fine horse."

Sally shook her head in some disgust and advised them, " 'Tis a cat."

"Of course it is." Lilly was unruffled. "I was only teasing Miss Elizabeth. I wanted to know if she knew what it was. She is forever getting cats and horses confused."

Little Sally giggled and waved her six-year-old's finger at them. "Aw then Miss Lilly, own up to it, ye didn't know."

136

Lilly mocked a heavy sigh. "Dunce that I am, I suppose that I did not."

"Well then, let this be a lesson to ye," said Sally returning to her crayons and paper.

Elizabeth laughed out loud and whispered to Lilly, "I think you have been roundly scolded."

"So I have." Lilly smiled. " 'Tis time I headed for Mrs. Brooks's tray." She indicated the tea tray set out on the side wall table.

"Oh, that sounds lovely." Elizabeth sighed as she followed Lilly to the repast.

Lilly poured, and as she handed Elizabeth her cup she eyed her thoughtfully for a moment. Her companion was a fairly attractive girl with a goodly height, yet a small frame. Elizabeth's disposition was sweet and her temper mild, but she walked about as if a dark cloud were overhead. Why?

"Elizabeth?"

"Yes?"

"What is wrong? Something has been troubling you, and I think I know you well enough to offer you my help if you need it."

Elizabeth turned away, and Lilly reached for her arm. "Don't draw away. I know we haven't been friends forever, but you may find me strongly loyal nonetheless."

Elizabeth scanned Lilly's face. She liked her and sensed that here could be a lifelong friend she could trust. She needed a confidante of her own age, someone with whom she could really talk. Her father did not understand and her mother did not wish to displease him. "You see . . ." She stopped and looked around and then in an even lower voice whispered, "I am in love."

"Ah," Lilly sighed worldly wise. "Does he not love you?"

"No, no. That is not it. I think he loves me as well."

"Then where is the rub?" Lilly scanned Elizabeth's face.

" 'Tis my father," responded Elizabeth tragically.

"Your father disapproves?"

"He doesn't even know about him, really, but yes, he would disapprove if he did know."

"I suppose I really am a dunce today. Explain Elizabeth, explain!" Lilly demanded impatiently.

" 'Tis so very complicated."

"Put it down in easy sentences," urged Lilly.

"I just don't know how to explain it all . . . where to begin. You see, my father—"

"Darlings," said Lady Augusta, coming into the room with her new protégé, Francis, who was holding her hand. He dropped it quickly as soon as he noticed some of the other children looking his way. Jess was skipping nearby and chatting with Francis as though he were his dearest comrade. A far sight from their encounter of the other day. Lilly eyed them with amusement and gave Augusta a bow. "Gussie, you are amazing!"

Lady Augusta laughed happily and then spied the tea tray. "Ah, refreshment." Augusta was soon followed by Mrs. Hawkins and Lady Sarah. The two women had a length of material between them and were deep in their plans for the fabric's use at the home.

It was obvious to Lilly that she could no longer have any private conversation with Elizabeth, so she whispered to her, "Do you ride, Lizzy?"

"Not very well." Liz pulled a face. "Though I have a nicely mannered gelding and can ride well enough in the park."

"Good, then meet me at the Serpentine in Hyde Park tomorrow at ten in the morning."

138

"Tomorrow it is—I should like that very much Lilly."

"Right then. 'Tis done." Lilly was determined to solve her new friend's problem, whatever it might prove to be.

Chapter Seventeen

Her life was a whirlwind of contradictions. Dedicated, hard-working and concerned by day at the orphanage, absurdly frivolous by night. 'Tis a double life she had said to her aunt, but Sarah's wisdom had taken over. Her aunt had put an arm about her shoulders and softly said, "We don't have to forgo our pleasures, my dear, to be dedicated. We seem to manage what we should. You'll do."

Right then. So here she was at the Merriweathers' ball, encased in a lovely gown of blue and silver, with Lord Raeburn twirling her round the ballroom to a lively waltz. She was enjoying herself immensely when she spotted Sir Anthony Meade entering the ballroom. "My lord, there he is now! You may go and do it at once!"

"What, puss, and leave you in the middle of the floor during this beautiful waltz? Never. Not gentlemanly, you know." He was grinning broadly down at her pretty face.

Lilly giggled and arched a look at him. "Well, I don't exactly mean this very minute. You may do it at the end of the waltz, my lord."

"May I, indeed?" returned the Earl. "How very sporting of you, my little dictator. No, I don't think so." He sounded maddeningly in control.

"What can you mean? You said you would do it."

"Did I?"

"You insinuated that you would."

"Insinuations are unreliable things," teased the Earl.

The lady's chin was up. "I was rather counting on you, but evidently I was wrong to do so. I shall have to ask some other friend to help me then."

He frowned. He should tell her to go and ask any damned soul she chose. Instead, he said, "Come now. You know no other could do the thing quite as neatly as I."

She directed a look at him. "Agreed. So then you will?"

"At my leisure and when the time is right," he found himself answering.

She pouted adorably, and he restrained himself from touching her lips with his own. She asked to be kissed. Every movement, every twinkle of her eyes, every smile begged a man to take her in his arms. He knew better. Did he not? Indeed, he was no fool!

"Seems to me," suggested the lady relentlessly, "the time is right."

"Right is it? What would you have me do? Stroll up to the unsuspecting fellow and say, 'Oh by the bye, in case there is an opening on your list, my aunt's god-daughter is an heiress.' " He firmly directed her by the waist as he moved her round the brightly lit room. "I don't think so, little one."

She laughed. "Well no, but—"

"Incorrigible minx. Leave it to me. I will do this thing you wish and I will walk away and watch the sport. This I promise you freely."

"You do?" She peeped up at him.

"I do what?" he asked her warily.

"Promise it freely?"

He chuckled. "Well, in truth, you have used unfair tactics."

"I have not." The lady was fired up. "What unfair tactics?"

"Your eyes, your lips, your soft smile," he said on a low seductive note.

Something in the sound of his voice rushed through her, and she felt a sudden heat. She lowered her eyes and attempted to regain control of herself. After all, he was a rogue. He was dallying for the fun of it. She knew better than to believe such words. The answer was to give as good as she got! She brought her eyes up to his face, and there was a sure invitation in those warm grey orbs as she huskily replied, " 'Tis no more, no less than what you do so well, my sweet handsome lord." As this last word was out, the fire in her eyes took the shape of a devil and did a little dance!

The Earl of Raeburn had been caught off guard. Her words, her tone enchanted him, while her eyes riveted him. There was no other like this woman-child. Her bold flirtation had taken him by storm, and while he was still struggling with forces unknown he suddenly realized she was at play. He threw back his head laughing. She was a tantalizing creature. He thought he had softened that hard shell she had surrounded herself with, but evidently he had not. She was not being trapped by his wiles! She was giving him back some of his own. "She-devil," he managed to whisper in her ear. He then took her chin and cupped it. "I shall do better in the future for I mean to keep this particular moment in my mind!"

She smiled sweetly. "But you *will* talk to Meade?"

He inclined his head. "It shall be as you wish, though

I am beginning to wonder if it is at all necessary?"
Raeburn was looking her over, and his tone was wry.

"How so? I don't know what you can mean?"

He indicated with a lift of his chin that someone was approaching, and Lilly half-turned to see Sir Anthony bearing down upon them. The Earl commented dryly, "The fellow seems to be throwing caution to the wind."

"Never mind him," said Lilly, all at once excited. "Why, I can hardly credit it."

Raeburn was obliged to turn round and was as surprised as Lilly to see an old friend. "Justin Reynolds, well . . . my, my."

Lilly frowned up at him. "What is that supposed to mean?"

"Justin Reynolds has not made an appearance for many, many months at anything near to a ball. Partly because he has been in mourning over his mother's death a good year ago and partly because of the work he has undertaken. I am just wondering what could have brought him here tonight?"

His answer came almost immediately, for the waltz had ended, allowing Justin Reynolds the opportunity to make directly for them. He was closely followed by Sir Anthony Meade. The Earl of Raeburn turned oddly quiet as he stood back to watch these proceedings.

The gentlemen in question took turns making their gallant bows to Lilly, though Meade had a moment's free time to whisper into her ear as the Earl clapped Reynolds on the back and warmly shook his hand. "It is good to see you out and about ol' boy!"

Reynolds was a pleasant-faced, pleasant-mannered man. His style was quiet, but there was no mistaking the masculinity behind the gentleness. He seemed out of sorts this evening, nevertheless, he responded happily to the Earl who was an old and dear friend. "Cameron, *certes,* but it is good to see you. I have been wanting to call on you. Forgive me, it has been a difficult year."

"I know." Raeburn was quick to change the subject. "That new mistress needs you more than your friends, I suppose."

"New mistress?" Reynolds puzzled and then the dawning came. "Ah, the orphanage. Indeed, it takes nearly all my time."

"Nearly, eh? Methinks the remainder of your time must be spent then with some new love?"

"What? Do you think a new love is anything to a trusted old friend?" bantered Reynolds.

"Not for me, but you? Well, Justin, you have always had your head in the clouds or in a book of poetry, so there is no saying where it might be now!" The Earl laughed.

"Blister it!" Sir Harry exclaimed; coming up to clap Reynolds on the shoulder and shake him affectionately. "I have a bone or two to pick with you, Justin! Where have you been keeping yourself?"

As the old friends became reacquainted with one another, Lilly managed to carry on quite an intense flirtation with Sir Anthony. Out of the corner of his eye, the Earl noticed and his mood blackened. He knew very well that it was make-believe, yet it was quite irritating all the same. Was Lilly still in love with Meade? Was she hoping to win him back with this lie of wealth? It could not—would not—serve. Did she know that?

Harry was waving a hand in disgust at Reynolds. "Mean to snub you ol' fellow." He turned to Lilly. "Lilly, my only true love, come waltz with me for I am sorely blue-deviled without you."

"Hold there," Reynolds ordered, surprising them all. "I was here first, and this waltz has already been promised to me."

"Do you take me for a flat?" retorted Harry on a snort. "When did you have the chance to obtain such a promise?"

"This morning, gapeseed," said Reynolds, reaching for Lilly's elbow.

Lilly laughed and would not call Reynolds a liar in front of them all. Quietly she gave him her gloved hand and allowed him to lead her out, peering adorably at the circle of men that had been around her.

As they moved in tune with the music Lilly scanned Reynolds' face before attempting to make conversation. "I did not expect to see you here tonight, Justin. You said you have not the patience for such frivolous things. In fact, we argued about the—"

He grinned sheepishly as he moved her round the floor. "I know, I know. I suppose I have come to see your point of view. 'Tis a valid one, after all. We can do more good by getting out into the Polite World and winning others over to our cause."

"Well, how nice. Now tell me the real reason you are here."

"I don't believe it!" Justin Reynolds seethed, suddenly turning into a madman right before Lilly's eyes. "Elizabeth promised she would not attend this ball, but she is here. 'Tis why I am here, I knew she had given me a false promise—I knew it."

Lilly was not totally surprised. She looked towards Elizabeth Hawkins, chatting with a number of dowagers and understood all. She had been thinking for quite some time that Justin Reynolds and Elizabeth might have a *tendre* for one another. Then the conversation she had had with Elizabeth that afternoon had made her doubt her eyes. After all, she could not believe that Mr. Hawkins would object to a match between his daughter and Justin Reynolds. That made absolutely no sense.

She studied Justin's face. "You asked Elizabeth not to come here? You don't want her here?" This made no sense either.

"She said she would not attend," he answered on a grim note. "Somehow, someone has made her change her mind."

"And this disturbs you?"

"Not her presence here, but the reason for it," he said between clenched teeth.

"Justin, I take it that you and Elizabeth have an understanding. However, I don't know what the deuce you are talking about."

As Justin twirled Lilly so he could better view his love, he saw Anthony Meade bowing over her hand. He watched in growing rage as Elizabeth Hawkins raised her eyes to Sir Anthony's handsome face and blushed shyly. Lilly, too, was able to see this, for Justin's steps had slowed to the point where they were hardly moving. Sudden enlightenment came. *Elizabeth Hawkins!* The Hawkins heiress. Sir Anthony's latest target. Elizabeth, whose mother was of the aristocracy and whose father was in trade! Why had she not seen this before? How could she have been so blind? Well, Meade was not going to break Elizabeth's heart! Not while Lilly was around to protect her new friend.

"Elizabeth deliberately misled me."

"I doubt it. She is an obedient daughter. Her parents probably insisted she attend this ball."

"I just don't understand her these days. I thought you might advise me as to how to go on. You and Elizabeth seem to be getting on so well. I thought she might have mentioned me . . . our situation to you?"

"No . . . At least, not exactly." Lilly shook her head. "There, now don't go looking so very glum. Silly man, just go engage her for the next dance."

146

As Justin Reynolds whirled Lilly round the floor, the Earl watched them with keen interest. There was no doubt that the pair were having a very intimate conversation. He could not help but note that at one point they almost stopped waltzing so engrossed were they in one another. Damnation, had Reynolds come because of an interest in Lilly? He felt supreme irritation as he watched Justin clutch Lilly's waist. Damn, just what did Justin think he was doing? It was deuced unseemly.

"They dance well together," said Lady Sarah softly. "Don't you think so?"

The Earl swallowed a growl. "Do they? I think the man too clumsy for our graceful Lilly."

Lady Sarah was surprised. "Indeed, I rather thought Justin quite good at his steps." She eyed the Earl. "Isn't Justin a friend of yours?"

"He is, but he won't do for Lilly," the Earl nearly snapped.

"Well, as to that, Augusta likes him very well and was good friends with his mother." Sarah shook her head. "Why wouldn't he do for Lilly?"

"Lilly will have half of London at her feet by the end of this season. She can do better than Justin Reynolds," said the Earl sharply.

Lady Sarah thought it prudent to refrain from further comment on the subject. She moved off thinking the Earl was obviously in an ill humour.

Chapter Eighteen

Lilly was looking smart in her riding habit of dark brown velvet with ivory lace at neck and cuffs. Her matching velvet hat, trimmed in the same lace, sat attractively on her dusky curls. She was sitting sidesaddle on the dark bay gelding Lord Wizbough had provided for her use while in London and was looking for the arrival of Elizabeth. She had not long to wait. Elizabeth, on a chestnut mare, rounded the bend in the bridle path and waved as she drew her horse up to face Lilly.

"Well and good morning, Miss Sassy of the Merriweather Ball!" said Lilly on a laugh.

Elizabeth blushed and objected. "Oh, please. I shall die of embarrassment. I only want to forget last evening."

"Dearest girl"—Lilly smiled—"you had two men at your feet. How can that be embarrassing?"

"Lilly . . . you don't understand. Justin—Mr. Reynolds. . . ." She stopped there, and her hand moved in the air as she looked for words to express her feelings.

"Stomped out of the ballroom and the Merriweather house in a fit of jealousy," finished Lilly in amusement. "It quite made me revise my opinion of him."

"Oh no, no . . ." Elizabeth stopped and looked at

148

Lilly sharply. "What do you mean? What opinion of him?"

Lilly heard the challenge in the question and concluded that her friend was very much involved with Justin Reynolds. She moved her horse up and touched Elizabeth's kid-gloved hand. "Liz, I like Justin . . . very much. I only meant that until last night I did not realize he was capable of so much . . . er . . . passion."

"Oh," breathed Liz, going quite dramatic. "He is all passion and romance, poetry and beauty—"

Lilly put up her hand. "Enough. 'Tis time you told me just what is going on? Last night, you and Justin nearly spit your words across the dance floor. 'Twas absurd. One should never try to carry on an argument while doing the Cotillion. It just can't work. Then, you were encouraging Sir Anthony. Truth, the sorry truth, seems to be that you appear to be leading both men on."

"No, Lilly, it isn't like that. I . . . I love Justin," declared the lady desperately.

"You love Justin?" Lilly shook her head. "Yet, I saw you with my own eyes, and you were not indifferent to Sir Anthony's charms."

Elizabeth Hawkins sighed. "He is quite diverting, and I do enjoy his attention, but he does not love me and I do not love him."

"Than what is going on?" demanded Lilly impatiently.

"Papa means me to wed Sir Anthony."

"Why?"

"Papa has never been accepted by my mother's people—by society. I have not been granted a voucher to Almack's yet, so marriage to Sir Anthony, Papa says, would change all that."

"As would marriage to Justin Reynolds." Lilly was

149

frowning. " 'Tis not quite the same. Sir Anthony is ti-tled, Justin is not. Sir Anthony's family name dates back to forever—and there is a family estate . . . in ruins per-haps but restorable. Papa likes the connection."

"Still, Justin Reynolds' family is from noble stock, and I believe there is some wealth behind *his* estates."

"Yes, and Justin's father insulted my father many years ago. Papa has a long memory. He refuses to allow Justin to court me. We only get to see one another at the orphanage," wailed Elizabeth.

"Oh, but that is dreadful," Lilly sympathized, and then her brows went up. "But that does not explain why you encourage Sir Anthony's attentions."

"Mother says that it pacifies Papa . . . that otherwise he might not even allow me to work at the orphanage . . . and . . . and I do not really encourage Sir Anthony."

"Yes, you do." Lilly was relentless. "I witnessed that myself."

"No . . . It is just that I do find it fun to flirt with him . . . 'tis . . ."—Elizabeth giggled then—"somewhat of a learning experience."

"Liz!" Lilly laughed. "I did not realize you have so much naughtiness stored up in you. We shall deal fa-mously well together, you and I." She thought a mo-ment and then pursed her lips. "I think I may be able to help you and poor Justin."

"I don't see how." Elizabeth sighed. "And Justin . . . perhaps he doesn't even want me anymore."

"Nonsense!"

"Yes, but, he was so angry—"

"Elizabeth," retorted Lilly. "You gave the man cause, did you not?"

"No, I did not." Elizabeth stood her ground.

"Well, you did, but never mind. We shall come about."

"How, Lilly?" She shook her head. "I just don't see how."

"One must stoop to devious methods. Your father must be brought round, and in the meantime, you and Justin must see one another in a more romantic setting. I mean really, Liz, you can't just go on meeting at the orphanage. It won't do!"

"Father will never be brought round to regard Justin as a suitor for my hand," Liz stated sadly.

"Well, as to that, your mother may help you in the end. I have a notion she thinks Justin is just the man for you."

"Yes, but—"

"Don't give me an argument. Courage, girl. Love must endure. Love must conquer. 'Tis what I know, what I feel, and Sir Anthony is the worst kind of cad."

"Oh, no. Do not say so," Liz objected on a laugh.

Lilly regarded her for a long moment. "Elizabeth, Sir Anthony is a fortune-seeker, he professes love, but he is most insincere. He connives and hurts people to get what he wants. I have first-hand knowledge of him—as does a friend of mine back in Lymington. You see, I knew him before you did."

"No? I have never thought him as bad as that." Elizabeth was horrified.

"He is worse than your wildest nightmares!" Lilly exclaimed. "If he could, he would take you, and use you till you had nothing left."

"Lilly . . . How can you say such things? He is so very charming, so handsome."

"Elizabeth, you do shock me. What a foolish girl you are. He is an Adonis with the heart of a devil—if heart he possesses."

Elizabeth sighed. "Perhaps . . . and you, Lilly, who will you have at the season's end?"

"I? Hmmm. I don't know. I haven't given the matter any thought."

"Sir Harry and Felix are forever butting heads over you," Elizabeth suggested curiously.

"They are not in earnest."

"Oh, but Harry is I think, and he is so very sweet."

"Sweet and gentle."

"Ah, but he is not the one that lights up your eyes," Elizabeth said knowingly.

"No, I suppose not, though in truth I don't know what that means. I don't know what love is or how it should feel. I thought I did once and it turned out to be . . . stardust."

"That may be so"—Elizabeth wagged a finger now—"but you seem more than just a little taken with that young Mr. Cobbett I saw you with last night, and *he* looks as though he absolutely worships you."

"Absurd girl. He is a boy." Lilly blushed, but added, "He is good fun, and handsome as well."

"Hmmm, I suppose no one can compete with your Earl of Raeburn?" Elizabeth was no fool.

Lilly nearly jumped out of her skin and did indeed move sharply enough in her saddle that her horse fidgeted. "The Earl? The Earl is not in the game, Elizabeth."

"No? Well, of course he is not," agreed Elizabeth. "Besides, Mother says he is still wearing his heart on his sleeve for Lady Anthea Melbourne."

"Lady Anthea?" Lilly thought of the woman she had seen only briefly at some rout or breakfast with Julian Melbourne. A creature who looked like a goddess with her china blue eyes and gold hair, but she was married to Julian. "I don't understand?"

"Mother says that Julian Melbourne and the Earl

were the best of friends until Anthea came between them."

"I don't believe it." Lilly's thoughts dived into confusion. "He wouldn't do that to a friend."

"The story goes that it was the lady who set them at one another. She seemed to want them both, and would have had the Earl had he not bowed out of the picture for Julian's sake. Mother does not like Lady Anthea."

"No? I never really spoke to her, but I did not like her smile." Lilly's voice trailed off as she thought of Anthea's china blue eyes gazing into the Earl's twinkling orbs. "I can't imagine the Earl with such a woman. I wouldn't think she was his style?"

"Ah, but, Lilly, she is precisely his style," returned Elizabeth, "Love moves one to do such heartbreaking things for the sake of the person one cares about. I know I shall never be the same girl I was before I met and fell in love with Justin."

The remainder of the morning they spent with their heads together, whispering excitedly about the future. When they parted it was on the best of terms, and each felt they had been friends for a lifetime.

In a cheery mood, Lilly entered the morning room of Lord Wizbough's house to find Justin Reynolds in polite conversation with her aunt. He jumped to his feet upon her entrance and came forward to place a kiss to her fingertips. "Lilly, finally," he said in heartfelt accents.

"And good morning to you, sir," she responded brightly before turning to her aunt to throw her a kiss and inquire after Lady Augusta, all the while wondering what Reynolds was about.

"She has gone off with young Francis to see the stables. He seems to be very interested in the horses. Mr.

Reynolds was kind enough to bring him over this morning. In fact, I am late, for I had promised to join them, and then we are to be off for the home. We are taking some of the older children to a cricket match in the park." Lady Sarah was already moving towards the door, though she turned to put up a finger. "I shall say good morning to you, Mr. Reynolds, and I trust you won't keep my niece too long." Thusly, she allowed them some privacy, assuring herself that such a nice young man would not take advantage.

Lilly smiled and turned to her guest. "Well then, Justin, whatever is the matter, and there is no use telling me 'tis nought when I can see something is dreadfully wrong."

He ran his hand through his fair hair distractedly. "Everything is wrong and my life is probably ruined."

Lilly raised her lovely brows. "Now Justin, you have a great many years ahead of you, so I will not believe that whatever is wrong can not be righted. We don't want you suffering into your dotage."

"Ay then, go ahead, make light of it, but my heart is breaking I tell you."

"Is it, why?"

"She is disgusted with me. I have made a cake of myself, and now she must think me vulgar."

"If you are referring to Elizabeth, it is no such thing." Lilly smiled.

"You smile, yet I tell you all is lost."

Lilly waved this off. "Nonsense, though I must tell you never try to hold any kind of discussion during the steps of a cotillion. 'Tis foolish."

"Yes, but—"

"You behaved badly because you were jealous." Lilly snapped her fingers in the air. "So much for that. You will not do so again."

154

"Yes, but, Lilly, Elizabeth said I was a boor, and she said our understanding was at an end."

"I am surprised she did not say it in harsher terms. You acted quite imprudently and in front of all her mother's friends. They have enough problems because of Elizabeth's father, they don't need such scenes. You should have known better." Lilly wagged a finger.

Justin Reynolds hung his head. "I am a fool and a sapskull."

It was now part of Lilly's plan to lull Elizabeth's father into a feeling of comfort by encouraging Elizabeth to flirt with Sir Anthony. Justin's passion on this score must be curbed. However, observing his distraction made her reach out impulsively for his hands, which she held tightly as she attempted to reassure him, "There now . . ." Lilly spoke softly, but her comforting was interrupted by the Wizbough butler's stentorian announcement, "Lord Raeburn!"

Absurdly guilty, Lilly withdrew from Reynolds and turned, blushing, to greet the Earl whose blue eyes were hard and glinting. "Justin." The Earl inclined his head, but gone was the friendship he had always felt for Reynolds. "How extraordinary. One does not see you for months on end, and then, lo, you are everywhere!"

Clearly there was a menacing tone in the Earl's voice. Lilly was surprised by it, and though Justin was slightly taken aback, he assumed it was merely disapproval at finding him alone with Augusta's godchild.

"Indeed, and I must be going. I have tallied from my duties too long already." Reynolds turned and bent to retrieve the hand Lilly had so quickly snatched away only a moment ago. "Until tomorrow." So saying, he was quickly gone.

Lilly watched him depart and then returned her attention to the Earl who was standing back, cool and

155

aloof. However, suddenly he came to her, taking a position beside her on the sofa. He reached out and held her ungloved fingers in his warm hands. She turned a bright shade of red, though she could find no immediate reason for this reaction. In her confusion, she pulled away from him, aware of the rush of sensations she was experiencing.

The Earl darkened. "Justin Reynolds may hold them, but the privilege is denied me?"

"*You* mean to tease me. Justin needed sympathy," she answered promptly, but as grey eyes met blue, she was surprised to see the flash of anger in his gaze.

"Sympathy? Devil take the man!" snorted the Earl. "How dare he hold your hand and take unfair advantage of you when you are unchaperoned?"

"Ah, so that explains it." The lady was suddenly feeling inexplicably low. "I have offended the proprieties. Well, it was not his fault. It was *I* who took his hands."

The Earl took her shoulders firmly. He hadn't thought. He had just reacted. There was a biting intensity in his voice. "It won't do, my girl. See to it that you keep your hands out of his in the future!"

Lilly was taken aback. Her chin went up defiantly. "My lord, you should not be dictating to me."

"Should I not? Test me then, love, test me." There was a threat in his voice as well as in his deep blue, glinting eyes.

They were not allowed to explore their tempers any further, however, for the door opened to abruptly admit Lord Wizbough. He was in an odd mood, but called out a greeting to his nephew before complaining. "Your aunt, Augusta, has cancelled me out for those sad little creatures of hers once more. I am here to thumb through my mail and then I'm off for the club."

"I shall join you, Uncle."

"Eh?" Lord Wizbough looked from Lilly to the Earl with narrowed eyes, "Oh, aye then . . . Blast the mail. Come along, lad."

The Earl bent to a stiff bow as he took his leave of Lilly, and Lord Wizbough winked at her before they left her to her own devices. Lilly looked after them for a moment before she went to see to her own mail at the writing desk. There was a letter there from Stuart that needed answering. Stuart, home, the hounds . . . all part of a world she had almost forgotten in this crazed land of London. Men? Odd beings to the last one. All of them were forever doing wild, mad things. Men, ha!

Chapter Nineteen

Lord Wizbough and the Earl of Raeburn spent a convivial time together. The Earl ranted about the mysteries of women while his uncle listened with growing interest. Much in harmony, they returned to the Wizbough town house some three hours later to discover that Lady Augusta was in something of a state. Wizzy immediately forgot his earlier grievances and forgave her recent neglect to go forward at once and take up his wife's hands. "My love, my dearest heart, what is it? What has happened?"

Augusta's frenzy was in part because she felt responsible for Lilly when Sarah was not about. She had expressly insisted that Sarah continue to enjoy her afternoon with an old acquaintance, saying that she would return to chaperone Lilly's afternoon. Return she did, to be told by the servants that Miss Lilly had gone off to meet Miss Elizabeth Hawkins. Very well, Augusta had felt satisfied. However, no sooner had she been told this, than Mrs. Hawkins and her daughter were announced.

She received them with some surprise and a great deal of misgiving. She had not wanted Mrs. Hawkins or Elizabeth to believe anything was amiss, so she had merely advised them that Lilly was out on an errand. They went off to do some shopping, and Augusta had been fretting ever since. There was a conclusion to be made here, for Augusta had noticed Sir Anthony flirting with Lilly the other night. She assumed the girl had gone off to meet the blackguard, and so she stated to her husband.

"There, there. What makes you think so love?" He shook his head. "I don't think Lilly gives a fig for the fellow, stap me, I don't."

"Yes, but she was in love with him . . . or at least she thought she was. Besides, 'tis just a feeling I have. 'Tis all Sarah's fault, for she has been addlebrained about the entire thing and has forbidden Meade's company to the girl. 'Tis just the sort of thing to make a woman want a man all the more." Augusta was now nearly wailing.

"All this fuss?" Wizzy waved a negligent hand in the air and chuckled. "No doubt Lilly will be here in a moment or two. Perhaps the servants misunderstood her message?"

The Earl was fairly certain that Lilly had arranged a clandestine meeting with Sir Anthony. She was certainly capable of doing so if she sought to pursue her plans. He said to his aunt, "I am sure Lilly did indeed go to the Hawkins residence and, finding them out, decided to take the long way home."

"She should not do so without her duenna in tow!" snapped Augusta.

"Well, if you like I shall go and have a look about, and if I find her before she presents herself here, you can depend on me to scold her roundly." The Earl suddenly itched to be off in search of Lilly.

"Oh, Cameron, thank you," his aunt fairly breathed out the words.

As the Earl closed the library door he caught a picture of the two within as his uncle sought to comfort his wife. The pair whispered infantile absurdities to one another. Love! Bah! he thought with a shake of his head. It was a most unwanted and unfathomable emotion. He was pleased to be entirely beyond its coils!

Lilly put up a hand to shade the bright sunlight as she scanned the park for a sign of Sir Anthony. Her grey eyes lit with quiet amusement as she observed him flirting outrageously with a couple of strolling young women wearing the uniforms of housemaids. She had agreed to meet him for a walk by the Serpentine. Everything was in motion. She had gone first to call on Elizabeth who was not at home, but she had done so to keep the lie out of her tale to Lady Augusta. There was no need to tell her godmother and her aunt absolutely everything?

Sir Anthony's vague blue eyes came away from the pretties and discovered Lilly walking towards him. Egad, he thought at once, she is a stunning piece of work. When he had finally taken her into his arms for a waltz at the Merriweathers' last evening he had thought he could very easily spend the rest of his life looking at her. It was a damnable shame she was penniless. He had been a bit surprised by the boldness of her flirtation. When they had engaged in that particular art form in the country he had found her a far more reticent participant than she was now. Well, no doubt that she had learned a thing or two in London, especially with the Earl of Raeburn forever at her side. That was another odd thing. Why was the Earl forever around her? No doubt, he wanted her in his bed? Well, Sir Anthony had every intention of taking her to his own and as quickly as he could. There were dangers there, and he would have to be careful. She was gentry, so he could be forced to marry her. However, he did not think her aunt wanted such a match, so if he proceeded cautiously he could take his pleasure and be off.

He went to her now and took up both her hands. "Darling Lilly, how lovely you are. Come, let us walk, for I have just been thinking that I would walk with you to the ends of the earth."

"Would you?" Lilly laughed. "Don't worry, I shan't ask it of you, for I have no desire to go that far."

"Lilly love, you make it quite difficult for a man to make love to you," returned Sir Anthony on an amused chuckle.

"Do I?" The lady turned coquettish. "And does that discourage you my handsome buck?"

"Indeed, it spurs me on," retorted Sir Anthony enlivened by her boldness.

The lady laughed and then stopped short as she neared the bridle path and saw Lord Raeburn briskly trotting his dapple grey gelding down it. "Ah," Lilly sighed, half in earnest. "We are undone."

"And that is another thing," Anthony answered frowning at this. "Why must we meet clandestinely like this, and why is that gentleman forever watching over you?"

" 'Tis a secret, the answer to your last question, and as for the first, my dearest Anthony, both my aunt and my godmother don't like you in the least." Lilly's grey eyes were sparkling.

"A secret? They don't like me?"

"It has been said you are a fortune hunter."

"But, darling, *you* have none."

"Ah, of course I don't." Lilly giggled unconvincingly.

Raeburn was upon them, and he raked Sir Anthony over with his hard blue eyes. Deftly he alighted from his horse, slipped the reins over the grey's head and led him cautiously towards the two so casually conversing. "Lillian Aulderbury, do me the pleasure of taking a seat on that bench under the birch tree to await my escort to where your godmother anxiously awaits your return."

His tone was sharp, but she could see that he had a twinkle for her in his wondrous blue eyes. Demurely she complied, giving him a quick almost saucy curtsey. From her bench she watched Raeburn take a stance with Sir Anthony, and she wondered what the two could be talking about.

The Earl's lips most certainly had formed a sneer. "I suppose then the word is out? We did so try to keep it all quiet. You see, Miss Aulderbury's aunt did not want every fortune hunter in London to be on the chase for Lilly."

"Fortune hunters? Lilly?" Sir Anthony pretended to be puzzled as he regarded the Earl.

The Earl sighed heavily as though the weight of the world was upon him. "Damned nuisance this whole thing. Promised my aunt to do what I could to see to it that no word leaked out, but those things never do keep mum. I trust, however, that you will say nought."

"Indeed, my word as a gentleman. I would never say that Miss Aulderbury had received a large inheritance . . . as I suppose it is?" Sir Anthony was fishing.

"As to that, she hasn't quite received it yet. My aunt and my uncle are still very much alive, you see, but at their ages there is never any telling . . . However, there is the fund from her mother's side as well," Raeburn blandly confided.

"I am honoured that you have chosen to confide—" Meade began.

"Confide in you? Don't be daft." Raeburn's sneer was more marked than ever. "I haven't been confiding in you. I have been explaining why *your* suit would not be acceptable to my aunt or to Lady Sarah." There was a dangerous glint in the Earl's blue eyes.

Sir Anthony took an affronted pose. "I take your meaning, my lord, and must inform you—"

"No, sir. It is I who must inform you that such meetings as these must stop." Then, as though removing a speck from his superfine coat, the Earl turned his attention away. He swung round on his heel, saying, "Now, I have kept Miss Aulderbury waiting long enough. I must return her to her godmother. Good day, Sir Anthony."

Lilly found her elbow firmly taken up as she rose from the bench. She shot a quick look back at Sir Anthony and knew by the way he was watching in a curiously thoughtful mood, just what the Earl had done. Raeburn had come through for her. She knew it, felt it, sensed it and demanded verbal confirmation, "My lord, you told him, didn't you?"

"Come along, brat," he said as he walked her briskly down the path, his horse in tow at their backs.

"Yes, but he thinks I am an heiress, doesn't he? I saw it in his face."

"How astute of you to notice. Had you noticed what he was at the outset, we would not now be involved in such antics!" he answered caustically.

She stopped him by clutching his arm and breathing out, "Oh, thank you, thank you."

"Make no mistake, little one, I warned him off."

She ignored this remark. "Did you actually say I was an heiress?"

"No. I said my aunt and uncle, as well as your aunt, did not want fortune hunters pounding down your door, so we were keeping your circumstances mum."

Lilly quite forgot herself and threw her arms round his waist. "Oh, you are wonderful. This is perfect."

He set her from him with his free hand. "Enough. You will have every scandal monger in the park whispering about us. 'Tis unseemly enough that you are here without even so much as a maid at your back." He wagged a finger at her. "Your godmother is greatly miffed with you and, I believe, quite distressed." His tone was serious. "I don't like that Lilly."

"I shall make it right and tight, see if I don't."

"How is that possible? She knows you were not with the Hawkins chit. She and her estimable mother were by the house, you see."

"Yes, I thought something like that might happen. 'Tis why I did go by the Hawkinses' house to call on Elizabeth. 'Tis no lie. That way, they will all know in the end that I was there. Then, not finding Elizabeth home, I took a nice walk in the park as it is such a lovely day . . . don't you think?" Her grey eyes twinkled.

Ruefully he responded, "What I think is that you are a minx, a devil-child and a dangerous piece of work!"

"Yes, perhaps, but you enjoyed leading Sir Anthony into the game. I saw it on your face."

"Did I? Perhaps." It was true in fact. Something inside the Earl wanted Meade to get a little of his own. The man had not been playing fair with his prey. A gentleman did not go about seducing innocent maids. Meade's intention was to seduce Lilly. It was obvious. Well, now perhaps he would fall into her trap!

"Yes, yes. I think, my lord, that you are greatly entertained." She looked up at him and touched his gloved hand with her fingers. "Thank you. Without your help, I would not have been able to go on with this."

He touched her nose. "Incorrigible child. I can't imagine you would give up at anything."

164

She dimpled. "Well, what a lovely compliment."

"Did you take it so?"

"Was it not meant as one?"

"Perhaps." He chuckled.

Thusly, much in accord with one another, they made the short walk home.

Chapter Twenty

Explaining away her morning's escapade had not proved to be an easy task. Lady Augusta was no fool. She listened quietly to Lilly's rapid series of word maneuvers, raised a brow and a hand to halt the flow. "Lilly, I think we know one another better than this."

Lilly felt like a villain, but what could she do? Tell the truth? Impossible. Lady Augusta and Aunt Sarah would never go along with her schemes. She averted her eyes, and waited for more.

"I am surprised at you, child. I had rather thought you were over Sir Anthony. I had believed your time in London had matured you, given you some insights. I can see that I was quite wrong. I am sadly disappointed."

"I don't give a fig for Sir Anthony," Lilly declared honestly.

Augusta was confused. She looked at Lilly and knew in that moment that her goddaughter was speaking the truth. "Then why, girl? What the deuce is going on?"

"Such language, Gussie." Lilly laughed. "Dearest, you and Aunt Sarah have nought to worry about. If it looks as though I am interested in Meade, it is only what he deserves. 'Tis nothing. Trust me. I know what I am doing, but I am not in the slightest attracted to Sir Anthony Meade."

"Yes, but—"

"Gussie, I shan't play the role of ninny. Not twice in one year!" Lady Augusta sighed. "Go on then. Go up and wash. We must be ready when Cameron comes for us. We have changed our plans and are attending the theatre at Covent Garden tonight." She looked at Lilly's face; which had considerably brightened. "Indeed, I told Sarah you would like the idea."

Lilly went to her godmother and put her arms round her neck and held her, a gesture prompted by strong affection. "Thank you, Gussie." Then, as she turned to leave the room, "Raeburn joins us, you say?"

"Indeed. Your Uncle Wizzy told him three women were getting to be more than he could handle and begged for his company."

"Oh." Lilly's smile vanished. "Of course, he comes at Wizzy's request." She left the room then hurriedly, and Gussie watched after her for a long thoughtful moment. Sarah was still at friends' for the afternoon. When she returned, should she tell her about Lilly's waywardness and worry her needlessly? The girl was playing some deep game, she knew her well enough to know that. What it could be was beyond her. Was it love for Sir Anthony Meade? That was folly. She shook her head over the notion. No. Lilly did not want that fellow, she felt this in her bones. What then? Just what was going on?

Covent Garden proved to be a delightful mixture of oddities. Intermixed with residential buildings was the market square, famous for its arrays of fruits, vegetables and flowers. Overlooking the market was the Opera

House. Farther down the avenue stood the theatre in all its rebuilt glory. Covent Garden's history was recounted to Lilly as the Earl of Raeburn led her along the avenue. Not far ahead of them, Lord Wizbough was merrily entertaining the ladies, and all appeared to be in high spirits.

Lilly, wide-eyed and awestruck by everything she saw, turned a shining visage to the Earl. "I am so looking forward to viewing Kean in action tonight." As an afterthought, she added, "Justin says he is the greatest actor in all of England."

The Earl stiffened, though he could not say why. "Justin says so, does he?" A short laugh and then, "Kean, indeed! For my part there is no greater actor than Kimble. Kean thinks himself the monarch of the stage when he is nought but an insignificant man with little grace, less countenance and even less voice!"

"Ah, you don't like Kean." Lilly nearly laughed. She noted that his eyes sparkled but were a deeper shade of blue when he was angry.

"Well, not as much as Justin does," snapped the Earl.

"Odd that. I rather thought you and Justin were friends."

"We are, but we don't always hold the same opinions."

She thought about this. "Byron said much the same thing the other night at the Merriweather ball. I was keeping him company for a space as the poor thing can not dance, and he was very caustic on the subject of Kean. He says Kean is a deformed runt of a man with a mind to match his body."

The Earl laughed. "Byron is not far off, and I would take *his* opinion before that of Justin Reynolds."

"And *I*, my lord, would take yours before any other,"

168

said Lilly, surprising herself as she realized the truth of this.

Odd that her compliment should so please him. Please him? It absolutely thrilled him. At that moment he had a sudden urge to scoop her up in his arms and hold her as his own. Her quaint little ways, so different from those of any other woman he had ever known, were beginning to entice him into feelings he had long ago set aside. This would have to stop, he told himself with a frown. However, Lilly dissolved such stern thoughts with a musical giggle and then said, "My lord, you look as though I just slapped you. Don't you like to hear compliments?"

He raised one brow, "Yes, just as anyone does, but I know better than to believe them."

She was surprised. "Don't you believe *me?*"

"Now how can I, my Queen of Prevaricators?" he teased.

She put up a chin. That is not fair. Meade is a cad. One must fight on his level."

"And fib to one's godmother?"

She blushed. "Grown people . . . guardians . . . just don't understand such things. 'Tis absurd to worry them with details."

He laughed outright and took her chin. "Brat!" He then took her hand once more. "Come along, and if you are a good girl, I shall treat you to some negus."

"Ohhhh . . . Then I shall certainly be very very bad," returned the lady saucily, for she did not care a fig for negus.

Chapter Twenty-One

Justin Reynolds was at his wits' end. He was nearly wild with distraction and wrung his hands as he attempted to reason with the woman of his heart. "But, Elizabeth . . . my dearest, my only love, you have misunderstood a simple—"

"I did not misunderstand. It was not at all simple. There was nothing simple about it. You are odious and deceiving. You are miserable and unfaithful." The usually gentle and meek Elizabeth Hawkins spat out the words. Then quickly before he could answer such accusations she accused him further, one hand shading her eyes. "You did not think I would be at Almack's because of my father. Well, you were wrong. Lady Augusta and my mother were able to win a voucher from the Jersey herself. Oh, I still can not believe what a fool I have been!"

"No, no my darling," Justin pleaded in an attempt to assuage her, but she was not hearing any excuses this morning.

"Stop it! Dreadful, dreadful man. You have betrayed and wronged me. Why were *you* at Almack's when you say you abhor such frivolous activities?" She crossed her arms over her middle. "Well?"

"Dearest—"

For some unknown reason this word enraged her. *"Dearest?* You call me dearest when you have come from the arms of another woman? You did not think I would be there, but Caroline Lamb was present and very much in your arms." She started to sob. "I saw you . . . I saw you kissing her!"

"I did not kiss her," retorted Justin hotly. "Let me explain."

"How can you? And you were kissing her. I saw you." This last came from trembling lips.

"I went to Almack's because I have a longstanding friendship with both the Jersey and Princess Esterhazy. I wanted them to send you and your mother vouchers, I knew it was something you wanted very much. That is why I was there. I had no idea Caroline Lamb would be there."

"But she was, wasn't she? And you managed to—"

"Lizzy dearest—"

"No. I shall not listen to you."

"I was not kissing Caro, at least not in the way you mean."

"Ha!"

"Darling, listen please. Caro and I have known each other for years. She is one of our best supporters at the orphanage. We are good friends, and her heart is breaking over Byron."

"She is an odious cheat. Her poor husband is a wonderful man." Elizabeth glared at him. "Evidently Byron's kisses are not enough for that one."

"She was only being playful . . ."

At this juncture Miss Hawkins lost all self-control. She picked up the nearest plump pillow and threw the pretty yellow thing at her beloved's head. "Cad! Boor! Cheat! Go to Caroline Lamb. You deserve each other."

"Indeed," said Justin taking affront. "And what of you?"

"Me?" The lady's hand went to her chest in some indignation.

"You, my love, you!"

"What can you mean?"

"You and Sir Anthony. You had eyes only for him. You hung on his every word, you—"

"Stop!" commanded the lady. "Sir Anthony was not kissing another woman when I arrived. In fact, I begin to think my father correct in his opinion of you and your family."

"Really? Well then, there is little left to say to one another."

"I want you to leave. Papa will be home soon, and I don't want him to find you here."

"I am going. Oh, yes. I am certainly going." Justin Reynolds, taking up his top hat with a flourish, stomped out of the drawing room. He turned at the door, and as his parting shot announced, "Perhaps Sir Anthony is the right choice for you." Upon this thrust, the unhappy suitor took his leave.

The lady turned away, listened for the closing of the door and then promptly burst into tears. How had all this happened? Her world seemed suddenly turned to ash.

Justin Reynolds was experiencing a devastating emotion. He had never felt just quite this way before. He loved and adored Elizabeth. He wanted to spend the rest of his life with her, wanted to call her his wife, to hear her call him husband. The notion thrilled him. Yet, he had left her. All was at an end.

Elizabeth had said some damnable things to him. Really, a man could not allow such unthinkable behavior in the woman he wanted to wed. This was no way to start, but he didn't want it to finish either. What to do? Did she really like Sir Anthony so very much?

His cogitations took him blindly down the avenue until he found himself standing on the steps of the Wizbough townhouse. He took them two at a time and was, some moments later, being admitted to the morning room where he found Lilly alone at the writing desk, quill in hand.

"Lilly," cried the distraught man, "I am undone."

Lilly's grey eyes opened wide with surprise. It was unlike the Wizbough butler to allow anyone to approach her unannounced when she was alone so Justin's arrival took her unawares. Secondly, she could see the man was more than just a bit blue-deviled, and could not imagine what could possibly have occurred since the Merriweather Ball to make matters between him and Elizabeth any worse than they had been.

"Justin, oh dear, whatever can be wrong now?" She got up from the desk and moved towards him.

Even in Justin's fog of despair it occurred to him that Lilly was looking lovely as ever in her pale green velvet morning gown. He was, after all, a man. Immediately he dismissed such wayward thoughts, however, and took up Lilly's fingers to lead her to the sofa. "All is at an end between Elizabeth and myself. She does not love me and I . . . I am no longer sure—"

"Nonsense." Lilly cut him off.

"No. It is true." The man dropped his head into his hands.

"Now, what is all this about? Start at the beginning, please."

"I did not think Elizabeth would be there. I had no idea . . . especially when I knew that you were going to

Covent Garden last evening, but I decided to go anyway to see what I could—"

"Go where?"

"Almack's. You see I thought I could use my influence with the Jersey to obtain vouchers for Elizabeth and her mother." He took a long dreg of air. "Apparently my offices in that regard were unnecessary, they were there, Mrs. Hawkins and her daughter."

"Indeed, my godmother and Mrs. Hawkins were friends in school. Elizabeth's mother is a Woodrow you know. Her family may have given her their backs when she married Hawkins, but she is still a Woodrow. Gussie went to Princess Esterhazy and Lady Jersey and presented her case. Since both women adore her they said they would issue vouchers for Mrs. Hawkins and her daughter, but Mr. Hawkins would not be admitted." Lilly shrugged, "In truth, if my husband were not allowed I would not go, but that is neither here nor there."

"Well, *I* was not informed of this circumstance," said Justin pettishly.

"Elizabeth can not have been angry at you because you were at Almack's?"

"Well no, but Lady Caroline Lamb and I are old . . . very good friends. Well . . . as to that . . . you don't know Lady Caro, but she is a bit playful."

"I know *of* Lady Caro, and I have seen her at play, Justin. It appeared to me that Lord Byron is not the only man she would gobble up if she could," Lilly commented dryly.

"Lilly!" objected Justin Reynolds, much shocked.

Lilly laughed and thought that the Earl might reprove her but actually he was rarely shocked by her many indiscreet, though truthful, utterances.

"Never mind. So, you and Lady Caroline Lamb were

. . . playful . . . which made Elizabeth jealous. 'Tis all nonsense."

"Worse than that." The man hung his head.

"Explain, Justin."

"Elizabeth saw me . . . kissing Caroline . . ."

"What?" shrieked Lilly. "Never say so! Well, dear me. Justin, I must say I am surprised at you. Why should you kiss Lady Caroline if you are in love with Elizabeth?"

"I didn't kiss her." Justin Reynolds was blushing like a schoolboy. "Caro is rather impetuous, and she, well, before I knew it she had at me you see." He saw Lilly's doubtful expression. "A gentleman can't throw a woman out of his arms just like that. It must be handled—"

"Absurd man," declared the lady. "Is that how you explained yourself to Elizabeth? 'Tis a wonder she did not put a bullet through your heart!" The words were only belied by the giggle in Lilly's voice. She saw Justin's miserable expression, however, and immediately took pity. Taking up the forbidden hands, she soothed, "There, there. She will get over it."

The Earl of Raeburn was in high spirits. His evening at Covent Garden had been more pleasurable than he had ever imagined it would be. Perhaps it was the play. Perhaps the atmosphere. Perhaps it was Lilly. She was good company. There was no denying that. She was becoming quite adept at flirting and was practicing with him, a style that was becoming all her own. Still, sometimes all at once, she would captivate him with some marvelously innocent utterance. In the next moment he would feel as though she were just one of the boys, for

175

she would rattle off some boxing cant, explaining that she had learned it from her friend Stuart in Lymington.

Lilly . . . He was forever thinking about Lilly. There was the undeniable fact that her grey eyes were warm and bright and had a habit of twinkling and teasing him. She was vibrant, finding so much in life to laugh at, her laugh was infectious. She was a minx, but soft and kind-hearted. She was—stop! This was absurd!

He shook his head over his foolishness, but set out nonetheless in a merry, high-spirited mood to call at the Wizbough house and perhaps invite the minx to ride with him in the park. It was a perfect morning for his open curricle, and he wanted to see if she had any skill with the ribbons.

The Wizbough's butler looked a bit harassed when the Earl advised him that he would show himself into the morning room and surprise Miss Lilly. However, there was nothing for it. One could never reason with the aristocracy. They were forever breaking their own rules. He stood aside.

Blissfully happy, the Earl opened the morning room doors and froze in place as he took in the scene before him. Justin Reynolds held Lilly's hands and appeared to be pulling her into his embrace. What the devil was this all about? He had an urge to take his friend by the collar and throw him into the street where he envisioned beating him to a pulp. He restrained himself deciding such a notion was idiotic. However, he could not still his anger, and his brow moved expressively upwards as his jaw set in a firm line. His voice, when it came, was steady and dry. "I hope, Miss Aulderbury that I am not *catching* you at an inconvenient time?"

Justin had already jumped away in what the Earl thought a very guilty move, and Lilly had turned a charming shade of pink. She quickly recovered her composure, though and smiled a warm welcome. "My lord, I am so glad you have come."

"Are you?" he returned in evident disbelief. "You amaze me. Where is my aunt and Lady Sarah?"

"They are shopping."

"Cameron." Justin nodded. "Well, I am afraid I must be off as I am due at the orphanage." Again he nodded at the Earl. To Lilly he inclined his head. "Thank you," he said softly.

The Earl waited only until the morning-room door closed before rounding on Lilly to ask in less than gentle tones, "Why in all that is wonderful must I forever find you with that man's hands in yours?" He was pointing towards the door Justin Reynolds had just exited through. "Tell me that, my girl!"

Lilly was taken aback by his heat. "I . . . I don't know what you mean or why you should be so vexed?"

"You don't know what I mean?" The Earl put away distance as he took long strides towards her. He pulled her to her feet. "Don't you?" The words came through clenched teeth, and then suddenly he was out of control and bending her into his arms as his mouth closed firmly on hers.

Lilly trembled as her lips parted to receive his kiss. She felt the wildness of his sudden passion as he drew her to him. Her knees weakening, she clung to the Earl. The hardness of his body thrilled her, and when his tongue moved to explore hers, she felt light-headed and weak. This was a kiss. This was a man. She had never felt like this before. The Earl, however, was in a fit of confusion. When he drew away from her it was to nearly spit out these words: "Does he kiss you like that? Did Meade kiss you like that?"

"No one has ever kissed me like that," Lilly managed to say on a whisper.

"You lead a man to it!" snapped the Earl.

"Do I?" His anger ruffled her. Her chin went up, and she turned to pull out of his embrace. He held her still and forced her to look at him. "Lilly, has he kissed you?"

"How dare you?" she demanded outraged. Her grey eyes glistened, but she refused to cry. She wouldn't. He was playing guardian for her aunt and godmother. He had such a sense of propriety in that regard that no doubt he had been moved to behave authoritatively. That certainly was what all this was about.

"How dare *you?*" he snapped back at her. "How dare you fall into my arms as you just did? How dare you return my kiss?"

Why was he doing this? His words slashed at her heart, and she defended herself against the tirade. "My lord, I dare what *you* dare. It was agreed between us. You are a rake. You just proved it. I won't be taken in. I have *not* been." She snapped her fingers in the air, thus dismissing the incident.

"No, my girl. You were asking to be kissed . . ."—it was a hiss—"and you liked it very well."

She blushed, but her grey eyes were glinting defiantly. "Evidently you felt the need to pursue your reputation. *I* gave in out of curiosity. You may leave to enjoy your pursuits elsewhere. I am not interested."

Certes! She goaded him beyond endurance. He did not stop to ask why all this nonsense should so infuriate him. "Dismissed am I? Ah, but, Lilly, there is so much more you may be curious about . . ."

"You are deliberately being provoking!" The lady wagged a finger at him. "You are insulting me. Very well, if I am still curious, I shall seek out my own teacher—in my own time!"

178

"Who then? Justin Reynolds?" The Earl sneered as he moved towards the door. "Well then, she-devil, have at him!"

Chapter Twenty-Two

Lilly stared without seeing as the Earl took his leave. She was stunned by his behavior. What had happened? Why had he acted so wild? They had been getting on so well together. They were nearly friends. She quickly collected herself as the Wizbough's man announced Elizabeth Hawkins.

Elizabeth swept into the room, and it was obvious that she was in a high state of agitation. She pulled roughly at her gloves, snapped them into the palm of her hand and demanded, "Lilly, I need you to take a turn around the park with me."

"Indeed," Lilly agreed, getting to her feet, "I think that will do us both some good." She then moved about the room collecting her chip bonnet, her blue silk spencer and blue kid gloves. She said as she went about, "Do you know, Liz, I think males have something missing—a very important something."

"Agreed," snapped Elizabeth. "Not a one of them has a brain!"

Lilly laughed. "No, you silly twit. They are very clever beings. That is not their problem at all."

"Oh, what then?"

"They don't know what they are about—emotionally

I mean. They are a very confused bunch of creatures, don't you think?"

"I think them a great deal worse than that, my pet," replied Liz caustically.

In perfect harmony, the two girls made their way to the park. They walked along, their heads bent in earnest conversation, until they reached the Serpentine. It was at this point that Elizabeth remarked, "I think, Lilly, I have lost him."

"If you are speaking of Justin Reynolds, you are speaking fustian."

"No, you were not there. You don't understand . . . how could you?"

"Nonsense. I know the whole," replied Lilly blandly. "I have already heard the entire tale from Justin himself only a short hour before you arrived."

Elizabeth stopped and turned sharp hazel eyes on her friend. "Justin was with *you?* He came from me . . . to you?"

"Well, in a manner of speaking." Lilly eyed her warily.

"Well!" snapped the lady. "Apparently he rushed right to you!"

"The man is miserable. He came for advice." Lilly sighed.

"He spoke to you about *our* private altercation."

"Which is no more than you want to do," Lilly snapped.

"That is quite different."

"Why?"

"You and I are friends."

"Justin and I, stupid girl, are friends, as well," returned Lilly.

Elizabeth pouted. " 'Tis not the same."

"No, but, Lizzy, why should it bother you?"

"Justin was a cad."

"My dear friend, you know this to be true: he is in love with you, Lilly said gently.

Elizabeth softened. "Is he? Do you really think he is still in love with me?"

"Lizzy, how can you ask?"

"He was kissing Lady Caro."

"Lady Caro is in love with Byron, who wants her not. All she was doing was regaining some of her hurt pride."

"Yes, well she should do so with someone else," said Lizzy hotly.

"I am sure she shall. Now give over, do. Justin is not a villain. You know that."

"Yes, but he makes no push to win Papa over. If he loved me he would not be wasting time kissing other women. Lilly, Lilly, are you listening?"

She was not. Her attention had shifted to the Earl who stood across the walkway in deep and earnest conversation with the golden-haired Lady Anthea. Lilly watched Lady Anthea's lashes skim her soft cheeks. The woman tossed her gold curls as she laughed over something the Earl had whispered. Then as he bent over the lady's hand, his deep blue eyes met Lilly's. She returned his look with one of contempt. Quickly she turned Elizabeth off the path and onto another.

"What is it?" Liz demanded as her friend spirited her away.

"Nought."

Elizabeth regarded her shrewdly. "Why should you run away from the Earl. That is what we are doing? Why?"

"Don't be absurd."

"Tell me, what is wrong?"

"Nothing, everything. I will tell you this Elizabeth

Hawkins; 'tis time we went home and chose our gowns for the Thornhill rout. Tonight we are going to dazzle them all!"

"Are we? I think I know what you have in your head, and frankly Lilly I am not sure."

"Yes, but I am, very sure 'tis time you turned Sir Anthony off and out. He must think you won't have him."

"Why?"

" 'Tis time he turned to me."

"Oh, very well," answered the lady almost reluctantly.

"Under your Papa's nose I shall make certain Sir Anthony dallies with me. It will be your job to make certain Justin shows himself to advantage."

"It isn't Justin Papa hates . . ."

"I know. He had some nonsensical feud with Justin's father. Well, my dear, Justin's poor father is gone, dead, buried as your father's feud should be." Lilly cut to the heart of the matter.

Elizabeth was a bit shocked, but then she sighed. "If only Papa will see it that way."

"Indeed. We shall have to make him," remarked Lilly brightly.

Cool night air swept into the ballroom during the Thornhill rout as one of the guests opened a garden door and stepped outside to get away from the crush of people that filled the unusually small room. The orchestra was too loud, but the abundance of champagne had so intoxicated most of the company that the music was acceptable. A heady group of young people laughed and followed one another through that same garden door and Lilly looked longingly their way for a moment. Never mind, she told herself, what she did indoors was necessary.

She looked ravishing with her dusky curls framing her piquant face in a most becoming and fashionable style. Her grey eyes sparkled with her mood and with the light given off by the hundreds of lit candles. Her figure wrapped in emerald green silk and lace, she presented a most alluring picture, and Sir Harry thought he would never be able to tear himself away. His carrot-colored head was not the only one with this thought. Males surrounded Lilly and hung on her every word.

The Earl entered the large salon and saw at once that his young tormenter had no need of his attentions, and remembering their earlier argument, he was pleased to give them elsewhere. For the next hour he never lacked for a pretty to play with, and he played with some intensity!

During this interesting spectacle he presented, Elizabeth arrived with both her parents, which was unusual as Mr. Hawkins was rarely invited to such affairs. Thornhill, however, was a close and dear friend of Mrs. Hawkins. At any rate soon after the Hawkinses arrived, Justin Reynolds and Sir Anthony, appeared. Lilly's eyes opened wide as the newcomers came upon the scene.

She was not the only person in the room that watched the unfolding of the plot. Lord Wizbough, who had for some days now taken a back seat out of a quiet understanding, nudged his wife to whisper, "We have a game at its best right now!" His eyes directed her to each player.

She frowned at him. "Whatever are you talking about, Wizzy?"

Lady Sarah noticed their whisperings and looked about. "Indeed, what is it you know that we don't?"

He smiled, "Just watch, 'tis very nearly Shakespeare before us." He was grinning widely, but on this parting line he chose to head towards the other end of the room, having been hailed by the small collection of his friends there.

Augusta frowned at her friend. "Whatever is Wizzy talking about?"

"I don't know precisely, but just look at Mr. Hawkins. He is not at all what I thought he would be. Gussie, he is very handsome, is he not?"

Elizabeth's father stood beside his wife, and it was obvious to all what had first attracted her to him. He was tall, lean and very good-looking. Though his hair was now completely white, this gave him distinction. He was extremely well dressed and was attentive to his wife as he escorted her to a group of ladies before he moved off to chat with a collection of his own friends. Though he seemed to pursue the entertainment at hand, an observer could see that he watched his daughter.

Sir Anthony had paid his respects to the entire Hawkins family at the entrance of the ballroom and had been surprised to find Elizabeth extremely cool and distant. He frowned over this as he moved on into the room. Then he spied Lilly. He quickly moved in on his next quarry. Well now, Lilly was an heiress. He was quite certain her fortune was no match for Elizabeth Hawkins, however, Elizabeth was elusive.

Lilly's hands went directly into Meade's as he presented himself, and she shocked Harry by allowing Meade to kiss her cheek. Harry looked on, as did Lilly's other admirers, in a confused state of annoyance. Lilly made no attempt to assuage their ruffled feathers, but continued to make Sir Anthony the center of attention. She did this with a sure skill, all the while sternly ignoring the Earl who seemed to be doing the same in her regard.

There was yet another man annoyed by Meade and Lilly, and he was not one of Lilly's admirers. Elizabeth's father watched Sir Anthony and Lilly with growing irritation. He moved to whisper in his daughter's ear, "Darling, there is a man you will surely lose if you continue to turn him up cold."

Liz pouted and showed her sire uncharacteristic rebellion. "Father, you don't know Sir Anthony as I do. He may have a title and old estates, but 'tis clear to me that he does not love me. He plays us, one against the other. He no longer appeals to me."

It may have been his looks that had captured his wife's heart all those years ago, but it was his good sense that had kept it for his own. He considered his daughter a moment and then said quietly, "Ah, is there another young man you are interested in, my dear?"

Elizabeth blanched. He was not supposed to ask that question. Lilly had not told her what to say to that. She improvised. "Nonsense. I just don't think I want Sir Anthony."

"I shall never force you to take a man you don't want," said Mr. Hawkins carefully. "You did seem to find young Meade to your liking?"

"Oh, Papa, what did I know then? He is very attractive, but now I think he is nought but a fortune hunter!" This was not what Lilly had told her to do, so she hurried on attempting to rectify her error. "I can't think why you should want him to court me when there are nice young men like ... like Justin Reynolds." Faith, how had she blurted it out like that? This was terrible. Lilly would be furious and would call her an idiot!

"Aha!" Good sense went to the winds. "So that is it! Justin Reynolds has poisoned your mind. You will never marry a Reynolds! Depend upon it!"

Elizabeth was not a spirited woman, and rarely faced up to her father, but she glared at him now. Love emboldens us, and so it was that she put up a defiant face.

186

"This is not the place, Father." So stating, she moved off to the protection of the one being who would calm her, and her mother put a comforting arm about her shoulders. She had been too far away to hear what Elizabeth and her father had been discussing, but she could tell from her husband's face and her daughter's set mouth, that things were muddled.

Mr. Hawkins would not be dismissed by his daughter in such a fashion. He strode up to them, but before he could speak, his wife put a restraining hand on his arm. Her soft smile touched him. "There now, Andrew, let it go for the moment."

He looked at his wife. She had the power to soften even his blackest mood. "I won't have her ogling that Reynolds fellow."

"You are very right," agreed his wife who was adept at saying just the right thing to him at such times. "However, I won't have anyone here talking about us." Her voice was gentle. "Besides, young love is a strong emotion. Don't pit yourself against it."

"Nonsense," he answered obstinately, for he would not be ruled by females, he told himself.

She smiled and glided off. "There is Augusta. I shall see you later, my only love."

He stood alone for a long moment and watched Sir Anthony courting Lillian Aulderbury. When he looked round for his daughter, she was nowhere to be seen. He pulled a face as he observed Lilly captivate Meade, stealing him right out from under his daughter's nose. She was a fine-looking girl and came from good stock. Well then, what was her living? he wondered. Nought to what he was settling on Elizabeth! If Meade were really a fortune hunter, he would not be chasing after Lillian Aulderbury who Hawkins was fairly certain, was no great heiress. He stood for a long moment contemplating the situation.

Reynolds gave up staring at Elizabeth when she began a meaningless flirtation with some young puppy. This she had done because Lady Caroline had come up behind Reynolds and given him what was very nearly a bear hug. He disentangled himself immediately and went to Lilly. Justin nodded at Anthony and reached for Lilly's satin-gloved hand.

"A moment, just a moment of your time."

"Upstart! Interloper! Take yourself off. You are very much *de trop*, Justin," declared Harry jovially. "Go on, you don't want me out of temper and calling you out. I am the very devil in a duel."

"Take a damper, Harry." Justin grinned. "Rest calmly in the knowledge that I promise to return the fair beauty presently."

Lilly's hands went to her nicely shaped hips. "Well! I shall have you know, gentlemen, I go where and when I please."

Justin bowed. "Forgive me, fairest maid, of course you do. Will you do me the honour of sparing me a private moment."

"Very prettily put." She wagged a finger at him. "Only a moment."

"Remember that, Justin, only a moment," Harry chided amiably.

The Earl of Raeburn saw everything. Lilly was separating Anthony from Elizabeth in front of Hawkins' nose, but why the deuce was she going off with Justin? Was she forming a *tendre* in that direction? Raeburn had always liked Justin Reynolds, but at the moment he could not summon up any charitable feelings for the man.

Elizabeth flirted with a youth she hardly knew, but she also watched Justin Reynolds as he went from Lady Caroline to Lilly. Her breath came in short quick starts, and she found herself flushing with anger. Nonetheless, she returned a bright smile to the young man blissfully relating an innocuous anecdote and advised him that she found him and his stories delightfully witty. The poor lad was so overcome that he lost all power of speech. Elizabeth sighed and returned to watching Justin.

Mr. Hawkins continued to watch his daughter with unabashed interest. Something was definitely being enacted right before his eyes. He was damned if he knew what the deuce it was, but 'twas something. His wife would have him forget his hatred of Reynolds' family. His daughter would have him consider Justin Reynolds a suitor. It was all beginning to fit. Ah! He watched Reynolds approach Lilly, and his brows rose with surprise. Well, damn the fellow for a flirt! It seemed to him, if a fellow was made of the right stuff, he wouldn't be with some chit instead of the girl he wanted. And feud or no feud, if Reynolds cared for Elizabeth, he should have made a push to meet with him. Just what was going on here?

Lord Wizbough watched the proceedings and did not have any trouble understanding what was going on. He was greatly amused and advised his wife to leave Lilly be when Augusta wanted to drag the girl away from Meade. "Yes, but Wizzy——"

"Never mind. Lilly doesn't want him."

"Really?" His wife's tone was dry. "She hides that quite well."

"Ay. She doesn't want Reynolds either."

"I suppose you know who she does want?"

"Yes, my dear wife, I do." It was all he would say on the subject before he drifted off again.

Augusta gave up. Throwing her hands in the air, she moved off to find a friend to help her forget her husband's very annoying attitude.

Meanwhile, Justin was nearly distracted as he demanded, "Lilly, did you not speak with Elizabeth?"

"Hush, you silly man. People will hear you," Lilly scolded softly. "Yes, I did, and she loves you, forgives you . . . so go to her!" Lilly had no notion that Mr. Hawkins was on the prowl.

"No," Justin replied flatly. "She hates me. Look at her with that boy. She means to taunt me."

"No less than you deserve. After all, Justin, you were kissing Lady Caroline." She was quickly losing patience, for she was suffering acutely with a heartache all her own.

"What shall I do?"

"Go to her. She will listen if only you go to her." Lilly shook her head. "Men are such fools about these matters. You want Elizabeth. You love Elizabeth. Right then, ninny, what are you doing with me? Go to her!"

"What if she won't have me?"

"If you tarry with me much longer, she won't. Go now immediately and tell her you are a fool and that you love her to distraction. 'Tis the truth, after all."

"Yes, oh yes. I do love her to distraction. She is the most wonderful woman alive!"

"Well, and I like that." Lilly laughed, but then quickly waved off his confusion. "Just so. 'Tis very proper that you should think so. Tell her!"

"What if she won't listen?"

Lilly wanted to slap his face. "Faith! This is absurd. Are you willing to lose by default?"

190

He bucked up his courage. "No, by God! I shall not lose Elizabeth!"

Thus, now a man with a purpose, he stalked his prey. Lilly sighed with relief and then turned to find the Earl towering above her. Her heart fluttered. "My lord . . ." she managed to say on a quiet note.

As though he had never kissed her, as though he had never shouted her down, as though the events of the day had never happened, he said with a half-smile, "You have been a busy girl. Sir Anthony is at hand, and Reynolds is at your feet, as are all those men-in-waiting."

She laughed. " 'Tis all nonsense, as you well know." A warm light had crept into her eyes.

He was drawn by the light, seduced by the heat, made nearly breathless by the nearness of her curved ruby lips. "Not at all. Sir Anthony has certainly switched to your quarter, and I quite suspect you have my old friend Justin nearly won."

"Sir Anthony has, I think, decided to throw in his towel and declare himself to me. As to Justin, we are friends and you are being absurd."

"Absurd? Why, you ungrateful brat. Without my aid to your plan, your precious villain would not now be on the verge of ruin."

She laughed. "Touché, my lord. Did I seem ungrateful?" Then, as an afterthought, added, "How can you say so? I did not even slap your face when you stole your kiss from me?"

He stiffened and then softened as her hand went to his and she quickly said, "There now, my lord . . . that is past, we shall call a truce, you and I."

"Indeed, we shall forget the day and proceed with the night," he responded on a low seductive note.

"Ah, you are dallying with me again. I am a female

and I suppose that means you can not help yourself." Lilly laughed, and it was a merry musical sound.

"Perhaps. Because I mean to steal another kiss," he answered and he sounded serious.

"Would you do that? Take advantage of a green girl from the country who might give her heart with that kiss?" she teased naughtily.

The twinkling of her grey eyes unmanned him. He felt himself no more than a schoolboy being taunted by a woman-child. "Indeed, I have not yet begged your forgiveness. Perhaps I should, but I think not. I enjoyed that kiss Lilly Aulderbury. I enjoyed it too much to say that I regret it."

"Well done, my lord. Surely now I should swoon into your arms so that you can claim the second one." She wagged a finger at him then, and her tone subtly changed. "The thing is: I am *not* a green girl any longer."

He laughed then and knew an urge to scoop her up and take that kiss. Instead, he said, "Never mind. Ah, look there. While I have been keeping you, your *friend* Elizabeth is flirting with your suitor, Justin Reynolds."

"God," Lilly declared. " 'Tis about time."

"What?" The Earl was genuinely surprised by her response. "You don't mind?"

Lilly giggled. " 'Tis the worldly way. I have become open-minded about such things."

He was momentarily at a loss. In pointing out Justin's flirtation with Miss Hawkins, he had meant to draw her fire. Her reaction confounded him. There was no other like his wild Lilly. He took her hand and slipped it through his arm. "I am famished. Let us go to dinner."

"Oh, yes . . . please," agreed the lady quite, quite happily.

Chapter Twenty-three

The Thornhill rout was turning out to be a lively affair. Not long after dinner was served buffet-style the small but noisy orchestra struck up a waltz in the ballroom, and a bevy of enthusiastic young people were soon dancing on the highly polished wood flooring as the sounds of a merry waltz filled the air.

Lilly was accosted by Sir Harry, who was very pleased with himself for having been agile enough to outmaneuver his rivals and obtain her hand for the first waltz of the night. His glee was short-lived, however, as he found his shoulder tapped and looked round to find Mr. Andrew Hawkins.

"I am afraid, young man, that I must pull rank on you and ask you to gracefully bow to age," said Hawkins quietly with only the hint of a smile.

Sir Harry had no choice. With as much grace as he could muster, he bowed himself off, winking at Lilly as he backed away. "I won't be far."

Mr. Hawkins addressed her as he led her into the steps of the dance. "Lilly, isn't it? You prefer it to your given name, Lillian?" He smiled benignly. "My daughter is much the same, preferring Liz to Elizabeth."

Lilly felt uncomfortable and wary, her every sense on

the alert. He appeared to be on the attack. Why? What was he thinking? She smiled. "Which does not meet with your approval?"

"It does not. You see her mother and I gave her the name of Elizabeth, as your parents gave you the name Lillian." He sighed as though greatly disturbed. "Children take it into their heads that they must strike out on their own at any cost. They have a need to make their own decisions, regardless of tradition and respect. That often drives them to excess. Age is what gives us wisdom. Children lack that, you see."

"Ah, but one must remember that most people marry when they are not much older than Elizabeth." She was smiling sweetly, belying the defiance of her words.

He was taken aback by her daring. His hazel eyes twinkled appreciatively. He could see why his daughter favored this girl. "Hmmm. I am sure there is a meaning behind such an obscure remark." He meant to frighten her.

"My meaning is clear, I think," returned Lilly, unabashed. "We are all of us individuals, with individual needs. You do not have to live with the name you chose for your daughter; she does. You will not have to live with the man she marries; she will." Lilly shrugged.

"Well, well." Mr. Hawkins was momentarily bereft of words. Children usually stood in awe of him, and after all he considered Lilly and Elizabeth no more than children. " 'Tis plain speaking then. Right, Miss Aulderbury. I had thought you were Elizabeth's good friend?"

"I am, sir."

"Then why do you steal her beau from under her nose?"

"I am not doing that, sir," answered Lilly, looking him right in the eye.

"Are you not?"

"No, I am not."

"We are speaking of Sir Anthony Meade."

"Are we?" Lilly was not quite sure whether she liked Elizabeth's father. She could see that he could be ruthless.

"Yes, girl, we are. Do you mean to have the fellow?"

"Mr. Hawkins, what I mean to do in regard to such a decision is something I will discuss with my aunt when and if such a decision must be made. More to the point, my aunt, who is very wise about such matters, does not wish me to marry Sir Anthony. Don't you find that interesting? And before you answer, another question in that framework, please? Why would you want such a fellow for Elizabeth?"

"You are impertinent," he said, and there was a glint of anger in his narrowed eyes. This is a girl to be reckoned with, he thought.

"Yes, I suppose I am," Lilly agreed amiably. She had held her own, but was thankful the waltz was coming to an end. She looked for and found Harry ready to claim her hand for the next dance. As she left Mr. Hawkins, she whispered softly to him. " 'Twas with all good intentions, sir."

Hawkins eyed her when she glided off with Sir Harry, and made a decision to investigate her position in society. Evidently, what he had been told was not totally correct. How could it be? A penniless girl could not afford the fashionable gown and jewels she was wearing. Lady Sarah's competence, he had been led to understand, was only modest. Sir Anthony may or may not be a fortune hunter, but it was understood that he had to make a marriage of convenience to bolster his dying estates. Why then did Meade pursue Lillian Aulderbury? Something here was not quite right, and he meant to get to the bottom of it!

Chapter Twenty-four

A heavy peltering of rain distorted the view from Lady Augusta's charming morning room. Lilly sighed and moved away from the panoramic window. Her aunt and Gussie had gone out to make last-minute arrangements for the ball Lord Wizbough and his lady were giving in Lilly's honour.

The heavy downpour had made it impossible for Lilly to ride. Since it was not her morning to work at the orphanage, she was feeling more than a little restless. The morning-room door opened, and Liz Hawkins came in, clucking her tongue as she removed her hooded cloak.

"Well, I nearly was soaked through to the skin just rushing up the steps to your door!" She smiled and dropped a kiss on Lilly's cheek before discarding her wet garment and taking a seat beside her friend. "There. I told your man I would see myself in. He didn't at all like it, but I was faster than he." Finding this amusing, she tittered in good humor.

"And good morning to you, noddy." Lilly laughed. "What brings you here in such dreadful weather?"

"I knew you must be home, and I had to see you." Liz breathed out the words excitedly. "I have so much to tell you."

"Then do so." Lilly was momentarily drawn out of her boredom. She had never seen Elizabeth in such a frenzy.

"Yes . . ." Liz smiled demurely and picked at her pink muslin. "Justin and I, well, everything is wonderful. At least, it will be if ever Mama can convince Papa to receive him." She shook her head and then wagged a finger. "Which brings me to the question. Papa and you? I was never so astounded, Lilly. There you were waltzing with *my* papa. Whatever were you talking about? What did he say? What did you say? Whatever it was, he was dreadfully bad tempered going home last evening and said that you were a saucy piece of work!"

"Did he?" Lilly smiled. "Then I am surprised he has allowed you to visit me this morning."

"Well, as to that you are *ton,* as are your aunt and Lady Augusta. He likes that," Elizabeth ingenuously added. "Besides, I would never give up your friendship."

"Did you tell him that?" Lilly marveled.

"I did and do you know what he answered?"

"I can well imagine." Lilly smiled ruefully.

"He told me not to be absurd, that impertinent though you may be, he liked you better than any other London miss he has had the misfortune to encounter during my first season." She shook her head in awe. "Does that make any sense to you?"

"Not a jot."

"Just so. Now, what shall we do?"

"In what regard, Lizzy love?"

"In my regard. Lilly, how shall we get Papa to allow Justin to court me?"

"Ah, that." Lilly shook her head, " 'Tis time for action. Your father is far too omniscient for my liking. I shall have to make adjustments to my first plan."

"What, oh what?" cried Elizabeth starting to tremble.

"We shall have to plan an elopement."

"No, Justin will never allow it." Liz shook her head.

"Not between you and Justin, noddy. An elopement between Sir Anthony and myself!"

Chapter Twenty-five

The Earl of Raeburn sat back in his leather-upholstered wing chair. His blue eyes were lost to another time, another place. An annoying realization was infiltrating his mind and demanding to be acknowledged. Lilly . . . She had been a wild country flower when she had arrived in London. Now she had society at her feet. Irrepressible as she was, she was a high-spirited child, a complicated woman, a desirable being in every conceivable way—and she filled all his thoughts, had crept up on them somehow. It was absurd.

The door opened, and his collie lifted her head. "Rest easy, girl. 'Tis only Harry." The Earl smiled a greeting to his red-headed friend.

"Cameron! We must talk."

The Earl watched Harry go into a sudden fit of pacing. "Indeed," he said. "Sit and then perhaps we may—you are making my poor Sheba weary with your to and fro, and I fear she may go for your leg."

Harry stopped and absently bent to pat the collie's head. "Right then. I've made a decision. Want you to be the first to know, though I must ask you to keep my confidence. If word leaks out, Felix will try to steal a march on me."

"Harry, sit." The Earl waited for his friend to drop into a nearby chair. "Now, what are you talking about?"

Harry leaned forward to say on a low note, "Mad about her. Nothing for it but to throw in the towel ol' boy."

The Earl suddenly knew, yet he had to hear it for himself. "Harry, what do you mean?"

"Get down on one knee and ask Lilly to be my wife." Harry gulped.

"What?" cried the Earl, jumping to his feet. "You can't be serious?" Harry was taken aback by his friend's reaction, but took it in stride and attempted to laugh. The sound came out as more of a squeak. "Didn't think I had it in me, did you ol' friend? Well, neither did I. But here I am nearly thirty. Must settle down, produce an heir. M'mother keeps on about it. Last of the line, you know." He shook his head. "Lilly is . . . she is—"

"Not going to be your wife!" returned the Earl scathingly. "What in thunder has gotten into you? You can not have thought this out."

Diverted by this accusation, Sir Harry reasonably offered the facts as he saw them. "Well, as to that, Cameron, I have thought it out, as I just explained. Last of my line. Duty 'n' all. Then there is Felix forever putting himself in Lilly's way. I am damn well sure he means to ask for her hand."

"You are a damn fool! That is no reason to throw away your life, your freedom."

"Well, but Lilly is such a perfect little sport. Thought about it, you know. I don't think she means to take away my freedom. She isn't the sort to want to hang onto my sleeve. Independent little thing. Like her . . . like her very much. She is forever in good spirits. Why, Cameron, she is very much like one of the boys."

201

"Harry, for pity's sake, give it up. You don't want to marry Lilly."

"Yes, I do."

"Harry, you have been in love half a dozen times in the last year alone," put in the Earl.

"Ay, so I have. Never thought of marrying any of those girls, though." Harry replied reasonably.

"That is because Felix didn't want any of the others," snapped the Earl, irritated beyond the norm.

"Well, and that isn't quite correct, Cameron," Harry returned thoughtfully. "He wanted that little Southby chit . . . what was her name?" He waved this off. "Never mind. Thing is, decided I will marry Lilly and be comfortable."

Absurdly, this pronouncement annoyed the Earl further. He turned quite red and now it was he who was pacing. "No, Harry. 'Tis all wrong. Turf and thunder, what do you mean to do? Go about having discreet little affairs, for you know you have a wandering eye."

"Don't be talking hum. You know me better than that. Once married, I mean to be faithful." This thought, however, made him fidget, for Harry did so like pretty women.

"Devil a bit! I have a lunatic for a friend," announced the Earl. "Let me tell you, Harry, she won't have you, and I forbid you from taking this notion of yours any further!"

Harry pulled himself up to his full height, which was considerable. Clearly he had taken umbrage. "You know nothing of the matter," he told the Earl on a superior note. "As it happens, Lilly will take me before she will take Felix."

"Will she, by God?" The Earl's irritation was leading him into dangerous emotions. "You think you know this for a fact, my dear noddy?"

"Ay, I do. Told me so."

"Lilly told you that she would have you?" the Earl cried in great disbelief.

"Well, not exactly, but she said she would have me before she would have Felix!"

"Harry, you will listen to me." The Earl was seething. "You will *not* apply for Lilly's hand. I forbid it."

"Will I not, by Jove?" Clearly Harry was offended. "Well, and we shall see." He moved to the wall table, took up his beaver hat, cane and gloves, then repeated as he opened the Earl's library door. "We shall just see!"

Sir Anthony strolled along the Serpentine, nodding to passing acquaintances and keeping a sharp eye out for Lilly. She had promised to be walking here on this day, though she had said she would have to have her godmother's maid in attendance. Such a fine little piece Lilly was, better than he had hoped to find. Fortune, beauty and chemistry. Life might indeed prove perfect. And there was still Elizabeth Hawkins. She, too, was pretty enough, and *her* fortune still drew him in her direction, but she did not seem quite interested in him any longer.

As though by magic Elizabeth appeared from a wooded sidepath. Beside her was Lilly, behind them a ladies' maid. He was at first more than a little startled to find these two women together. He was aware that they were acquainted, but he had not expected to find them in company today. He put on his most charming smile and tipped his hat gallantly as they approached him. "Good morning, ladies. I was just thinking it is a lovely morning, but as it turns out, it has turned out to be a perfect one."

"Sir Anthony." Lilly smiled coquettishly. "As ever delightfully flattering." She looked at Elizabeth, who was doing her act very well. Elizabeth simply nodded a greeting. Lilly put up a hand and called to a passing acquaintance. "La, there is Cecilia Brent. Do excuse me just a moment, love." She touched Elizabeth's hand. "I must go and speak with Cecilia for a minute or two." Thus, Lilly, maintaining a sophisticated reserve, rushed off to accost the surprised Miss Brent.

Sir Anthony gave Elizabeth a soft smile. "So, Elizabeth, finally we have a moment alone."

"Indeed, but it is a moment alone with Lilly that you want, sir. I am no fool." She hurried on before he could speak. She had rehearsed the words with Lilly so often that she knew them well, and Anthony had given her a perfect opening. "I knew just how it would be once word got out that Lilly was the Wizbough heiress. Her family wanted it kept secret, but such things do have a dreadful way of getting to the gossip mongers." Elizabeth released a long sigh. "Never mind, sir. I quite understand." She sent a sly look in his direction. "The question is, will you win her before Justin Reynolds does?"

Sir Anthony knew better than to give away his game to one of his chief prospects. Until Lilly was safely his, he was not allowing Miss Hawkins to escape his wiles, "Elizabeth, you are wrong. I have no interest in Lilly. We are good friends, believe me."

Satisfied with her performance, Elizabeth took it one step further. It was imperative that he believe his chances in her regard were undone. "As to that, Sir Anthony, it is of no consequence to me." He could have no doubt as to her meaning as he looked into her cold eyes. This one would not have him.

Lilly returned, chattering and making very little sense, but he was aware of her vivaciousness, especially as they

204

rounded the corner and found Justin Reynolds pulling his team up to the curbing. Reynolds waved and immediately invited the ladies to join him for a ride. As Lilly accepted, Elizabeth turned and gave Sir Anthony a "you see" look that made Lilly whisper, "My, I did not realize just how cunning you could be?"

Elizabeth giggled. "I have learned the art from an expert, my dear."

Justin was in high spirits as he drove his female companions round the park. As Elizabeth had been called for by Lilly and her maid, she was taken home first. She gave her love a long meaningful look and mentioned that she would be visiting the orphanage with her mother later that day. Justin quietly answered that he, too, would be there.

Lilly laughed and exclaimed, "La, but any more of this and I shall be sick! Quick, Elizabeth, in the house with you before your Papa sees us all together."

It was some moments later that Justin had Lilly at home. As he aided her to alight and she turned to thank him, she became aware of a pair of grim blue eyes bearing down on her. For no reason at all she experienced a guilty rush. "My lord, good morning. Are you here to visit Gussie? I don't think she is at home. She and my aunt are out shopping, and Uncle Wizzy is away on estate business."

"I am here to see you," said the Earl pointedly as he bent his head over her extended hand. To his friend, he nodded. "Justin. So glad to see you getting away so often from your duties at the orphanage. We must take a bumper of ale together soon, and you can bring me up to date on its progress."

Justin warmly agreed to this and then gave Lilly a final smile before climbing back onto his perch and taking up the reins from his tiger. He clicked his horses forward and was off. The Earl watched him a moment before he turned to take Lilly's arm and quietly inquire, "Has Harry visited with you this morning?

Lilly eyed him curiously. "No . . . at least, I don't know. I have been out all morning."

The front doors opened seconds after the Earl released the large brass knocker. He then led Lilly to the study and waited until they were within the cozy chamber before continuing. "Then no doubt he has been here with my uncle."

"No, I don't think so. Uncle Wizzy is off for the day with his man of business." Lilly frowned at Raeburn. "Why all the concern about Harry?"

There was only a small flame in the grate. The Earl went to it and took up the poker to play with the embers. This done, he threw on another log before he turned to answer Lilly. "There, that should do," he remarked about the fire.

"Should it? I am ever so pleased, but now that 'tis done, perhaps you might answer my question? What is all this about Harry? Is he all right?"

"The thing is, Harry is my dearest friend," the Earl replied slowly. "I can't help thinking this is in part your fault, Lilly."

"My fault?" Lilly's hands went to her hips. "Well, of course. Here is Lillian Aulderbury. There is a fault floating about. We must quickly pin it on Lilly! Very fine, my lord."

"Harry means to ask for your hand in marriage," Raeburn blurted out, running a hand through his locks.

Lilly was genuinely incredulous. "Never say so. 'Tis impossible. Harry and I get on so well!"

"Precisely so. He says you are a great sport, like one of the boys, and he imagines he will be a comfortable husband with you as wife," retorted the Earl in great disgust.

"Oh? Something in the sound of the word should have warned the Earl to take heed, but he pushed onward.

"Ay, here is the poor man declaring his love for you to me this morning and insisting that he will marry you. I told him he was a fool, of course."

"Then you don't think I qualify for Harry?" Again the tone.

"Nonsense. That is not the issue. You two are not suited."

"Are we not?"

"No. Harry will fall in love with another pretty face next week . . . next month, that is why!" snapped Raeburn.

"Is that what I am? Another pretty face?" Lilly had an urge to kick Raeburn in the shins.

"That has nought to do with anything. You are not in love with Harry. You will never be in love with Harry, and you two won't suit!"

Goaded, Lilly replied, "Ah, but I disagree. We are, as I have said, good friends. 'Tis important in a society marriage that the husband and wife be friends, don't you think? Harry and I laugh at nearly all the same things, and we enjoy many of the same sports. I think we could deal famously together!" Lilly's grey eyes glinted.

"Do you think so, by thunder!" He did not really want an answer. The Earl's temper was now out of control. His blue eyes were sparkling dangerously with storm shafts of light. He had her delicate shoulders in his grip, and he was bending her to him. He didn't know what he was doing as he brought her into his fierce embrace and covered her mouth with his own. He came up from that kiss to whisper in her ear, "Lilly . . . that second kiss was due. 'Tis now time for a third . . ."

Lilly made no attempt to pull out of his hold. She wanted him. His mouth closed on hers once more, and his tongue teased for entry. She responded to its touch, to the pressure of his sensuous lips, to the sensations he aroused in her. She loved being in his arms. She wanted these feelings to go on forever.

He wasn't thinking. She felt so good. She felt so right. He had to have her . . . but she was an innocent maid. In his mind he repeated the words. She was an innocent. What was he doing? Devil a bit. He stopped himself. He couldn't breathe, he was so pent up with desire, but he pulled away from Lilly sharply. Certes, he was going to go mad. His voice seemed not to come from him as he heard himself growl, "Will you fold into Harry's arms as you just did into mine?" He shook his head. "I don't think so."

His hot passion had stirred her own, but now Lilly was confused, flustered, hurt. "Harry does not try to take advantage of me," she said in a small voice.

"But I do."

"You did just kiss me, my lord. In fact, you are getting into the habit of picking a terrible fight with me and then kissing me. What must I think?"

He couldn't think clearly himself. How could he tell her what to think? Damnation! He suddenly felt trapped. He had to get out. He had to get away, yet he couldn't make himself leave. The door opened at his back to admit Lord Wizbough, who came into the study grumbling about some business matter. Wizzy was quick to size up the situation and casually remark, "Ah, I interrupt?"

"No, no, Uncle." the Earl answered immediately. "I was just leaving." So announcing, he was quick to make his escape. Lord Wizbough moved to Lilly and put a comforting arm about her shoulders, for he could see she was about to cry. "There, there, child. We shall come about."

As it turned out, Sir Harry had fooled them all. He had left the Earl and marched straight to Kensington, where he stood staunchly before the Wizbough house. "Up the steps, Harry," he told himself out loud. "Go on. Your mind is made up, and you don't mean to let Cameron scare you off." Somehow though, his feet would not move. "Marriage. Ol' fellow . . . that's the ticket."

A passerby looked at him strangely and he nearly took those steps, but again his feet would not move and his legs seemed to be in stocks. Better think this through, said a quiet voice in his brain. Not ready. If Lilly sees you now, she will never say yes. Better wait.

He listened to this voice, turned away immediately, his feet and legs now back in working order, and promptly marched off as fast as he could without running. The farther he got, the more he thought he should spend a few days with a friend in the country.

Thus, when Cameron called on his friend later in the day, he was told that Harry was not at home, not in London. Raeburn found this surprising, but proceeded to his club to cool his temper and get Lilly and her wondrous-tasting kiss, her brilliant eyes, her perfect smile out of his mind.

Damnation! This wasn't like him. He couldn't concentrate on the cards. He was bored with his friends. He hadn't even been able to work on his speech about the corn laws for the meeting in the House of Lords. Bah! This had to stop!

* * *

Lilly allowed Lord Wizbough to comfort her for only a few moments before she drew herself up straight and sniffed without speaking. She was infuriated with the Earl's behavior, distressed with herself for her own, unsure of how to go on.

Lord Wizbough had an idea. "Lilly, at times like these I often take a good long walk. It helps to clear the mind."

"Yes . . . I shall do so."

"Indeed. Walk the Serpentine if you like—I think I saw that Meade fellow heading in that direction—but take your maid along with you." Wizzy was now playing his own deep game.

She gave her godfather a kiss on the cheek. "You are wonderful, Uncle Wizzy!"

So saying she plopped her bonnet on her head, pulled on her Spencer and apologized to her maid, who was in no mood for a long walk. Off they went, and strolling leisurely about she did indeed find Sir Anthony. He bent over her fingers and came up to admit on a low seductive note, "I have been walking about forever, hoping to find you here."

"How nice," was all Lilly was able to respond.

"What is it, my love?"

"I have just had a row with Raeburn, nothing more."

"Shall I slay the fellow? Tell me, what is your will?"

The man is an idiot, she thought as she looked at him. There was not a sincere bone in his body. She said wryly, "Would that *I* could slay the fellow, but never mind."

"He disapproves of me," said Meade thoughtfully. "Is that it? Have you been arguing over me?"

Lilly took the opportunity. "They think you are after my fortune."

He did not shrink from the challenge. "I know of no fortune. I want you, only you."

"Really?"

"Darling, how can you question that? I adore you."

"Then we shall have to elope and soon. Reynolds is forever at my door, and Sir Harry . . . I don't think my uncle will say no to everyone, especially when he is worrying about you." She had taken the initiative and done the proposing. She was tired of the game. It was time to bring matters to a close.

"Elope?" said Meade, feeling the word over in his mind. "Yes, that is perfect. Lilly, my dearest love, will you fly with me then?"

"I have just said so," she answered almost impatiently.

"My dear girl," he said, squeezing her hands, "I shall make all the necessary arrangements. I must go quickly and obtain a Special Licence." He shifted his eyes to Lilly's maid who was standing idly by, chatting with another young girl also in service. "Does she suspect?"

"No, no, but Anthony, I don't want to travel too far. Can we find a local country magistrate . . . minister?"

"Well, yes . . . It can be arranged, but why?"

"Elizabeth. I mean to bring her for company."

"My love. *I* will bear you company," said the gallant in some confusion.

"Yes, but Elizabeth will provide propriety . . . just in case," Lilly returned obstinately.

"I don't understand."

"Well, we might break down . . . or the minister might change his mind and we should have to find another. No, I wouldn't like spending a night with you —until we are married. Elizabeth must come."

211

He was not pleased, but it appeared that he had no choice. Reluctantly, he conceded. "Very well, it will be as you wish."

She smiled and bid him good day, saying only that she did not wish her maid to become suspicious and report to her aunt. As she walked off, Lilly smiled to herself. Things were certainly falling into place!

At least some things were . . .

Chapter Twenty-six

Lilly had not reckoned with Mr. Hawkins' full potential as an adversary. He had set his man of business to discover Lilly's social and financial status. He was looking into Lord Wizbough's holdings, and though confidential documents were concerned, he managed to bribe his way into learning the contents of these papers as well as the will of his lordship and of Lady Augusta. Now Hawkins sat in his study reading and rereading the report compiled by his very efficent man.

Lillian Aulderbury was certainly mentioned handsomely in both Lady Augusta's and Lord Wizbough's current wills. Lady Sarah's competence, too, would fall her way, but that was only a modest living. These combined incomes would keep Lillian Aulderbury quite comfortable in the future, however, she would not be wealthy. He set down the report, eyed his man, and then requested verbal confirmation.

"You are certain that there is no mistake? Lillian Aulderbury is not a great heiress and could not possibly revive Meade's estates with her future inheritance?"

"I am certain, Mr. Hawkins. However, I, too, was told that such a rumour was circulating. Lord Wizbough recently heard the rumour when he was at his club, and he shouted it down. Said it was all a hum, but there surely are those who speculate that it still could be true."

"Is there a new will being drawn in her favor?"

"No, Mr. Hawkins, there is not. The Earl of Raeburn is the next in line to inherit Lady Augusta's main holdings as well as those of Lord Wizbough."

"Then it appears Sir Anthony courts Lillian Aulderbury under a misapprehension."

"Apparently, sir."

"Well, we must set that right." Mr. Hawkins gazed at nothing in particular as he thought this out. Meade was aristocracy at its most charming. He was just what his daughter needed to win her complete approval by the *beau monde*. Perhaps Meade was marrying for convenience, but in time he would fall in love with Elizabeth. How could he not? She was a darling girl that any man must love. Her father, easily believed this, as well as that Elizabeth would love Meade in the end. She must, for he would not have her wed to a Reynolds. He could not forget that part of the past. "Indeed," he said finally, "I think I will jot off a note to Meade and ask him to attend me in the morning so that I may properly inform him of the facts!"

"Very good, sir."

On the other side of the door, Mr. Hawkins' darling daughter stood up straight and wrung her hands. She had never listened at her father's door before, but then he had never before tried to ruin her life, so she reasoned that they were even. She had heard the words he had had with her mother earlier and knew he was doing something dreadful. She was familiar with her father's style from many years of watching him. They were un-

214

done! All their careful planning . . . No, she would not be taken away from Justin! She must get to Lilly at once.

Elizabeth grabbed her bonnet and cloak. The butler, an old and favored retainer, hesitated to inquire, but thought perhaps he should. "Miss Elizabeth, is there perhaps a message for your mother?"

Careful, she warned herself. No one can be trusted. "Only that no matter what happens, she must not worry, that is all." Thus, in a youthful frenzy she was off!

Unaware that his beloved was rushing hotfoot to Lillian, Justin was anxiously attempting to convince Lilly to accompany him to visit Elizabeth and her mother at her home. It was his hope still to win over Mr. Hawkins with honest, plain speaking. Lilly wagged a finger at him and soundly told him not to be foolish. "Elizabeth's father won't receive you in the usual manner, not while he thinks he can have Meade." Lilly sighed. "You see, he just does not perceive Sir Anthony in the same light that we do."

"Very well then, we shall go and visit with Elizabeth's mother. Perhaps she—"

"Mrs. Hawkins has known you now for many, many months. She has had the opportunity to become aware of all your wonderful characteristics through your mutual association at the 'home.' She is already on your side." Lilly spoke in a worldly-wise tone; however, she was wondering why the Earl had not come by for his usual morning call. She did so very much want to see him.

"Yes, perhaps, but—"

"Shhh. Calm yourself. If you wish to visit with Elizabeth, I can send a note round as usual and ask her to visit me." Lilly was very irritated with Justin Reynolds at that moment.

The door opened and Elizabeth stood like a stock to wail in horrified accents, "Lilly . . ." Then, spying her beloved, "Justin, something dreadful has happened. We are undone!"

Lilly's eyes opened wide. "Faith, Elizabeth, what are you talking about?"

" 'Tis my father," she wailed as she plopped on to the yellow damask sofa and pulled at Justin's hand so he might join her there.

"Oh, no. Never say he means to take you out of town?" Lilly was momentarily distracted.

"Worse than that," cried Elizabeth. "He has had *you* investigated. I overheard him with his man of business; Lilly, he knows you are not an heiress! What are we to do? He will never let me marry Justin." Elizabeth shook her head. "He has sent a note to Meade, asking him to attend him in the morning!"

Lilly was surprised and just a little amused. "Well, well . . . imagine that. Your father is a very shrewd fellow. I wonder what made him suspicious of my circumstances?"

"What difference can that possibly make? My father is everything everyone says he is. Cruel, calculating and . . . and I . . . I hate him!"

"Elizabeth," objected Mr. Reynolds, taking her shoulders. "You must not say such things."

Elizabeth burst into tears. "Justin, you don't know the whole. We, that is, Lilly and I, had a plan we were working on. You see, we were going to have Sir Anthony abduct Lilly. That way my father would see what a ruthless villain he is, but now everything is miserably undone."

Justin was shocked by his beloved's disclosure. He had

216

no idea what the two girls had been about and did not at all approve. He looked at Lilly and was about to scold her, but she was already on the move towards the bellrope. "Lilly, tell me this is not true?" he pleaded.

"Oh, but it is true, Justin, though we shall not be thwarted in our efforts because of this little setback." Lilly gave the rope a good yank and then went to the writing desk, where she picked up a quill but did not bother to sit as she penned a note:

Dearest Anthony,
It seems that Mr. Hawkins overheard Elizabeth and me talking about our upcoming plans. He means to see you and give you a good lecture. He also means to visit with my aunt and advise her of the whole. If we are to elope, we must hurry. Come with a post chaise to Mayfair Gate in one hour as I will be longingly awaiting you.

Lilly

"Ha!" declared Lillian Aulderbury. "That should do it!"

"Lilly, what have you done?" demanded Justin.

"Hush now, we haven't time. Elizabeth and I must go the Mayfair Gate. You must fetch your carriage and be ready to follow us at a discreet distance. I am fairly certain we shall be traveling to Edinbridge. When I met Anthony this morning for a quick chat in the park, he mentioned that he had obtained the Special Licence and directions to a vicar in Edinbridge that performs such marriages for some outrageous fee."

"This is moving too fast. Why are we doing this? I feel very strongly, Elizabeth, that it is certainly not the way to handle the situation with your father."

Lilly intervened. "Justin. We do not have a choice.

217

Just look at the matter the way it stands. Mr. Hawkins made it his business to know mine. He knows now beyond a shadow of a doubt that Anthony is courting me for my inheritance, which means he knows what Anthony is; still he means for him to marry his daughter!" She shook her head. "He can not be thinking straight. 'Tis time someone woke him up."

"Yes, but what am I to do?"

"Rush to the rescue. Make sure you stop the wedding and then see Liz safely home. You will be a hero, and Mr. Hawkins will see the error of his ways."

Justin was still doubtful, but his darling and Lilly were ushering him out of the house with the command to be at the Mayfair Gate as quickly as he could.

Lilly then took a moment to put quill to paper once more.

> Dearest loves,
> Don't worry. Elizabeth is with me and though we might be very late, it will all be fine, I do promise.
> Always your
> loving Lilly

Setting this sealed note on the desk, she took up her bonnet of blue silk, placed it on her black curls and tied a matching cloak round her shoulders. "Well then, Elizabeth, my girl, we are off."

"Lilly . . . will it work? If it doesn't we shall be ruined." Elizabeth wrung her hands nervously and pushed at a stray fair tress.

"It will succeed," Lilly assuaged.

"Yes, but if it doesn't they will banish us to the country . . . to die alone," Elizabeth wailed mournfully.

"No, silly child." Elizabeth could be a dunce at times, Lillian thought, but she took another moment to explain. "Gretna Green would be a last choice. Eloping to Gretna Green would hurt you in the eyes of the *beau monde,* and I don't want that for you, Elizabeth, but if your father gives you no choice, 'tis what you shall do with Justin."

Elizabeth brightened. "Oh yes. I would go anywhere with Justin, and I wouldn't give a fig for the *beau monde,* but, Lilly, what will you do?"

Lilly sighed and was about to shrug this off when the door opened and the Earl filled the frame with his large, masculine and infinitely handsome self. "Ah," he commented quietly, "Off, are we?"

Lilly's heart was suddenly throbbing, and her cheeks flamed. She could scarcely meet those twinkling, blue eyes as they raked her over with a look that nearly made her faint. When last they had parted she had known beyond a shadow of a doubt what love was, how it felt, who was the object of that feeling. It was Cameron, Earl of Raeburn. She loved him, though it was probably hopeless.

"Out, my lord. We must go for a fitting."

"Right then. I have my carriage outside; I will drive you both."

"Oh, no. We don't want to bother you," Lilly demurred.

"Bother?" He had already bent over Elizabeth's gloved fingers and was now taking Lilly's wrist to his lips. "It would give me great pleasure. Come, allow me the treat of two lovely ladies at my side."

"No, no. We need the exercise." Lilly was now desperate, but grey eyes met and held blue. Faith, he drew on her every feeling. She loved him beyond hope for herself. She lowered her gaze. "Really, my lord, we must be going."

He did not release the hand he still held, but instead

219

touched her gloved fingers to his lips heedless of the astonished Elizabeth who stood watching with her mouth agape.

"I will let you go for now, if you promise me an hour or two later this afternoon."

"Today?" Lilly did not make promises she could not keep.

"Indeed, today," he answered softly. He was aware, all too aware that he was experiencing a schoolboy thrill because he held her hand. He had stayed away a couple of days, had run from her and that second kiss which was an endorsement of the first. He had wanted to get control of himself. Then he'd seen her earlier in the morning, strolling with Anthony, and he'd known he wanted an end to the games—all of them!

"Perhaps you could come to dinner?" Lilly countered. "We are dining in tonight and have no plans for the evening." She peeped up at him. "We could play ducks and drakes."

He laughed. "Ducks and drakes, indeed!" A slight frown marred his shining smile. "Is your afternoon too busy for you to spare me a moment?"

She blushed, for she had come to the full realization that she adored this rakehell, the Earl of Raeburn. Though she had berated herself for having a penchant for libertines, there it was. She was in love, and this time it was different, encompassing. She couldn't imagine life as having any meaning without him in it. However, she had an obligation to Liz and Justin. Getting back at Anthony, making an accounting with him, seemed unimportant these days and was only a part of her plan for Liz and Justin. Her heart whispered, "Tell him, tell him, tell him." Then her mind cautioned her about doing so. "I am never too busy for you," she answered

220

softly. "However, you would find yourself bored with all our tiresome errands."

"I could never find myself bored when in your company," he responded on a low hungry note.

Elizabeth Hawkins' mouth opened even wider as the dawning lit her eyes. These two were in love! Why had she not seen it before? The Earl looked to her as though he was not going to give up easily, however, and they were running out of time. Hurriedly she interrupted them.

"My lord, I am so very sorry. 'Tis my fault you see. I need Lilly to attend me on some very personal matters . . ."

What was this? No fittings? Personal matters? Clearly he could no longer detain them. Graciously he bowed himself off. "Very well then . . ." He turned to Lilly and kissed the hand he still held. "Dinner, it is."

Elizabeth took her friend's elbow and urged her away, breaking the spell between the two lovers. "Come, Lilly. Again, forgive me, my lord, but we must be off . . . we are so very late."

Lilly looked back at the threshold. "Do you remain here, my lord?"

"Ah, child, I think I will await my uncle."

"Oh." Lilly's face fell in an absurd contrast to the inner joy she was feeling. When word got out, he might hear that she had gone off with Sir Anthony. There was no doubt that such word would get about. Would he know better? Please . . . He must.

The Earl watched them depart. There was a secretive air to the two. They were certainly up to something. He moved about the room and noticed the sealed envelope on the desk. He looked at it and saw that it was addressed to Lady Sarah and was written by Lilly. Just what was his minx up to now?

Chapter Twenty-seven

Sir Anthony's leased bachelor establishment reposed quietly on a small back street in Belgravia. His last extravagant expenditure. Appearances. One must keep up appearances. His rooms, however, were small and sparsely furnished. He sat now in the study and held the Special Licence in his hand thoughtfully contemplating his immediate future.

The licence and the vicar had proved to be costly commodities, but this would be offset when he could call Lilly and her fortune his own. Lilly . . . He was almost as pleased at the notion of Lilly as his wife as he was about the fact that he would soon be a wealthy man. His future bride was a lovely creature, and her bubbling good nature had endeared her to him. Indeed, his affection for Lilly was quite real. Right then, what the deuce was wrong? Something was. Every instinct warned him of danger. What could it be?

His valet, who also served as his butler, appeared at the doorway with a silver salver and the information that a letter, hand-delivered, had just arrived from the Hawkinses' house. The man then excused himself as the door knocker was once again requiring a response.

Anthony looked down at the sealed letter on the silver

tray and frowned as he picked it up. It was addressed to him and was from Elizabeth's father. What the devil? He looked up as his man appeared once more, this time with a sealed note in hand. "Sir, this appears to be urgent, as Miss Aulderbury's servant requested you see its contents at once."

Anthony got up from his desk chair and met his man halfway. All his senses were wary. He thanked his valet and told him to wait while he opened the missive and read its contents. Frowning, he took the notepaper to the street window and reread the hurriedly scribbled words. Briefly he glanced over at the note from Mr. Hawkins, which still rested on the silver salver on his desk. Well, well, just what was going on?

Quickly he made his decision, for there was no time to stall. He must meet Lilly and drive to Edinbridge without further delay. To be stopped now would mean all was lost. He could see Lilly and her fortune being snapped away. He would be at a loss then, as Elizabeth Hawkins was no longer in the picture. Elizabeth had made it clear that, whether her father willed it or no, she would not have him.

"Pack my overnight portmanteau, my man, and hail me a hackney as speedily as you can!" His voice was testy with irritation. He would take the hackney to the livery, hire a post chaise and rush to Mayfair Gate for Lilly. By the morrow she and her fortune would be his! He looked towards Hawkins' letter, started out, thought better of it and returned to slip the missive into his inner pocket.

"Lilly, we can't walk all the way to the Mayfair Gate," complained Elizabeth. "I am exhausted."

"You need the exercise." Lilly laughed, "We shall be

223

cooped up in a carriage for a good part of the day you know." She shrugged. "Besides, I haven't a sou on me. I forgot my purse."

"Well, I haven't forgotten mine," Elizabeth declared triumphantly, "Please, Lilly . . . please can we hail a coach?"

"Oh, very well then, but you know we might have to wait about as I don't know if Sir Anthony will be there yet. He will have to go first to hire a conveyance," Lilly mused out loud.

Elizabeth suddenly was fearful. "What if he wasn't home to get your letter. Worse, what if he received Papa's first?"

"If he received your father's letter, well, we can only speculate. There is a good chance that your father's note only requested him to come by at some given time. If that is so, then my note will cover that problem. If he wasn't home . . . well, then we may have a goodly wait."

"Oh, no," wailed Elizabeth, and then, "There . . . a cab. Lilly."

The girls hailed the hackney and clambered within. After Lilly requested to be taken to the Mayfair Gate, they were off, Elizabeth voicing her fears and Lilly chiding her for cowardice.

Lord Wizbough entered his study to find his nephew awaiting him, and one of his thick white brows went up. "You here, Cameron? Well, well."

The Earl eyed him suspiciously. "Well, well, what?"

Lord Wizbough chuckled. "Glad to see you ol' boy, nothing more."

"Ay, what do you take me for, a flat?" the Earl demanded amicably, "What are you thinking? What is that grin on your face?"

"There there . . ." soothed his uncle, as if speaking to a young boy, "you'll come about in spite of that testy godchild of Gussie's."

"I don't take your meaning," returned the Earl on a wary note.

"You want her, admit it, lad. You're done up, you've met your match, your heart has been fair pinked and your soul is chained forever." His lordship shrugged. "Happens to the best of us."

"I don't know what the devil you are talking about!" thundered the Earl, heating up. He had never been one to open his heart, it made him feel vulnerable, which was difficult to tolerate.

"Don't you?" Wizzy shook his head. "Me, well, I've seen it coming. You never had a chance."

The Earl paced about in a frenzy, "The thing is, something is wrong. I think that little minx is up to some mischief she won't be able to handle on her own. Don't want to see her hurt."

"No. I don't imagine you do. What sort of mischief?" pursued Lord Wizbough calmly.

"She left you a note. Perhaps you should read it," suggested the Earl hopefully. It was driving him mad.

"Eh, a note?" Lord Wizbough moved over to his desk and took his spectacles from a drawer. "No . . . This is addressed to Lilly's aunt. Not for me to open." He set the letter down again.

The Earl was on the verge of snatching it up and ripping it open.

"I tell you, we can't wait for them to return and open the damned thing. Something is wrong."

The logic of this was taken into consideration, but Lord Wizbough did not rush willy-nilly into anything. Experience had given him wisdom. "Look, Cameron, what we need is some coffee and a bite to eat. We'll take our refreshment by the fire, and I will read you the speech I mean to give next week in the House. By the time we've finished rewriting the blasted thing, Gussie and Sarah will be home."

The Earl was frustrated and threw himself into a chair. "Oh, very well!"

Mr. Hawkins was satisfied with his morning's work and went in search of his daughter in the hope that she would forget her grievance with him and join him for lunch. He was told by the servants that she had gone out alone. "What then, no message for me?"

"No, sir. Miss said only to tell her mother that she was not to worry about her."

"What does that mean?" Mr. Hawkins asked in resonant tones.

His wife walked in at that moment, and as she took off her bonnet, her husband rounded on her to advise her that her daughter had left her an obscure message. Mrs. Hawkins responded quietly and somberly that she did not like the sound of such a message.

"You don't like the sound of that?" demanded her irate husband. "What precisely do you mean, madam?"

He was a strong man. His strength, his boldness, his power had always made her warm with pride, but just now she found his attitude insufferable. She squared up for the fight, and her hands went to her plump hips as she assumed a most unladylike stance. "I mean that you have driven our daughter to point non plus!" His wife caught his attention with the spitfire response so unlike her habitual serenity. She drove home her point. "You made her believe that you were going to force her into a marriage with Meade. She loves Justin Reynolds!" She paced about and ran her hands through her tousled, fair

226

hair. "And if you have made our daughter run from us, I shall never, never forgive you, sir!"

"What is this? What are you saying, my dear?" He had her shoulders in his grip. He adored his wife and certainly did not want to see her so distraught. He knew she had sacrificed much when she had married him, and it had been his goal to provide her with her every need.

"I am saying that Justin Reynolds is a wonderful young gentleman—and our daughter loves him."

"No. He is the son of—"

"Of a man you long ago encountered and despised. He knows it, so does Elizabeth. Still they want each other. 'Tis time you put aside your awful feud. It has nought to do with Elizabeth and Justin."

He shook his head, "If he is anything like his father—

"You won't know that, can't know that until you have met the lad, given him a chance. Please, my love. My father was in the wrong, and now, so are you."

Usually he couldn't deny his wife anything, yet his hatred had roots that were deep. "No." The word irritated him. He felt—knew—that he was wrong. Yet the word came again: "No!"

"Darling, she will marry no one else. It is Reynolds she loves."

"She will not marry Reynolds! Do you understand me, madam?" he ranted, his mind and heart beating a wardrum and driving out logic.

She looked at him, released a sob and fled the room. She did not know where Elizabeth was, but intuition made her afraid. If her daughter and Reynolds had eloped, Elizabeth would be ruined in society, for she already had a father who was in trade. Justin would not do that to Elizabeth, would he? Young love knew very little about rules. Elizabeth would be ostracized . . . No.

Quickly she took up cloak and gloves. Lillian Aulderbury. She would know what Elizabeth was doing. Perhaps all this was for nought. Perhaps Elizabeth was only visiting with Lilly and therefore did not feel the need to have a maid in tow? She left the house and hailed a hackney, so much faster than sending to the stables for her coach.

Indoors, her husband paced to and fro in the study. It was all his fault . . . No, it was the fault of that dratted Lillian Aulderbury for putting notions into his Elizabeth's head. That was it! He would talk to Lilly's people and get to the bottom of this! He left the house almost behind his wife.

Chapter Twenty-eight

"Lilly, I am very frightened," Elizabeth said suddenly.

They were standing at the Mayfair Gate just outside Hyde Park and they had been waiting there for nearly twenty minutes. "Why?" asked Lilly absently. She appeared calm, but her insides were threatening a revolt.

"We have been here so long. Someone will see us."

"That will be excellent, child."

"How so?"

"If someone sees us get into a hired post chaise with Sir Anthony, then it will confirm the story that he has abducted us."

"No, it will appear that we went willingly. Oh, this is not going to work."

"It will. As we get into the coach, I will turn and push you into Anthony's arms. He will help you, keep you from falling; but you will be very clumsy and it will look very much like a struggle. It will be convincing. Really very convincing."

She looked doubtful. "I don't know . . ."

"Never mind. I think he is here." Lilly indicated an approaching vehicle.

"Faith, look at that coach," Elizabeth exclaimed.

The vehicle was weather-beaten, and the wheels

looked quite worn. The two horses that pulled it were certainly tired old cobs who looked as though they would not make it through the park let alone any great way.

Lilly eyed Sir Anthony whimsically as he alighted from the coach. "In *this*"—a wave of her hand took in the conveyance—"we shall be travelling all the way to Edinbridge?"

"Forgive me." Sir Anthony raised her gloved hand to his lips, managing to guide Elizabeth closer with his free hand, not at all embarrassed by the fact that until recently he had been heatedly courting her. He urged the women within the carriage's aged confines. "We must hurry . . ."

Lilly made a great deal out of climbing within, and instead of then taking her seat, she turned in the carriage's doorway, saw with some pleasure and surprise that Sir Harry was eyeing them as he walked down the avenue. "Oh look," she cried in mock distress, successfully distracting Sir Anthony, "we have been seen!" She then gave her friend a good push so that Elizabeth had all she could do not to fall backwards on Sir Anthony. Elizabeth yelped. As Sir Anthony attempted to put a steadying hold on her, Elizabeth made a great show of demanding to be released. Lilly nearly burst into laughter as Sir Anthony struggled to help Elizabeth into the coach. Sir Harry put up his stick and called out, "I say . . . !"

Lilly took Elizabeth's hand and called out, "Help me!"

Sir Harry quickened his steps. "What in thunder is going on?" he demanded.

Sir Anthony clambored within, and the coach was off. He sat down to face his bride-to-be and her dear friend

230

with a rueful frown. "Now that was nearly a disaster, and blister it, Lilly, what did you mean calling for help?"

"I wasn't calling for help," said Lilly, looking puzzled.

"You said, for all the world to hear, 'Help me!' " retorted the harassed young man.

"No, no. I was telling Elizabeth to help me, for what did she do when I gave her my hand but stand there like a stock."

Elizabeth turned an outraged countenance upon her friend before remembering her part and slumping back against the torn leather upholstery to declare, " 'Tis musty and dreadful in here."

The coach was already beginning to rumble through the city streets, so Lilly took a moment to look back out of the window. She saw with some satisfaction that Sir Harry was hailing a hackney. There was no sign of Justin, and she could only hope that he was not far behind!

Justin stopped at the bank, pleased with himself for having the presence of mind to do so. After all, Lilly's schemes might certainly go awry, and then they could all be without a sou between them! Well, he knew better than that. When he returned to his lodgings he attempted several notes to Lady Sarah. In the end, he hurriedly penned the following:

Dear Lady Sarah,
It is my sad office to inform you that I have reason to believe Sir Anthony has abducted Lilly and Elizabeth Hawkins. He has planned a clandestine wedding, to be performed at the vicarage in Edinbridge.
Please rest assured that I have no intention of al-

lowing such a disastrous ceremony to take place. Trust me in this,

                    I am your very obedient servant,
                    Justin Reynolds

Justin Reynolds winced as he reread what he had penned. It was insufferable. He had told an outrageous lie—in part. There was, of course, no abduction, though Anthony did plan a clandestine wedding. Lilly's aunt was sure to wonder how he knew all this? Yes, well, in the end perhaps all would be explained . . . at the happy conclusion. Laden with guilt, he put this note into a servant's hands and gave strict instructions with regards to its disposition. He then called for his closed carriage and his set of matched, sturdy bay geldings to pull it. Sharply he then told his driver to take him to the Mayfair Gate.

His arrival exactly coincided with Lilly's artful scene, and he hung out of his carriage door a moment, unsure whether he should run the distance and land Sir Anthony a facer for shoving his beloved Elizabeth within the post chaise so roughly.

No doubt Lilly had somehow contrived this entire scenario for the benefit of passersby in the park. He then spotted Sir Harry running towards them, and his brow went up. Well, well, Lilly really did have luck on her side. Perhaps all this might yet work. He had thought it an unsavory scheme, distasteful, but eloping to Gretna Green was even worse. He could not ruin his dear Elizabeth by wedding her at Gretna. This alternative did seem like the only feasible plan. Right then. He began to help things along, spur them on by playing a part. He told his driver to follow Anthony's hired chaise, and as the man did so, he called out, "Harry! Harry! Don't worry. I'm after them and will have them back safe!"

"It's Lilly and Elizabeth," Harry shouted, beside himself. "Take me up, Justin! I'll go with you."

"No time, Harry—get word to their people!"

"But take me up, Justin ... thunder and turf!" Harry nearly spat as Reynolds' coach tore off. What in blazes was going on? Why was Sir Anthony abducting two girls? Why Lilly? He would have his blood! Harry stood for a moment, dumbfounded, and stared after Justin's departing equipage. Ay, you're after them, thought Harry, when it should have been me! He turned and hailed a passing hackney.

Sarah and Gussie entered the study, both bubbling with excitement about their morning's work. They had taken Francis and some of the other older boys who seemed to have an interest in horses to the livery, where the Wizbough head groom had given them a practical lesson about those great animals, livery tack and its accessories. The boys had taken to the horses and the lesson with great enthusiasm. Both Augusta and Sarah were pleased about this. However, they were quick to note the harassed look the Earl wore as he jumped up to greet them.

"You're here!" declared Raeburn as he went forward to snatch up Lilly's note and present it to Lady Sarah. "Good. Please read this immediately."

"And good afternoon to you, Cameron," teased Lady Sarah.

"Forgive me, but I have been anxiously awaiting your arrival," he offered in faltering accents. He felt the fool.

"Really?" Lady Sarah was surprised.

"Why, Cameron?" Augusta's brows went up. "Whatever is wrong?"

Lady Sarah had already opened Lilly's letter and read

the few lines. She put up a hand. "What can this mean?" She turned to Augusta. "Lilly has gone off somewhere with Elizabeth Hawkins and means to be late."

"Gone off? Gone off where?" demanded Augusta.

"Drat the girl!" declared the Earl, beside himself. "I knew she was up to something. I knew it."

"How did you know it? And what do you mean?" Sarah was concerned but not yet frightened.

The study door opened and the Wizbough butler announced Mrs. Hawkins; however, she was already through the door before her name met the air. Augusta went forward at once, hands outstretched. "Amelia . . ."

"Please, tell me Elizabeth is here with Lilly," cried the woman, already distraught from her fears.

"No, she is not," said Sarah. "And we have just been wondering where those two monkeys could be." Lady Sarah was trying to make light of the situation, for she could see that Mrs. Hawkins was on the verge of tears.

"No, oh no . . . She has eloped with—" The door once more opened and Mr. Hawkins stomped into the room.

"Ah-ha!" he said.

All eyes turned to him and awaited further comment. It came.

"They are not here, are they?"

Lord Wizbough went forward and put out a welcoming hand. "I take it you are Mr. Hawkins. Do come in so that we may discuss this matter in private." He motioned for the butler to close the door.

"Mr. Hawkins," his wife cried, "what are you doing here?"

"The same thing you are doing, my dear." He was angry, but curtailed his temper. "Looking for our daughter." He turned to the assembled company.

"Apparently, her friend, Miss Aulderbury, is missing as well?"

"Well, as to that, Lilly has left us a note." Augusta was attempting to assuage his ruffled feathers, though she was now seriously worried.

"A note, you say?" Mr. Hawkins put out a hand. "If you please, I should appreciate it if you would allow me to peruse this note."

Timms had been serving Lord Wizbough and Lady Augusta for thirty years. He was quite sincerely attached to his employers and had a special feeling for Miss Lilly as well. It was obvious to his trained eye that a great deal was amiss. He reentered the study and cleared his throat resonantly to announce that he had an urgent missive for Lady Sarah.

"Urgent, you say?" inquired Lord Wizbough.

"Indeed, my lord. Mr. Reynolds' man advised me that her immediate attention to his master's note was required."

"Thank you, Timms," said Lady Sarah, taking up Justin Reynolds' penned note and breaking the seal. The room went silent, and the Earl gritted his teeth. Justin Reynolds again? What had Reynolds to do with all of this?

After a moment Sarah looked to Augusta. "Gussie, this is very distressing, very distressing . . ."

"What in thunder?" demanded the Earl, going to her side and taking the note from her. Quickly he read the letter and then turned to his uncle. His brows were drawn together, for it didn't quite make sense. "What the devil is this all about? Uncle, Justin writes that Sir Anthony has abducted the girls and that he is off to rescue them."

"What?" shrieked Mr. Hawkins distracted. "Both of them? What the bloody hell does he want with both of them?"

His wife sank into a nearby chair. Augusta put a comforting arm about Sarah. "This is absurd."

"I don't understand this . . ." Mrs. Hawkins' voice was scarcely audible. "What can he be thinking of?"

"Perhaps he only wanted one of them," suggested Lord Wizbough, who seemed greatly amused, "and found he could not have one without the other?"

The Earl frowned at his uncle. "Ay, and how is it that Justin Reynolds knows where they are off to? Too smoky by half, Uncle."

"Agreed. It bears looking into, don't you think?" suggested Wizbough reasonably.

Once more the study door opened, and in its doorway stood a frenzied Sir Harry. "I have come," he announced to the assembled company and then discovering the Earl, he said, "Cameron, you here? Good. Need you ol' boy." He looked round and noted that Mr. and Mrs. Hawkins were present and staring blankly at him, and was happy for the Earl's company. Determinedly, he marched over to the wall table, poured himself a snifter of brandy and swigged it right down as though it were no stronger than ale! He then further astonished everyone by turning to announce, "Abduction! Right before my very eyes! Called them to a halt. Called Justin to a halt! No one paid me any mind. He has shepherded our Lilly away and that other one . . . what is her name?"

"Elizabeth Hawkins!" snapped the other one's' father.

"Yes, that's it. How came you to know that?" Harry inquired, momentarily diverted by curiosity as he had never had the pleasure of meeting Mr. Hawkins face to face.

"Harry, you actually saw Sir Anthony abduct them?" inquired Augusta before anyone else could speak.

"Ay, that I did. Lilly called for help—heard her, saw her. Horrible, horrible. Tried to catch them . . . then there was Justin . . . Chased them. He refused to take me up. Know what I think?" He turned to the Earl. "Wants Lilly for himself. Means to rescue her and marry her himself!"

The Earl turned to his uncle. "Justin sends a note before the abduction took place . . . What, sir, is going on do you think?"

"An interesting question, and we both know that only Lilly has that particular answer, don't we, Cameron?"

The Earl reread Justin's missive. Had Justin and Lilly been planning something that went awry? Perhaps Justin meant to marry Lilly? Was Lilly attached to the blasted fellow already? Was it too late for him? Devil a bit! This notion nearly drove him into a frenzy. He would see Justin, his good friend dead before he would allow him to steal Lilly away. That was love. When he and his friend had been rivals over Anthea, he had stepped aside in the name of friendship. He would not step aside in the name of anything where Lilly was concerned. She was meant for him. She was his heart. With sudden clarity he knew this. He started from the room, taking up hat and gloves and turning to announce, "I shall have Lilly safely back by dinner, mark me!"

Lord Wizbough, who had just poured himself and Mr. Hawkins snifters of brandy, now raised his glass to his nephew. "I have no doubt of that, no doubt whatsoever."

"Yes, but my daughter . . . ?" cried Mrs. Hawkins.

"Your daughter is in excellent hands . . . or she soon will be," answered Lord Wizbough quietly, as he watched his nephew depart.

237

Harry started after the Earl, a solid objection on his lips, but he was roundly told to return to his brandy. "There is no need for you to join me in this, Harry. I mean to ride hard and fast and in the end Lilly will marry no man save myself!"

Harry was stunned, too stunned to reply to this until after the Earl had gone. Then he breathed out, "My word . . ."

Lord Wizbough smiled benignly. "Precisely."

Chapter Twenty-nine

"There! Look, Anthony, we are approaching a posting house," Lilly cried thankfully as they came upon a weather-beaten but still inviting sign that welcomed travelers to the Red Bull Inn. When he did not answer she persisted. "Anthony, please . . . I am so very famished, and I am sure Elizabeth is too." Her foot touched her friend's. "Aren't you, Elizabeth?"

"Famished," agreed Elizabeth, wishing she were home. The ride was bumpy, the interior of the coach was odiously damp and she found Sir Anthony's insincerity detestable.

Anthony objected. "Yes, but we have only another hour or so to push on. Can you not wait till we get to Edinbridge?"

"Anthony, we haven't eaten or had tea, and I need to stretch my legs," argued Lilly.

"I am astonished that you have an appetite. I'd have thought you would be too nervous to eat . . . considering our upcoming nuptials?"

"Anthony, I am too hungry to be nervous. If you want me nervous, you shall have to feed me first." Lilly would not be deterred. She had to be certain that Justin was still close behind. After all, any mishap could have

239

occurred. His horse could have lost a shoe, or if he was traveling by coach, a wheel might have loosened or some other freakish thing. She had to stall for time, just in case.

In fact, she was quite proud of her foresight. She was feeling very good, bright and clever. Had she not engineered all this? Indeed, she was a power to be reckoned with. True love would soon win out, Anthony would have been taught a lesson and she . . . she would return to London in love with a rakehell! Clever she might be, but that did not stop a wayward heart. Whatever the Earl was, she knew she would love him for the rest of her life. This seemed such a hopeless situation that she forced herself to turn her thoughts away and considered instead the inn's cobbled courtyard. It was a neat-looking establishment, freshly painted and with ivy growing up its two stories in swags of green. It was surrounded by spring flowers in tidy gardens and by evergreens. A wagonload of hay reposed interestingly near the stone barn, and several urchins were at various tasks. Two came running to meet the coach.

Anthony alighted and turned to help the ladies. Lilly was met by the brisk breeze and fresh scent. "Lovely, such a quaint place." She turned to Elizabeth. "There, Lizzy, you will feel better presently. What we need is hot tea and cake."

"Where is Justin, do you suppose?" Liz asked on a hurried whisper.

"At our backs. He won't want to be seen, so I think he will approach the inn cautiously."

As it happened, Justin Reynolds was not far behind. His driver, who had been with him for some years, had wondered why they were following the hired post chaise, but had finally put it down to some eccentric turn his employer had taken. This was certainly odd, for young Mr. Reynolds, as he had always thought of him since he'd come to work for him ten years ago, had no time for the habitual absurdities of the aristocracy. Nonetheless, when the hired carriage had turned into the posting house and his employer had requested that they pull up short and remain on the road, he did as he was asked without question. There they stood for some ten trying minutes.

Justin was at an impasse. What to do? He didn't want to pull into the posting inn directly on Anthony's heels, for surely then the man would suspect things were not as they seemed. What should he do? Sir Anthony would no doubt see the ladies to a private parlor for their refreshments. He could have his driver wheel his equipage into the courtyard and quietly take up a corner table in the main galley. There was nothing else for it. He couldn't keep his carriage here in the middle of the road. He signalled for his driver to take him into the Red Bull Inn.

The Earl took his fastest, fittest hunter, a bay gelding from his stables, hopped nimbly onto the horse's back and made his way out of London onto the Post Road heading for Edinbridge. He thanked Justin's sense of propriety for his having advised them of the destination. How Justin knew of it, though, was something the Earl could only guess at. Had Lilly entrusted Justin with this information? Perhaps she expected Justin to come to her rescue. The notion struck like a slash across the heart.

He slowed his horse to a walk to allow the spirited blood to collect its wind before being urged onward again. He would fast gain on Anthony's hired coach.

The man had perhaps only one hour on him, and he was in a cumbersome hired vehicle being pulled, no doubt, by a set of tired old cobs. Would Anthony discover Lilly's duplicity and, thinking her an heiress, try to force marriage on her? Or would Justin arrive in time to rescue her and win her heart and hand? Such a notion drove the Earl back to a frenzied speed. Lilly would be wife to no man other than himself!

How had he allowed things to come to such a pass? How had he allowed this slip of a girl, this scampish hoyden, this vixen, this oddly mannered country child to ensnare his heart, his mind, his spirit? Certes, but he loved her! "Lilly . . . please . . . don't . . ." he whispered out loud. His horse's ears pricked up at catching the distress in his voice. "We have got to hurry Rough-Play; there is no time!" he told the animal as he spurred him on.

As Justin had supposed, Sir Anthony situated his ladies and himself in a private parlor. There he impatiently partook of refreshments with Lilly and Elizabeth, who behaved as though they were on a country outing. He was a bit surprised by this. Lilly, though a runaway bride, was certainly not at all concerned. Or was she? He did catch her looking round more than once. Well, no doubt she was worried about being followed? As they ran out of tea, cakes, bread 'n' butter and time, he excused himself and went to see to the fare with the innkeeper.

He found this worthy in the main galley, serving a gentleman in a far corner. Sir Anthony saw at once that it was Justin Reynolds, and he whirled quickly out of the room before he could be seen. What the devil was Reynolds doing here? He frowned and wondered if the man had spotted him. No, he couldn't have, for if so, he would certainly have called out a greeting.

The innkeeper appeared and Sir Anthony reached absently into his inner pocket for coin, touching the note from Mr. Hawkins he had put there earlier. He settled his bill and then brought out the note.

Instinct moved him to seek an outside corner, where he opened the sealed missive and silently read:

Dear Sir:
A false rumour regarding the extent of Lilly Aulderbury's inheritance has evidently been circulated, for what purpose we may only guess.
Please come and see me tomorrow morning so that we may discuss the matter.

A. Hawkins

Sir Anthony's brows rose. Lilly was not an heiress? Why would she want him to think she was? But ... Lord Raeburn was the one who had led him to believe that. Damnation! Blister it! He had been duped. Hawkins wanted him to marry Elizabeth! Elizabeth wanted Justin Reynolds. Reynolds was here! That was it. Instinct had been warning him of something. Here it was, all so very clear. Well, well, darling Lilly, you won't get to see Edinbridge today, but Elizabeth will! He moved towards the private parlour, in some anger and with sure purpose.

Justin had seen him. Justin had also seen how quickly Anthony had retreated. It could mean nothing, yet perhaps he should move about quietly and see what was towards? He would wait a moment, give Anthony time to return to the girls. Slowly, cautiously, he made his way down the hallway to the private dining chamber and listened at the door. There was no one within. It was too quiet. He opened the door a crack to confirm his suspicions. They were gone. He hurried from the inn just in time to see Anthony viciously push Elizabeth into the carriage and close the door before Lilly could follow her within. What the deuce? Justin Reynolds' heart skipped a beat in fear as he rushed at them.

"Justin, he is abducting Liz—he knows!" cried Lilly, furiously running after the slowly lumbering coach.

"Driver!" demanded Justin. "Stop your coach, do you hear! I shall have your blood! Stop the coach!" He continued to shout as he gave chase on foot.

The driver of Anthony's coach had been well paid for just such an eventuality. He wasn't afraid of the conservatively dressed gentleman running after them. He had been promised another gold coin when they reached their destination. That was what he wanted. He never even blinked as he hastily drove his carriage out of the yard.

Justin couldn't catch up. His temper was out of control and so, for a moment, was his reason. He stood in helpless fury, kicking at the dirt and cursing Sir Anthony for a coward and a blackguard whom he would see hanged. Lilly pulled at his sleeve, "Justin . . . please. You can send him to perdition when we catch up to him. He means to marry Elizabeth—or compromise her—so we must catch up to him."

Justin heard her through the storm in his head and turned without another word to hurl this order at his driver. "I will drive myself!" Then to Lilly, he said, "Get in. This, young lady, is all your fault! How did I allow such a scheme?"

"Well! If you hadn't allowed yourself to be seen, he would never have read Mr. Hawkins' letter," she snapped as she clambored within Justin's carriage and stuck her head out to watch him climb up beside the driver and take the reins, giving a harsh command to his horses. She fell back into the coach as it lurched forward and prayed they would reach Elizabeth in time.

They were moving at a threatening pace, and though Lilly was not really frightened of speed, she knew that Justin's respectable coach had not been designed for this kind of driving over such badly rutted roads. Just as she was worrying about this circumstance she found herself thrown on her side and nearly knocked out when her head struck the front board of the interior.

Justin was at the door and looking anxiously within not long afterwards. "Lilly . . . Lilly, are you hurt?"

"No, not really," Lilly assured him. "What happened?"

Justin blushed a bright red. "I . . . I hit a rut. The carriage swerved into the drainage ditch before I had the horses managed."

"Oh, no. The wheels?"

"Not broken. Just hold on while my man and I pull the horses forward and get us out of this mess."

This was slow, careful going as they did not want to break a wheel in the process. The ditch ran the length of the road, and Justin and his driver were sadly muddied before the carriage was set right. The bays, prime bloods, fidgeted during this episode, but their training overcame their nervousness and they helped the men along, finally pulling the carriage out of the water ditch. A goodly twenty minutes were lost, but even so, Justin thought it prudent to take the coach forward at a slower pace.

Lilly sat back against the fine brown leather upholstery and folded her arms across her chest. Would the Earl come to her rescue? If he loved her, would he save her from such a situation? She wondered if he truly loved her. Sometimes there was such a look in his blue eyes, but she had been fooled before. Yet, she was wiser now, and something in her heart, instinct perhaps, felt something from his. Was she wrong? Was it wishful thinking? Or . . . was it love?

Sir Anthony Meade knew that Reynolds' carriage carried by Justin's sturdy, prime goers could easily overtake his own hired chaise. Thus, he devised a plan to take a more roundabout route to throw Justin off the scent. Lilly knew, of course, that he was headed for Edinbridge, but she did not know where in Edinbridge. By the time she found him, the deed would be done and Elizabeth Hawkins with all her wealth would be his wife!

However, when another hour went by and there was no sign of Justin Reynolds at his back, Meade decided to head straight for the vicarage. He looked at Elizabeth cowering in her corner, and sneered. "Don't look so frightened, my dear. You may recall that you once invited my attentions."

"No, I never did!" Elizabeth was moved to sit upright and fume.

"Ah, did you not? Well then, you will learn to invite them . . . and soon. I shall have an obedient wife who will bear my children and whose father will pay for the privilege of my name!"

"I will never marry you," Elizabeth cried. "I will tell the vicar you have abducted me. He will never perform—"

"Ah, but the vicar is *my* man, paid for this time with *my* money. I will further explain that I have compromised your reputation, and he will feel it is his moral obligation to wed us. You will see."

"No! Justin will come . . . He will stop you." Elizabeth was weeping now.

"He will not be in time."

Elizabeth's weeping increased immediately, as did its intensity. Meade grimaced to hear her. Finally he put up a hand. "Stop it, silly chit. What good does it do you?"

When she did not acquiesce to his command he put up a warning finger. "Listen to me, Elizabeth. I am not under normal circumstances a violent man, but when goaded I hold no scruples with regards to having my wishes obeyed. A woman is but man's chattel. I believe in punishing or rewarding her for her behavior. Am I understood?"

Elizabeth sniffed back a tear. "You are odious. Justin and Lilly will come—they will."

To prove the truth of his words Sir Anthony Meade lifted his open hand and slapped her face hard enough to leave a red stain. Elizabeth had never been hit in all her life. She went silent with shock.

"There," said Meade heartlessly, "that is better." He had but one hope now if he was to come about. He had to be safely married to this chit or create enough of a scandal trying to wed her so that her father would have no choice but to allow the marriage to proceed to save her name. Ay then, there was still a trick or two he had under his fashionable sleeve.

Justin Reynolds slowed his carriage just outside town upon seeing a young man walking along the road with his sheepdog.

"I say there, can you tell me where the town vicar is located?"

Lilly put her face to the window and frowned. There could be more than one in the area. There was no saying that the vicar Anthony spoke of dwelled right in Edinbridge. Indeed, the lad pulled at his wool, peaked cap and returned the question with another. "Well now, sir, there be two. There be Reverend Taupe just inside the village, and then there is Vicar Poole some two miles back off country lane number three."

"Thank you," said Justin and started for town. He had no choice he would have to try the closer one first. However, when they arrived at the richly appointed ministry with its handsomely landscaped gardens and its quietly designed buildings, he could not imagine that this reverend had been paid to perform so questionable a service. He gave the reins to his driver and started for the gate, but Lilly called him back,

"Justin, we are wasting time. This is not the right place."

"We don't know that. His hired coach could be somewhere out of sight."

"Justin, please . . . I just know this is not the place. We must hurry."

He was inclined to agree, but shook his head. "I must first try." Some moments later he was again on the driver's seat, and while Lilly stomped with frustration inside the carriage he made his way back out of town once more.

"Please Vicar Poole . . ." Elizabeth was stalling for time. Her cheek still smarted from Meade's hard hand, but he would not dare hit her here at the ministry. "This man has abducted me. He is forcing a marriage on me that I do not want."

The vicar blushed to hear such talk. Sir Anthony had already explained her circumstances. She was a bold piece who had stolen away to be with him and had now changed her mind. Sir Anthony was attempting to do the right thing by her and her family. Very proper indeed! Terrible, terrible, these young people with their loose morals. She spends a night with a man and then says him nay? Outrageous! Perhaps she didn't even know what she was saying. Women were forever coming out with the oddest things when they were distraught. Meade had suggested that she need not be in the room while he and the vicar signed all the final documents.

Elizabeth watched them go through the motions and suddenly realized what was taking place, "Stop! What do you think you are doing? You can not. 'Tis not even legal! I—"

Meade took her shoulders. "Careful Elizabeth. I will not punish you now, but I most certainly will do so when we are alone. Mark me!"

Upon hearing those words, Elizabeth felt weak, her knees gave and she started to collapse.

"Terrible ... terrible ... what will my housekeeper think?" exclaimed the vicar as he stared down at the young woman who lay in a faint.

Sir Anthony made an attempt to scoop her up, but in spite of her thin frame he found it a herculean task to maneuver her dead weight to the sofa. Finally he dragged her and in gradual stages lifted her to the couch's height. Somewhat out of breath he then returned once more to the vicar. "Shall we proceed, sir?"

The door burst open, and though the housekeeper seemed to be objecting to the new arrivals, no one paid her any heed as Justin Reynolds and Lilly Aulderbury stormed the room. Lilly discovered Elizabeth in a faint on the sofa and cried, "Elizabeth! Oh, my dear, what has he done to you?" By that time she had reached her friend to find her cheek still quite red.

Justin was beside her in a trice, and discovering his dear heart disheveled and only just waking from a faint to sob in Lilly's arms, he lost control of his usually calm temper. When Elizabeth pointed to Meade and said that he had struck her, Justin turned upon the man, outraged. Lilly saw murder in his stance and hurried to spring between him and Meade. Anthony grabbed her and, putting a firm arm beneath her chin, dragged her backwards towards the door. "I shall break her neck, Reynolds, for I don't mean to be trapped in this matter!" Meade threatened as Justin still went towards him.

Justin stood his ground. "Damn your eyes! I'll have—"

"What?" Meade was in a rage. He had been thwarted, and this was a game he could not afford to lose. "What will you have? If you take another step, I shall have this tart's neck! Desperate men do desperate things."

"You will go to prison, sir," Lilly declared.

"I could, but I would have to explain to the court that you and Elizabeth enticed me for a lark. Think of the scandal?"

"You could do that," said a strong familiar male voice at Anthony's back, "but I could kill you now and save us all a great deal of future trouble." And then on a growl, "Release my Lilly at once!"

Anthony felt the hard round shape of a horse pistol's nozzle in the middle of his back. Having recognized Raeburn's steely voice, he put up his hands and then dropped them to his sides as Lilly bounced away and clapped her hands like a child.

"You have come." The words came out on a joyful gurgle as she rushed the Earl and threw her arms round his waist and repeated, "You have come."

He took a moment to look down at her beauteous face and then softly asked, "Did you doubt that I would?"

"Yes, yes. For so long I have doubted so many things . . ." Lilly held him tighter.

He felt a thrill he could not deny. Zounds! Was it possible to love anyone the way he loved her? Was it possible that she loved him? "There now, little one. Go and sit for a moment with Elizabeth. I think that Anthony and I must go outdoors to settle our differences."

"All of you go outdoors!" the vicar ordered, finally finding his voice. "Madmen . . . every last one of you . . . mad!"

The Earl rounded on him viciously. "Your part in this, my good man, is not at all innocent. That young lady was abducted, and you were about to perform an illegal wedding. She is under age!" He then returned to Meade, but Justin was already moving in Meade's direction, declaring that he had a score to settle with the fellow first.

"Do you, by God! I think not. No one will pick up the cudgels for the sake of my Lilly, save myself, Justin. Do you take my meaning?"

Justin frowned at him. "That may be so, but as it happens he needs some bloodletting on account of *my* Elizabeth."

The Earl regarded him for a stunned moment as dawning arrived. However, Meade took this opportunity to rush the door. The Earl was upon him almost at once, turning him to face his fist which pummeled him hard and fast. Meade went reeling backwards and he fell against a wall table, but the Earl pulled him up by his coat and landed him yet another facer before throwing him outdoors.

Justin hurriedly followed them and heard Meade wailing for a bargain to be struck. "Listen to me . . . listen." Meade wiped at the blood pouring out of his nose.

"There is a way we can settle this . . . so that I shall no longer trouble you."

" 'Tis my turn," said Justin, itching to brutalize the fellow.

Lilly and Elizabeth comforted one another within as Justin and the Earl exacted their revenge. Finally Lilly could stand it no longer and got to her feet. It was at this juncture that Justin reentered the house, and she went forward as Elizabeth put out a hand for Justin's attention.

"Wait . . . Where is the Earl?" Lilly inquired anxiously as Justin took Elizabeth into his arms.

"Outside," Justin answered briefly as he kissed Elizabeth's forehead and murmured, "Poor dear . . . poor love."

Lilly flew towards the door even though Justin called after her, "Lilly! Lilly, you are to remain with us!"

Lillian Aulderbury never even gave him a second glance. She hurried outdoors and called for the Earl. He heard her and came round the stable building to catch her up in his arms. "There, there, little brat, what are you about? You should be with Elizabeth."

"I . . . I was worried." She peered at him, all too aware of the sensations he aroused in her.

"Worried about me?" He grinned. "Did you not think I could handle my man?"

"Oh, yes. I was worried that you might have killed him."

He laughed. "Ah, you meant to save the devil?"

"No, not exactly." Then she saw the twinkle in his blue eyes and slapped his arm. "You odious thing. I meant to save you from gaol."

He kissed her then, long, hot and sweetly. When his

lips came apart from hers it was to whisper her name. She pressed herself to him and requested to know, "Do you love me, my lord?"

"Love you? I adore you."

"Yes, but do you love me? Truly?"

"Truly, completely, devotedly, madly. Lilly, I love you."

It was a moment before she remembered Sir Anthony and inquired about his status. The Earl grinned and flicked her nose. "I have sent him . . . up north."

She wrinkled her nose. "Up north? Cameron . . . dearest, you *have* murdered him, haven't you?"

"I should have done so, but no. I gave him his walking papers."

"Explain," demanded his lady love.

" 'Tis very simple. I gave him a voucher to disappear for several months."

"What?" shrieked Lilly. "You paid him to go away? I thought you would drive him through, lay him low, beat him to a pulp!"

He laughed. "Indeed, my bloodthirsty girl, I . . . er . . . had some of his blood, and then secured his promise to leave London for other parts where he might pursue some more willing heiress at his leisure." The Earl touched her chin. "You see, he could muck up our lives with some unwanted gossip."

"What gossip? We have done nothing."

"There is the question of your fortune," the Earl replied gravely, "It became a widely spread rumour in polite circles that you are an heiress. Such things do get about. He meant to declare it a hum that you started. Now no one will be the wiser, for when you are my wife, you will be an heiress." His face was devoid of expression, but there was a deep and vibrant feeling in his voice and eyes.

"Your wife? Oh . . . your wife," Lilly sighed. "But you have not asked me. You have not had my reply," she teased.

"Brat. You will be my wife, if only to save that doubtful reputation of yours. After all, you can't go about the countryside kissing Earls in barnyards without marrying one of them, and this one had better be the only one you kiss."

"And marry," added Lilly, sighing once more. "What about Justin and Elizabeth?"

"With Meade out of the way, Mr. Hawkins might be persuaded to see things in a new and better light. I think he might agree to have his daughter married to Reynolds at a double wedding? What think you? It will make quite a social stir."

"My lord, my lord, that is brilliant! Oh, you are Cameron the Great!" declared Miss Aulderbury with fervent glee. "You have arranged everything right and tight!"

"Everything, my wild Lilly," he whispered as he took her up very rightly, very tightly, into his arms.

A Memorable Collection of Regency Romances

BY ANTHEA MALCOLM AND VALERIE KING

THE COUNTERFEIT HEART   (3425, $3.95/$4.95)
by Anthea Malcolm
Nicola Crawford was hardly surprised when her cousin's betrothed disappeared on some mysterious quest. Anyone engaged to such an unromantic, but handsome man was bound to run off sooner or later. Nicola could never entrust her heart to such a conventional, but so deucedly handsome man. . . .

THE COURTING OF PHILIPPA   (2714, $3.95/$4.95)
by Anthea Malcolm
Miss Philippa was a very successful author of romantic novels. Thus she was chagrined to be snubbed by the handsome writer Henry Ashton whose own books she admired. And when she learned he considered love stories completely beneath his notice, she vowed to teach him a thing or two about the subject of love. . . .

THE WIDOW'S GAMBIT   (2357, $3.50/$4.50)
by Anthea Malcolm
The eldest of the orphaned Neville sisters needed a chaperone for a London season. So the ever-resourceful Livia added several years to her age, invented a deceased husband, and became the respectable Widow Royce. She was certain she'd never regret abandoning her girlhood until she met dashing Nicholas Warwick. . . .

A DARING WAGER   (2558, $3.95/$4.95)
by Valerie King
Ellie Dearborne's penchant for gaming had finally led her to ruin. It seemed like such a lark, wagering her devious cousin George that she would obtain the snuffboxes of three of society's most dashing peers in one month's time. She could easily succeed, too, were it not for that exasperating Lord Ravenworth. . . .

THE WILLFUL WIDOW   (3323, $3.95/$4.95)
by Valerie King
The lovely young widow, Mrs. Henrietta Harte, was not all inclined to pursue the sort of romantic folly the persistent King Brandish had in mind. She had to concentrate on marrying off her penniless sisters and managing her spendthrift mama. Surely Mr. Brandish could fit in with her plans somehow . . .

Available wherever paperbacks are sold, or order direct from the Publisher. Send cover price plus 50¢ per copy for mailing and handling to Zebra Books, Dept. 4443, 475 Park Avenue South, New York, N.Y. 10016. Residents of New York and Tennessee must include sales tax. DO NOT SEND CASH. For a free Zebra/ Pinnacle catalog please write to the above address.

MAKE THE
ROMANCE CONNECTION

Z-TALK
Online

Come talk to your favorite authors and get the inside scoop on everything that's going on in the world of romance publishing, from the only online service that's designed exclusively for the publishing industry.

With Z-Talk Online Information Service, the most innovative and exciting computer bulletin board around, you can:

- ♥ CHAT "LIVE" WITH AUTHORS, FELLOW ROMANCE READERS, AND OTHER MEMBERS OF THE ROMANCE PUBLISHING COMMUNITY.

- ♥ FIND OUT ABOUT UPCOMING TITLES BEFORE THEY'RE RELEASED.

- ♥ DOWNLOAD THOUSANDS OF FILES AND GAMES.

- ♥ READ REVIEWS OF ROMANCE TITLES.

- ♥ HAVE UNLIMITED USE OF E-MAIL.

- ♥ POST MESSAGES ON OUR DOZENS OF TOPIC BOARDS.

All it takes is a computer and a modem to get online with Z-Talk. Set your modem to 8/N/1, and dial 212-545-1120. If you need help, call the System Operator, at 212-889-2299, ext. 260. There's a two week free trial period. After that, annual membership is only $ 60.00.

See you online!

KENSINGTON PUBLISHING CORP.